THE
SUPER
Sunny
MURDER
CLUB

Mysteries are all around us. The world, and the people in it, are a fascinating series of puzzles to solve, and you don't have to look far to find a problem that needs unpacking. What was in that letter your parent just opened? Why is your sibling acting so strangely? Why is your teacher suddenly obsessed with horses? Every one of us is a detective, whether we acknowledge it or not.

But it's especially fun to be given a set of made-up mysteries to solve. No real-world consequences, no annoyed adults, no interfering police. Just you and your brain as you try to work out what on earth could have happened.

This book gives you thirteen opportunities to do just that. Last time we brought you a set of chilly, festive crimes. This time you're baking in the sun, on a summer holiday mystery tour that will take you from a tropical resort to a caravan park, an airport to a pick-your-own farm. You'll go to weddings, plays and dance competitions, meet monsters (both real and metaphorical), chase down treasure and fall into worlds very different to our own. You'll meet new detectives and reconnect with old friends from our first collection, and together you'll come up against terrifyingly cunning and tricky criminals. But you're smart enough to outwit them all, right? I believe in you.

So happy sleuthing, Detectives.
Enjoy your cruel summer

Robin S x

I can remember long, hot summers spent at home when I was growing up, bored and nothing interesting to do. My world and being me often felt not that great and so books were a fantastic escape, and trips to the library were just the best. Nothing beat escaping into a book and I especially loved the feeling of solving a mystery story, putting the puzzle together and seeing how the pieces fit.

I realise that I always related to the characters in stories who were a little bit different. I didn't know why back then but I've realised it's because I'm a little bit different too and I'm really proud of that because it's helped me to become a writer.

Stories show us that we might be different to each other, but we also might be the same, in big ways and small. We might appear to be one thing but we can also be many amazing things all at once.

I'm incredibly proud of the amazing cast of characters our brilliant authors have created in this collection of sizzling summer mysteries because they are each different in their own ways too. They all have their own quirks, interests, skills and personalities. What they share is a determination to find the truth and when I was reading the stories, I found myself loving each detective for so many reasons. Which one will be your favourite, I wonder? Happy reading!

Serena x

First published in Great Britain 2024 by Farshore
An imprint of HarperCollins*Publishers*
1 London Bridge Street, London SE1 9GF

farshore.co.uk

HarperCollins*Publishers*
Macken House, 39/40 Mayor Street Upper Dublin 1, D01 C9W8, Ireland

ISBN 978 0 00 865176 3
Printed and bound in the UK using 100% renewable electricity at CPI Group (UK) Ltd
1

THE SUPER Sunny MURDER CLUB

Farshore

Edited by
SERENA PATEL & ROBIN STEVENS
Illustrated by HARRY WOODGATE

CONTENTS

ROBIN STEVENS

THE MURDER AT MYSTERY AND MAYHEM

TOP SECRET

PROPERTY OF THE SUPER SUNNY MURDER CLUB

THE MURDER AT MYSTERY AND MAYHEM

By Robin Stevens

That was the first time I met Why. We'd only been in Stow-in-the-Grove for three hours when my mum dragged me into Mystery and Mayhem, looking for another one of her *really important books*.

My mum is doing a PhD, which means she hasn't left school even though she's very old (forty-five – I'm eleven, I haven't left school either). She's obsessed with someone called E. Ellison Beckett, who is even older (one hundred and thirty-seven, technically dead) and wrote murder-mystery stories and books about *real* crimes, way back before the internet was even invented and you couldn't just Google any crime you wanted. My mum's spent so long talking and reading and thinking about E. Ellison Beckett that she's somehow managed to make the *extremely awesome crimes* E. Ellison wrote about seem completely boring.

1

So she was in Mystery and Mayhem – and in Stow-on-the-Grove, and I was in Stow-on-the-Grove even though it was my summer holidays and all my friends from school were in New York or Greece or Cornwall or somewhere good – because of E. Ellison Beckett. My dad's given up trying to do anything. He just goes on very long walks. Stow-on-the-Grove is a town (in the middle of nowhere!) full of second-hand bookshops, and Mystery and Mayhem's a shop that only sells books about horrible crimes. You see why Mum thought she'd like it.

She was looking for an E. Ellison Beckett biography she'd never been able to find before, and I was looking for absolutely anything interesting to happen at all – and that's when I met Why.

Mum gasped when she saw Mystery and Mayhem for the first time, and I did too. It's got murals all across the storefront – horrible hounds and demons with glowing red eyes and murderers rising out of banks of fog. Then you go inside and the murals follow you. There's a white chalk outline of a body splayed across the floor and the walls (at least the parts of the walls that aren't covered with shelves and shelves of fat red- and green-bound books) are painted with knives and poison bottles and the spooky heads of famous murder-mystery authors. I could see another room beyond the room we were in and a staircase going up to the left. Someone (Why's mum, I

found out later) was halfway up that stair.
books around. 'Welcome!' she called down to
just see one of her feet in a sensible boot on the
nothing else. 'Talk to Why! They'll help you!'

Why was sitting behind the till. They were wearing big, shiny aviator sunglasses and a Hawaiian-print shirt and chewing a toothpick. Their feet, in dirty Converse trainers, were up on the desk and they were reading a book called *The Case of the Drowning Duck*.

'Hi. I'm Why,' said Why, and I could see when they opened their mouth that one of their front teeth was chipped half off. From what I could see of their face behind their dark glasses and their scruffy hair, they looked about my age, maybe a year older.

'Hi,' I said shyly, rubbing at the sequins on my T-shirt so the picture changed from a unicorn to an ice cream. I felt underdressed.

'This is Gracie,' said my mum, who isn't good at noticing how people are feeling. 'I'm Marion. Where's your early-twentieth-century biography section?'

Why waved the toothpick at the smaller room behind the one we were in, and my mum rushed off, eyes gleaming. We were left alone.

'Hi,' I said again.

'Er, hi,' said Why, obviously bored of me. My stomach clenched.

'I can do three backflips in a row,' I said, because I can.

'Nice,' said Why. 'I tried to climb over a roof in the dark.'

'Did you do it?' I asked.

'Mostly,' said Why, pointing to their missing tooth with a shrug. 'Hey, do you want to kidnap a cat?'

It turned out the cat belonged to the shop across the road – 'And also to us!' said Why angrily. 'We share him! But Mr Novak's locked him in his back room and he won't let him out. I've been trying to get him all week. That's why I climbed the roof, to get in through the top window. But it hasn't worked.'

They stood guard while I wriggled through the tiny window at the back of the other store (I'm a gymnast, I'm quite good at it), where I found an enormous black and white cat asleep on a chair. I shoved him through the window into Why's arms as he hissed furiously, and then I climbed out after him. I think I left some sequins on the windowsill.

'This is Cain,' said Why happily, rubbing their cheek against the cat's face. 'Brilliant. All I needed was a partner in crime. Hey, you're not going home, are you?'

I blushed. 'I'm here for a week,' I said. 'On holiday.'

'To *here*?' said Why sceptically.

I said, 'I know,' and we both grinned at each other.

'It's not so bad,' said Why. 'If you like books.'

'I do actually like books,' I admitted.

And that's how Why and I became friends.

And then there was a murder.

When I got a call from the Mystery and Mayhem shop telephone on our third day in Stow-on-the-Grove (Why's still not allowed a mobile of their own), I was expecting Why to tell me to come over for tea. But instead they yelled, 'Gracie, there's been a murder!' and hung up the phone.

I thought it was a game. I said, 'Mum, Dad, I'm going to see Why. I'll be back in an hour.'

Mum was reading a book called *Crime and its Detection* that smelled of mould, and didn't look up. Dad was cooking in the kitchen. 'Are they all right?' he called out to me.

'Fine!' I said. 'See you soon!' Then I put on my flip-flops and grabbed my phone and went running down the street.

When I got to Mystery and Mayhem, I still thought it was a game. There was white-and-blue police tape across the front door, and someone in a police uniform walking about inside. Why was waiting for me at the front door. They had on a grey trench coat that was too big for them, and too hot for the day, and they were chewing on their toothpick.

'Hey, Why. I didn't know there was a murder mystery on today!' I said.

'There isn't,' said Why. 'There's been an actual murder, like I said.'

'Oh!' I said, feeling stupid. 'Really?'

'*Really*,' said Why. 'Someone's actually dead!'

'Well, what are we going to do about it?' I asked.

'We're going to detect it, of course,' said Why with a shrug. 'First, let me tell you what happened.'

But before I get into that, I need to tell you some more things about the bookshop.

The first thing to say is that Why's mum runs it. She's renting the shop from Mr Novak across the road, whose bookshop is much bigger and nicer and not as full of dusty mannequins and fake knives and paintings of ghosts. He's really mean about Mystery and Mayhem, because he'd rather the space was filled with a *normal* store that sold *normal* books to *normal* customers (which means people who aren't like my mum). Mrs Why (her name's Petronella) doesn't care at all about being normal, or about paying the rent on time, but her assistant Sadie is always trying to keep Mr Novak happy and keep customers coming into the shop. She re-shelves the books so the ones with titles like *The Bloody Murder at Hangman's House* aren't as obvious, and she puts bouquets of fake flowers in the window (around the actual knife used in the 1985 film adaptation of E. Ellison Beckett's book *Death at Last*). She even bakes cupcakes decorated with tiny little spun-sugar magnifying glasses and hands them out to people.

The second thing to say is that Mystery and Mayhem is actually more popular than Mr Novak thinks. If you are weird, like my mum, you've heard all about it. Some people come from other countries just to visit the shop, because the weirdest thing about it, weirder than the painting of the Hound of the Baskervilles with blood dripping from its fangs, or the life-sized cardboard cut-out of E. Ellison Beckett's detective, Thomas Smoke, is that it isn't on the internet. Like, at all. It's not on any social media because Mrs Why doesn't like technology. It doesn't even have a website. So if you want to buy a book – and it does have some of the rarest books in the world, written for people who are weird like my mum – you have to actually come to Stow-on-the-Grove to look for it. And that means that people do. They never know what they're going to find, but they do know that if they don't buy it that day, it probably won't be there again. It'll be gone forever. This makes everyone who's weird like my mum *really* weird about Mystery and Mayhem.

And the last thing you should know is that Mystery and Mayhem has two rooms on the ground floor. Between them is a staircase that goes up to another room on the first floor. The staircase is decorated with even stranger stuff – a display of weapons, and a mannequin sitting at a tea table set with poisoned cakes and chocolates and cups of tea, and a box full of fake body parts, and photos of famous houses where murders happened, and a quote from Thomas Smoke: *The truth is always there, and if you ignore what you think you know, you will see it.*

There's a storeroom on the first floor, on the other side of the stairs, where all of the extra books are kept. That's where Sadie and Mrs Why and Why go to take breaks when they're working. Customers can't get in there. The only way in or out of the shop is the main door downstairs at the front. If you're up on the first floor, the only way out is to come down the stairs – or jump from the window, I suppose, but that's a bit much.

The reason I'm saying all this is because of what Why told me. You need to know what I knew then, otherwise this won't make sense.

It all happened that morning. A customer came in, right after the shop opened at nine. He was a collector, one of those people who came from another country to buy murder books, and he'd been in Stow-on-the-Grove for days because he'd heard that Mrs Why was about to get in a first edition of a really special book. And that day she did. She unpacked it and the customer, Mr Rustin, looked at it and he wanted it. Of course he did!

But then he asked the price, and Mrs Why told him (a lot of money!), and he got upset. He said he'd have to think about it – even though *obviously* he wanted it. There wasn't another book like this in the whole world. He went over to Mr Novak's shop across the road, but Mrs Why and Sadie both saw him peering out through the glass longingly at them like Cain when he was stuck in Mr Novak's back room.

It all got too much for him at nine thirty, and Mr Rustin came back into Mystery and Mayhem, along with a tourist who wanted to look at the Agatha Christie section. The book was sitting behind the till, and Mr Rustin asked if he could take it upstairs, to look at it and decide if he wanted to buy it. Mrs Why said yes, because he wasn't exactly going to be able to run away with it, was he? So he took the book upstairs to have a read. There's a big comfy chair with a reading light up there, which you need this summer. It keeps on raining like it's not summer at all.

Mrs Why had to go then, because she had a meeting with her bank about the rent, which Mr Novak was putting up again. She left Sadie in the shop, organising the ghost story section and making a new display. Why stopped by at about ten – it wasn't their day to help, but they wanted to take another book to read, and then they started talking to Sadie about the ending of *The Swifts*. Then Mrs Why came back, just before ten thirty, feeling anxious about the rent, and Why wandered off into the village to see Mrs Patel's dog, who'd just had puppies. Mr Rustin was still upstairs, chatting to someone on the phone.

Sadie'd already tidied up the shop, and sorted out the till, and made the new window display and taken nice photos of it to upload on her own Instagram (she's very efficient and very good with technology for an adult). Mrs Why was just beginning to look through a new box of books that'd come in from the wholesalers, Cain sniffing around her, and Sadie had just gone out to get coffee – when they both heard the most horrible noise from upstairs.

It was like a scream, but the worst scream either of them had ever heard in their lives. It trailed off into a howl and then a horrible gurgle. Sadie ran back inside – she was only halfway down the street – and she and Mrs Why looked at each other, and then Sadie threw down her phone and Mrs Why dropped the book she was holding and they both raced for the stairs.

Sadie got up them first – I told you she's efficient. Mrs Why came panting up behind her. The light was off in the upstairs room – the lamp had been knocked over – and the chair was pushed sideways. And on the floor behind the chair was Mr Rustin's body.

Sadie rushed over and knelt next to him. He was very

still. Mrs Why stood in the doorway gasping in horror, the book in her arms (she'd found it on the floor, just beside the door) and Sadie looked up and said, 'Quick, Petronella – go get Mr Novak! He's hurt!'

'Why Mr Novak?' I asked at this point, and Why said, 'He knows first aid. Sadie didn't know what had happened – she just found him on the floor and thought he'd fallen over. So anyway, Mum ran off to get Mr Novak.'

Mrs Why went running down the stairs and across the street and pounded on Mr Novak's door – which was silly since the shop was open. She scared the customers and then had to explain that someone had fallen down in her bookshop. But she couldn't find Mr Novak. It was like something in a horror film – she was looking and looking, and she couldn't find him. He wasn't in any of the normal places he should have been and she was getting more and more panicky.

'Why didn't she just call an ambulance?' I asked, and Why said, 'Well, that's Mum. She doesn't think like that. She gets stuck on an idea, and since she'd been told to find Mr Novak she just kept on going until she found him. You know. Plus, she'd left her phone at home that morning.'

I nodded. My mum's like that too sometimes. She forgets to think normally, when she's focused on something, and sometimes she doesn't text me back all day. Once I asked her if I could go to a picnic with Evie's family at 9 a.m. and she sent back *yes* at 5 p.m., after we were already home again.

She finally found Mr Novak having a coffee at the Cuddly Kettle and told him what had happened. Mr Novak jumped up, spilling his coffee, and as soon as he'd cleaned himself off they both ran back to Mystery and Mayhem, where Sadie was still with Mr Rustin.

She'd turned him over and tried to give him CPR (she watched a video on her phone, but she couldn't really understand it) and even mouth to mouth ('Ugh!' said Why. 'He was really old!'), but none of it helped. Mr Rustin was dead.

Mrs Why kept sobbing that if she'd just found Mr Novak quicker he might have been able to save him. But then Mr Novak took a look at Mr Rustin's body and telephoned an ambulance, and when the ambulance crew arrived they took a look at Mr Rustin's body and telephoned the police, and when the police arrived and took a look at Mr Rustin's body they turned to Mrs Why and said, 'This man has been murdered.'

Which was when Why came back from looking at the puppies. ('They weren't even very good!' they said angrily. 'Their eyes weren't open yet, so they just looked like little sausages with legs. And I missed a murder!')

'How did the police know he'd been murdered?' I asked, and Why said, 'Because he was strangled. You can tell.'

'That's disgusting,' I said. I knew about strangulation from my mum's books, but I wish I didn't.

'Anyway, that's why I've got my coat on,' said Why, sweating in it. For once it wasn't raining. 'This is my detection coat, and we're going to detect, Gracie.'

It always means something, when someone says your name. It feels special. I looked at Why, with their hands shoved into their coat pockets and their big sunglasses on their nose, and I said, 'All right, Why. Let's detect.'

So we went to the Cuddly Kettle to plan our next steps, and to find out more about Mr Rustin. I got out my notebook with a pineapple on it, and my pen that looks like a dragon, and wrote down:

THE MURDER OF MR RUSTIN

'Time of death: 11 a.m. ish,' said Why, chewing on their toothpick intently. 'Place of death: the first floor of Mystery and Mayhem. Method of death: STRANGULATION.'

'How do you spell "strangulation"?' I asked, writing.

'Are they making you do a murder-mystery play?' Joel from the Cuddly Kettle asked me as he brought over our hot chocolate.

'Joel, this is real life,' said Why, pushing their sunglasses up their nose. 'Mr Rustin's been murdered.'

'No!' said Joel, putting down the hot chocolate with

a crash. 'He's been coming in here all week. What happened? Who did it?'

'That's what we're trying to work out,' explained Why. 'Do you have any leads?'

'No, apart from he's been coming in here all week,' said Joel. 'And I didn't do it. I've been here all morning. I've got an alibi. Oh, listen – I did see him talking to Mr Novak earlier, just after we opened. Mr Novak came over to his table and they got really serious. I heard Mr Novak say that he had something to give him, he just needed to wait, and then I didn't hear any more.'

'So Mr Novak's a suspect,' said Why, when Joel had rushed away to tell the other regulars about the murder. 'If they were talking this morning. Who else? Sadie and Mum have alibis, don't they? They were both downstairs when the murder happened.'

'You know,' said someone at the table next to us. We turned to look – it was a tourist, a woman with long hair and an intense expression. 'Strangulation is a crime of passion. It takes a really long time to do it, so you've gotta *want* to. It means the murderer knew the victim!'

'Hello,' said Why, narrowing their eyes. 'I'm Why and this is Gracie. Who are you?'

'Chelsea Green,' said the woman, sticking out her hand. 'I'm from Long Island. I'm here on vacation and I couldn't help but overhear what you two said. About strangulation. For your play.'

'It's not a play!' said Why crossly.

'There's been an actual murder,' I explained. 'At Mystery and Mayhem.'

'Really?' said Chelsea Green. 'I was in there this morning. Wait – who's been murdered?'

'Mr Rustin,' I said.

'No!' gasped Chelsea. 'Archie? But – I know him! We're friends – it's a small world, collecting detective fiction. This is awful! Excuse me –'

And she jumped up from her chair and ran out of the Cuddly Kettle.

Why and I turned to each other. 'She was the tourist who came in this morning. She's definitely a suspect!' said Why. I could see the chip in their tooth.

'She's really suspicious,' I agreed. 'Maybe she wanted the book he was going to buy!'

Suspects, I wrote down. *Mr Novak. Chelsea Green.*

Then something hit me. I know a lot about murders, way more than I should. My mum says it's fine, and my dad says it's unfortunate. I think it's useful, especially given the situation we were in.

Mr Rustin had been up on the first floor. Sadie and Mrs Why had seen him go up, and Why and Sadie had heard him on the telephone, and Sadie had just left Mrs Why when they heard the murder. That gave them all alibis (even Why, which I was glad about), but it also meant that there couldn't have been anyone else up there with him. And Why'd told me that Sadie and Mrs Why went running upstairs (up the only stairs in the shop!) as fast as they could to find his body on its own.

Which meant that this wasn't just a normal murder.

'Why!' I said. 'This is a locked-room murder mystery!'

If you don't know, which you might not if you don't have a weird mum like I do, a locked-room mystery means a crime that seems impossible. The dead body's alone in a room that's locked (usually) or at least very hard to get in to (always). Maybe the only door or window is being watched all the time. Maybe the room's totally sealed. So how did someone get in? How could the crime have possibly happened? That's the question.

And that's the crime we had to solve.

'We have to go look at the crime scene now!' said Why, and they jumped up from our table and went running out of the Cuddly Kettle, just like Chelsea Green had. I followed them. Then I ran past them, because I'm a much faster runner than they are. They've got short legs and arms and I'm a gymnast. Also, they were wearing their big coat, which slowed them down even more.

So I got to the door of Mystery and Mayhem first.

It was still blocked off by white-and-blue police tape, and there were people walking around inside.

Which is how I ended up clinging on to the gutter of Mystery and Mayhem while Why waved up at me from the street. We'd stolen Sadie's phone (Why's mum won't let them have one yet, like I said) and Sadie's fancy headphones that stick into your ears without wires, and Why had Sadie's phone up to their mouth, hissing instructions at me. I knew they were really mad they couldn't come with me, but no one could possibly get up to the window unless they were *extremely* good at climbing, like I am. Which really did make this a locked-room mystery.

The window was a tiny bit open, so I pushed it up with my foot and wiggled inside. Luckily, it was empty. Not so luckily, Mr Rustin's body was still there.

'WHAT CAN YOU SEE?' said Why in my ear.

I got out my phone and started to take photos. I feel bad for the detectives in old murder mysteries, because they have to remember what they see, when they're sneaking around places they shouldn't be. But I've got everything stored in the cloud. I looked away while I took a photo of Mr Rustin, and then I looked at the photo, because a photo's easier to look at than real life. He was sprawled out on the floor, head towards the window and feet towards the door. He was staring at the ceiling, but that didn't mean anything. Sadie had given him CPR, so she'd moved the body.

The old velvet chair was over on its side, like someone had dived at Mr Rustin and knocked it over, and the lamp had been pushed off the little table next to the reading chair. Its fringed shade was tipped sideways, but its bulb, when I looked, hadn't broken. It was still plugged in to the wall with a big, thick white plug that looked strange in the old-fashioned book-filled room. It's got dark green walls with more creepy murals, and it hasn't been dusted for a long time.

Then I saw something next to the lamp's plug. I said the room hadn't been dusted, but there was a mark in the dust, like something circular and flat, a bit bigger than my fist, had been put down on it and then moved away again. I took a picture of it and said to Why, 'I've found a clue.'

'WHAT IS IT?' hissed Why. I described it and they said, 'Take pictures. Hey, Gracie! Careful! Someone's coming! You need to get out!'

I panicked. I might sound like I knew what I was doing, but actually I hate breaking rules. It makes me feel sick. I shoved my phone into my pocket, ran to the window as fast as I could and swung back out onto the gutter, sliding down so fast that I hurt my hands.

A white van had pulled up, and some people dressed

all in white suits like thumbs in gloves were getting out. 'Hey!' one of them yelled at me. 'What are you doing?'

'*Run*,' said Why to me. We ran.

I showed Why all the photos I'd taken, and we added my clues to our document.

'Now what do we do?' I asked.

'Are you writing a book?' said Dad, peering at my notes. Why and I were sitting at the kitchen table of our rented house, since Why's mum was at the police station helping the police with their enquiries. Why had chewed through three toothpicks so I could tell they were worried. 'Here, what do you think of these flapjacks?'

'No, it's real life,' I said, chewing on the flapjack, which was pretty good. Dad's got good at cooking while Mum's been working on her PhD. 'There's been a murder.'

'Not you too!' said Dad, and I could tell he still didn't believe me. 'Well, even I know this. You've got suspects and clues here, so what you need now are some motives. How about a jealous ex? Or revenge? Or money? Or –'

'Thanks, Dad,' I said, sighing.

'He's right, though,' said Why, when Dad had gone back to his cooking.

'I know,' I said. That was the worst part.

'Chelsea Green knew Mr Rustin,' said Why. 'Maybe

he did something awful to her – stole a book she wanted from her – and she killed him out of revenge? She knows loads about crime; she proved it. So she's a good suspect. And Mr Novak might have wanted to stop Mr Rustin from buying a book from Mum. Or maybe he wanted Mr Rustin to buy one of *his* books, so he tried to persuade him, and he wouldn't, so he *killed* him.'

'I don't know,' I said doubtfully. 'He didn't really know him, did he? Why would you kill someone you don't know?'

Why made a face. 'It's not great,' they said. 'Gracie, what about Mum? She was alone in the shop when it happened. What if the police think it was her?'

'She wouldn't have had time!' I said. 'Strangulation takes a while, that's what Chelsea Green said. Actually, how did anyone have time? Your mum and Sadie heard the noise and then they went running upstairs immediately. No one was in the room with Mr Rustin. How did it even happen?'

'That,' said Why, chewing on their fifth toothpick, 'is a very good question. It must have happened, because he's dead, but *how*? It's impossible.'

I took a deep breath. '*The truth is always there –*' I started.

'*Don't* say it,' said Why. 'Fine. It's a locked-room mystery, and we both know that they're not really impossible at all. They can't be, unless a ghost did it, and I don't believe in ghosts.'

'Don't you?' I asked.

'Not at all,' said Why. 'They're silly. So, if it wasn't a ghost, what else could have happened? It can't have been the window, because neither of our suspects are as good at climbing as you, and you almost didn't manage it. And it can't have been the stairs, because Mum was there and she didn't see anyone. Wait, so it *is* impossible!'

'It can't be!' I said, even though I kind of thought it might be. 'No, wait, what if – what if someone hid on the stairs? What if they hid . . . Why, I know! They might have hidden behind the mannequin! Look, I took some photos of the top of the stairs and . . . it's moved, hasn't it? It wasn't in that position before?'

We both bent over my phone.

The mannequin's a man in a suit, with a hat and a beard that's always sort of falling off him. Before, he'd been positioned like he was about to drink a cup of poisoned tea, but now, in my photos, his arms were down on his lap, and his head was listing a little on one side. He'd *definitely* been moved.

The top of the stairs is pretty dark, and if Mrs Why and Sadie were focused on getting into the top room on the left, they wouldn't have looked right at all. Someone could absolutely have moved the mannequin and sat there in his place, holding still while they rushed past.

I thought this was it.

'Well, if we're looking for someone who was hiding at the top of the stairs *after* the murder, it can't be Mr Novak,' said Why. 'He was in the Cuddly Kettle when Mum came to find him. That means – we've solved it! It has to be Chelsea Green!'

So off we went to confront Chelsea Green, just like in all the detective novels.

We were both very excited. Why was wiggling in their detective coat.

But Chelsea Green, when we found her in Lost in a Good Book, just laughed at us when we told her what she'd done.

'That's so smart!' she said. 'It should be in a book. But, sweeties –'

'I'm not a sweetie,' said Why.

'– *kids*, there's no way I had time to do that. I came by this morning, sure, but right after that I had to head off again. My wife broke her arm hiking yesterday evening and she's been in hospital all night. I went to check in on her – bring her some nicer breakfast – and I'd just gotten back to the Cuddly Kettle when I saw you two writing your play. It'll all be on camera at the hospital, if you want to check it out. That's what I told the police. I'm sorry. I mean, I'm not sorry, because I didn't kill him. But you know what I mean.'

'That's our suspects, all gone!' said Why, when we were outside again. 'So it's impossible again! Maybe I should believe in ghosts.'

'You shouldn't,' I said, although I wasn't sure I was right. 'This has to have been a person.'

'But no one could have done it! There isn't time!' said Why.

And I realised they were right. There *wasn't* time. In the story Why had told me, the scream had happened and then a minute later Mrs Why and Sadie had run up the stairs to find Mr Rustin on the floor. But it takes ages to strangle someone, a lot more than a minute. No one could possibly have killed Mr Rustin and left again before Mrs Why and Sadie arrived. There was something wrong.

As I was thinking that, Sadie came running up to us. 'Why!' she called. 'There you are! Can you come with me? Your mum needs you down at the station.'

Why looked at me as they were led away, and I felt my stomach clench with anxiety. What if it *was* Why's mum, somehow? What if it wasn't, and someone was framing her? What could I do?

I went home, because I couldn't think of anywhere else

to go. Dad was in the kitchen making stew for dinner. It's so rainy this summer that's all you want to eat.

I got out my phone and started scrolling through the photos of the crime scene again.

I zoomed in to the circular dustless gap on the floor next to the big white plug socket. There was a snaky patch next to it that might have been a cord . . .

'Oh, I want one of those,' said Dad behind me. I jumped.

'One of what?' I asked. 'Dust?'

'Don't be silly, Gracie. A smart plug! In the picture, there. The big white one. You can turn things plugged into it on and off with your phone, if you've got the app. It's really clever.'

And then, just like *that*, I knew the answer.

I ran all the way back to Mystery and Mayhem, my flip-flops splashing in puddles. The tape was still up outside, but the door was open and Why was sitting behind the till. They were wiping their eyes, but when they looked up and saw it was me they dropped their dark glasses down over their face.

'What do you want?' they asked in a muffled voice.

'Why, I know what happened!' I cried. 'What's wrong?'

'Mum's been arrested,' said Why. 'They think she did

it. But she wouldn't have!'

'She didn't,' I said. 'She was framed. Sadie did.'

'No, she didn't!' said Why. 'She was outside when they heard the scream!'

'I know,' I said. 'But she was on her phone, wasn't she? That's how she did it.'

This is what I worked out. If you're like Mrs Why, and you hate technology, you won't know this. But if you're like my dad, you will. If you're good at technology, you can connect up your phone to smart speakers and smart plugs, and then you can play noises and turn lights on and off whenever you want.

And that's what Sadie did. She was alone in the shop for a while, remember? After Mrs Why had gone to her meeting and before Why arrived to get their book. In that time, she went upstairs and got Mr Rustin to hide in that storeroom on the other side of the stairs. Then she went into the main upstairs room and set up the smart plug and the smart speaker. The speaker could play noises she'd pre-recorded, of Mr Rustin walking around and talking on the phone, and the plug could switch the light on and off. And she did something else too – she took the mannequin from the stairs and laid it face down on the floor.

So everything was ready when Mrs Why came back. Sadie pretended to leave, and then she turned off the light on her phone, and played a noise of screaming and crashing. Then she ran upstairs with Mrs Why, crouched over the mannequin and told Mrs Why to go and get help. Then, once Mrs Why had gone, she put the mannequin back, unplugged the speaker and called the real Mr Rustin into the room, where she strangled him so she could be standing over an actual dead body when Mrs Why came back. She must have forgotten about the smart plug though.

I was really proud of myself.

But Why looked confused.

'It doesn't make sense,' they said. 'What if Mum had found Mr Novak faster? Sadie wouldn't have had time to do all that. And why would Mr Rustin just sit in the storeroom? He'd have heard the noise.'

'Well,' I said, because that was true. 'Well –'

Then Why's eyes widened. 'Unless,' they said, '*Mr Novak helped?* He wasn't in his shop, was he? He was all the way across town in the Cuddly Kettle. And then he spilled his coffee when Mum found him, so he couldn't come back with her quickly. What if he was giving Sadie more time? And what you said about the recording – Sadie needed to record a man's voice talking, so it would sound like Mr Rustin. That might have been Mr Novak!'

We stared at each other.

'But what about Mr Rustin?' I asked. 'Why didn't he come out of the storeroom when he heard the noise?'

And Why suddenly grinned. 'Cupcakes,' they said. 'Sadie's cupcakes. I bet she put poison in one of them and gave it to Mr Rustin. It knocked him out, and she dragged him into the storeroom until Mum was out of the way. Then she brought him back out and strangled him. And she and Mr Rustin did it so that Mum would be framed, and they could take over the shop together and make it *respectable*. Gracie, we did it!'

'We did it, Why!' I cried. 'We worked it out!'

And we had. When we told the police, they didn't believe us at first – adults never do – but then they tested Mr Novak's blood and found a sedative (something to send you to sleep) in his body, and more sedative in the remains of a cupcake in the shop's bin. And they found text messages between Mr Novak and Sadie on her phone, and voice recordings, and a smart speaker in the boot of her car. She'd just forgotten to take out the smart plug, like I thought, or to smash the bulb of the lamp the way it would have broken if it had really fallen over during a struggle. So they had everything they needed to arrest them. And Mrs Why got released, and she and Why came round to our holiday rental and told my mum and dad all of this, and they couldn't believe their ears.

'I solved it, really,' said my dad. 'See? Technology's important, which is why I should definitely buy one of those smart plugs.'

'*No,*' said my mum. 'If anything, this proves that having a good grounding in the classics is what's important. Look at what Gracie's done!'

Why and I beamed at each other. 'Can we stay longer?' I asked.

'I thought you didn't want to be here!' said my mum.

'I changed my mind,' I said. 'After all, you never know what might happen next.'

MURDER
ON THE
DANCEFLOOR

TOP SECRET

MURDER ON THE DANCEFLOOR

By Abiola Bello

3.30 P.M.

Roe swayed as she got off Inferno, a high-speed roller coaster and her favourite ride at Astro Towers. She was having the best day ever! A whole day on rides with her best friends and dance crew, Masquerade. Roe still couldn't believe that Masquerade had been invited to perform at Astro Towers' 20th anniversary! It was a massive deal. Tomorrow she would be dancing in front of thousands of people. And the showcase was to be live-streamed on YouTube, which meant that the whole world could see her dancing!

'What shall we go on next?' her twin Roman asked, looking around the packed theme park.

'How about the bumper cars?' Justin suggested. He was the tallest in the group and was able to spot the rides the quickest.

'I need a second,' Maria said, her olive-skinned face looking a little green. David handed her his bottle of water, which she took gratefully.

Finally feeling balanced again, Roe looked at her phone. They only had thirty minutes until they had to meet their dance teacher, Jada, for the performers' meeting. Even though just being here was amazing, the best bit was that Duke Collins was the headline act! Masquerade had been huge fans of Duke ever since he won *Britain's Got Talent* with his slick dance moves. Roe and Roman would spend hours trying to copy his complex floorwork and his overall swag. He had cancelled his last few performances due to being unwell but tomorrow they would finally see him perform in person.

So far they had managed three roller coasters and a maze of horrors since they had arrived that morning – which was pretty good considering how long the queues had been – as well as cheesy chips, Coke and lots of ice water. It was the hottest day of the year and Roe had already sweated out her T-shirt. She had even caught a tan, which made her brown skin a shade darker. Roe glanced at Maria, who was still looking poorly, and figured another roller coaster would be the end of her. Then she spotted the perfect ride . . .

'What about No Man's Land? I think it's where you have to beat the zombies.'

'I'll sit this one out, but you guys go,' Maria said.

'I'll stay with her.' David shuddered. 'I hate zombies.'

They waved goodbye and Roe, Roman, August and Justin went to join the short queue.

'Do you think it's super scary?' August asked Roe. She looked nervously at the dark tunnel they had to walk through.

But before Roe could respond, a loud female voice behind them said, 'How did this happen? The email said I was meant to be the headline act, not Duke.'

She turned around to see two short mixed-raced girls with big, curly dark hair wearing matching crop tops, baggy combat trousers and high-top trainers. Roe recognised them instantly. They were the Fallon sisters – Aaliyah and Asia. Both of them were amazing professional dancers who had performed at some of the same shows as Masquerade. At first glance anyone would think they were twins, but Aaliyah was some years older.

'I know,' Asia said. 'We have to talk to Mr Stewart about this. I thought Duke was ill?'

'Duke's not even that talented.' Aaliyah screwed up her face. 'Someone's going to pay for that mistake.'

Roe was surprised by Aaliyah's tone. She always came across so bubbly and fun on social media. The Fallon sisters noticed Roe and her friends staring at them and Aaliyah raised her eyebrows.

'Can we help you?' she snapped.

Roe quickly spun around and the others followed suit, but she could feel Aaliyah's eyes boring into her back.

No Man's Land wasn't as scary or fun as Roe hoped. It didn't help that the sisters ended up being in the same group as them and Aaliyah spent the whole time moaning about Duke and the performance tomorrow. Asia seemed nice enough but nothing she could say could calm Aaliyah down.

Roe was grateful to get away from them, and thankfully Maria was feeling a lot better when they got back. The group all headed over to meet Jada for the performers' meeting. They arrived at the massive stage where several acts were waiting around, and Roe was surprised to see Jada talking to the Fallon sisters.

'Guys, over here!' Jada waved them over.

'Is she friends with *them*?' Justin frowned.

'She probably just knows them from dance,' Roe said. There was no way her lovely dance teacher could be anything more than acquaintances with the sisters.

'Duke isn't even supposed to be here,' Roe heard Aaliyah say as they got closer. 'Funny how he's cancelled every performance, but somehow he's OK for this one. Ridiculous!'

'This is my crew,' Jada said quickly, her hazel eyes sparkled in the sun. 'You lot know Aaliyah and Asia.

They're dancing tomorrow as well.'

Masquerade waved back politely. Studying them closely, Roe could see more differences between them. Asia had longer hair and Aaliyah had a narrower face.

'Twins?' Aaliyah asked, pointing at Roe and Roman, who did look more alike today with their locs tied up into a bun and the same white T-shirt with jeans.

'Yep, although I'm the eldest,' Roman said, puffing out his chest.

'You wish,' Roe hissed. She was two minutes older.

Asia laughed and Aaliyah gave them a strained smile. Roe wondered if she also had an issue with twins.

All the performers were called to the front of the stage, where the organiser Sophie Cruz was running through tomorrow's event. It was a mix of singers and dancers. Roe tuned out as she searched for Duke Collins. She gasped when she spotted him near the back in dark sunglasses, a baggy T-shirt and basketball shorts. Despite the hot summer, his skin was pale – almost ghostly. He always had an athletic build, but he looked skinnier than usual. Maybe he was still recovering from being unwell.

Duke was looking down at his phone. A Black lady with her curls in a bun handed him a water bottle with his initials on and Duke began to drink. Roe recognised her from Duke's social media – his manager, Annie. She used to be a really great dancer until she injured her back when she was teaching a dance workshop and had to retire.

'Guys, he's there,' Roe whispered. 'Don't all look at once!'

But of course everyone in Masquerade turned at the same time. Duke at that point lifted his head and gave them a weak smile.

'It's Duke!' August squealed, making Jada shush her, but it also drew the attention of the Fallon sisters and Aaliyah glared at him.

'He looks really ill,' Maria whispered. 'I hope he's OK to dance tomorrow.'

'See you all at the performers' party tonight!' Sophie finished and everyone applauded her.

Roe was determined to speak to Duke at the party and hopefully get a selfie.

4.30 P.M.

After the meeting, Jada told them to go upstairs to their room and rest until the party later that evening.

'Absolutely no trouble, guys,' Jada said, eyeing them all. 'We are guests, so let's be professional.'

Roe was sharing with August and Maria. Maria wanted a quick nap and August wanted to finish the series she was watching. But Roe was giddy with excitement about talking to Duke Collins later and couldn't relax. She wondered if Roman wanted to sneak out and try and find Duke's room? They could just say hello . . .

Roe knocked on the boys' bedroom a few doors down but when she opened the door, they were too busy playing an online fighting game.

'I'll catch you later,' Roman said, not even bothering to look up.

Roe sighed. She knew Jada wouldn't be happy if she was walking around by herself. Just as she was heading back to her room, from the corner of her eye Roe saw someone in a black hoodie walk hurriedly across the corridor. Roe frowned – *Who was that?* It was way too hot to be in a jumper. Without thinking, Roe ran along the corridor, determined to see the person, but when she got to the end and looked from left to right, no one was there. Something gold sparkled on the floor. Roe picked it up and studied it. It was a gold necklace with an *A* on it. She frowned and pocketed it.

'I think I might give the party tonight a miss,' a deep voice said from around the corner.

Roe put her head round to see Duke and Annie walking towards one of the bedroom doors. He was so close! On the floor was a pretty bouquet of blue and white blossoms.

'Must be from a fan.' Annie picked the flowers up from

the floor. 'Come to the party for a little bit.'

'I just feel a bit light-headed. Ugh! And my stomach's bubbling like I'm going to vomit . . .'

'Oh no, really?' Annie said. 'Maybe you haven't eaten enough today. I'll order you some soup and, don't worry, I'll make sure it's just right.'

Duke smiled. 'Thanks, Annie. What would I do without you?'

They went inside the bedroom. Roe prayed that Duke would make it to the party tonight.

5.30 P.M.

When Maria woke up from her nap, Roe told her and August about the person in black. Then she handed Maria the necklace, because Maria's mother owned a jeweller's and Maria spent lots of time there.

Maria eyeballed it and said, 'I need a glass of water.'

August hurried to the bathroom and returned with an empty glass that they used to hold their toothbrushes, but it was now filled with water. Maria dropped the necklace into the glass and it sank to the bottom.

'It's real gold!' Maria said. She pulled a lock of curly hair from the water that had unravelled from the chain.

'Well, that should be easy to narrow down,' August said, looking at the hair strand. 'There's only a few performers here with curly hair like mine.'

Roe couldn't help but think of Aaliyah's dark curls as she took back the necklace. *But why would she be creeping around all dressed in black?*

Someone knocked on the door and Roe put the necklace behind her back.

Jada poked her head round. 'Hey, girls, can you start getting ready for the party?'

'OK,' the girls chorused. Jada smiled and closed the door.

'Shouldn't we tell Jada about the necklace?' Maria asked.

'Hmm, not yet,' Roe said. Something in her gut told her that this necklace could be important and Roe's gut was never wrong.

6 P.M.

Roe, Maria and August walked with Jada and the rest of Masquerade down to the function room where the party was being held. Roe was in a yellow summer dress that looked beautiful against her dark skin. It was a nice change from wearing a T-shirt and shorts, although she kept her trainers on. The best part was the dress had pockets in the side so the necklace was safely tucked away.

They could hear the bass of the music before they even

entered the room, which was full of the performers, the organiser Sophie Cruz, as well as various other people who Roe assumed were the team working on the show. The DJ was in the corner and there were gold balloons everywhere with *20th Anniversary* printed on them, a very pretty floral wall, which would be perfect for pictures, and a table full of food and drink. The multicoloured disco lights made the room appear red then blue then green as it switched every other second.

'This is so cool!' Roe said.

'OK, guys.' Jada huddled them around her. She looked stunning in a pink floral jumpsuit and, like Roe, her dark skin had caught the sun. 'Make sure to eat some food, stay hydrated as it's very warm in here and be polite to everyone.'

'Yes, Jada,' Masquerade chorused.

'I'm gonna say hi to a few people. Do not wander off,' she said before she left.

'I want to film everything for my nonna,' August said, getting out her phone.

'This party is sick!' Roman said, looking around. He eyed the table greedily. 'I want to check out the food.'

'I'll come,' Roe said, not because she was hungry but because the table with food and drink had a great view of the dance floor. Maybe she could see if someone was looking for a necklace. She spotted Aaliyah and Asia who were talking to Annie and Mr Stewart, the manager of

Astro Towers, who was in a black suit even though it was boiling hot.

The spread was amazing – chicken drumsticks, mini burgers, a range of sandwiches, crispy halloumi sticks, sausage rolls, fruit, biscuits, cake, crisps and jugs of ice-cold water, juice and wine for the adults. Roe watched amused as her brother loaded up his plastic plate. As she reached for the juice her hand clashed against someone else's.

'I'm so sorry,' the deep voice said.

Roman made a weird noise beside her as Roe turned around and caught her breath. It was Duke Collins! He was wearing a blue shirt that matched his eyes and smart black trousers, but he looked exhausted and had dark circles under his eyes. In his hand was the water bottle from earlier.

'I'm Duke.' Duke held out a hand.

Roe swallowed and shook it. 'I'm Monroe but everyone calls me Roe. And this is my twin brother Roman.'

'We're such big fans of yours!' Roman held out his plate to him. 'Want some?'

Duke smiled. 'Oh, thanks!' He took a crispy halloumi stick. 'Being a twin must be very cool.'

'Hmm, it's OK,' Roe and Roman said at the same time before pointing at each other and shouting, 'Jinx!' which made Duke laugh.

August walked towards them, and they waved as she filmed them before she wandered off.

Duke frowned and mumbled to himself, 'Why am I over here again?'

Roe and Roman looked at each other. Roe remembered that he had complained about feeling light-headed. Maybe that was affecting his memory.

Duke continued to look confused and then suddenly laughed and hit his forehead. 'I can't even remember. It must be the heat making me confused. Hey, you're part of Masquerade, right? Jada's group?'

He knows who we are! Roe wanted to scream out loud.

Duke ate the halloumi stick, closing his eyes as he savoured it. Roe had hundreds of questions for him but just then the Fallon sisters, Mr Stewart and Annie walked over. Annie had a plait on one side of her hair with blue and white flowers weaved into it.

'Duke,' Aaliyah said sharply, and Duke winced like he had been hit. 'I want to talk to you.'

'Please don't yell at him,' Annie said as she flashed a look at Aaliyah. 'Duke,' she said softly, almost like she was speaking to a child. 'There seems to be a problem – what are you eating?'

'My friend Roman gave me a snack.' Duke winked at Roman who grinned. 'What's up?'

'Duke, I'm so sorry,' Mr Stewart began until Aaliyah

huffed and said, 'You should be apologising to me!'

Roman began to fill their glasses up slowly so they could eavesdrop on the conversation, but everyone was talking over one another.

'OK, let's all have a drink and calm down,' Asia said but no one listened to her. Asia sighed and her eyes widened when she spotted Roe and Roman.

'We weren't listening,' Roman said quickly and Roe rolled her eyes. Honestly! Could he not play it cool?

Thankfully Asia smiled. 'Can you pass me a drink, please?' she asked and Roman gave her a glass of juice.

Words like 'traitor' and 'untalented' buzzed in the air and Duke closed his eyes with his face screwed up. It was the face Roe made whenever she had a pounding headache.

'This is ridiculous,' Annie snapped as she made her way over to the drinks.

'They're pretty.' Roe pointed at the flowers in Annie's hair. 'What are they?'

'Thanks.' Annie smiled. 'Hydrangeas. Are you two excited to perform tomorrow?'

'Yes! But I can't wait to see Duke. I know all of his routines,' Roman said excitedly.

'Maybe you should headline the show instead, Roman,' Roe teased and Roman laughed.

Annie looked curiously at the drinks already poured

but she didn't take one.

'What's wrong with the ones I made,' Roman whispered to Roe.

Roe shrugged. 'Grown-ups are weird sometimes.'

Aaliyah was still talking, Mr Stewart kept wiping his sweaty brow continuously and Duke stood in silence looking like he wanted to be anywhere else than there.

It was clear this argument wasn't going to end soon, and the last thing Roe needed was Jada seeing them so close to the commotion. So she grabbed Roman's hand, the plate of food he had made and led him to the dance floor to join the rest of Masquerade, who were oblivious to what had been going on as they had been dancing to song after song.

'Do you know the Randy J TikTok dance?' Justin challenged Roe.

'Duh!' Roe said, all thoughts of the argument forgotten.

Roe and Justin got in position and began doing the choreography and everyone was cheering them on. August was filming them with a massive grin on her face when suddenly her eyes went wide and she covered her mouth. Roe followed her gaze and her heart froze when she saw Duke Collins stumbling towards them, clutching his throat, like he was choking. His face had turned blue, his eyes bulging out of his head.

Duke caught Roe's eyes before he looked to her left

at Roman and pointed a shaky finger at him before he dropped a glass that smashed on the floor. Duke fell to his knees and collapsed right in the middle of the dance floor.

There was a moment when everything was still and then the hall erupted into screams. Mr Stewart was calling someone on his phone. Annie ran over to Duke with tears falling down her face. She bent down, cradled him and felt his pulse.

'He's dead!' she wailed. Then she looked up at Roman. 'And you poisoned him!'

6.30 P.M.

Everything happened so fast. Jada ordered them to go to their rooms, but then Mr Stewart intervened and said Roman had to stay because he was being accused of putting poison in Duke's drink and the police were on the way. Roman burst into tears and Roe's head was spinning.

Roman? Murder? Poison? None of it made any sense. *What would Mum and Dad say if Roman went to prison? Is he going to prison?*

'Roe, we have to go,' David said softly, tugging on her arm, but Roe shook her head.

'I can't leave him,' she protested.

'I'll sort this, Roe, I promise,' Jada said with a fierceness in her eyes. 'Just go to your room.'

Roe walked in a daze as David guided her out of the room and down the corridor. They all piled into the girls room. August and Maria were sniffling, their eyes red from crying, and there was a sombre mood in the room, but Roe couldn't sit still. She paced up and down trying to understand what had just happened and how Roman was in the firing line. All he had done was give Duke a snack, but Roman had eaten the snacks as well. He'd made drinks, but she had watched him so of course nothing was in them, and then they'd left to go dance with their friends. So why was Roman being accused of murder?

Roe felt a lump in her throat as she thought of her brother. He must be terrified.

'Roman didn't do this,' Justin said. His long legs stretched out as he sat on August's bed. 'Why would they think he did?'

'And poison! We're kids! How would we even get that?' Maria asked, shaking her head.

'Roe?' David called, and Roe stopped walking and looked at him. 'We need to help Roman. Can you tell us everything that happened?'

'I-I . . .' Roe began but suddenly her mind was blank. All she could think about was that the other half of her was in trouble and she needed to be there with him.

'Come on, Roe – think!' David said. 'We can't help him unless you tell us.'

David was right. Someone had poisoned Duke and there was no way her brother was getting accused of it. Roe nodded. She focused and remembered what had happened, which she relayed to everyone.

'It's obviously Aaliyah,' Justin said once Roe was finished. 'She's had it in for Duke since we got here.'

'But I didn't see her give him a drink,' Roe said. 'Actually, I didn't see anyone give Duke a drink.'

Everyone fell silent.

'Who did you see pour drinks apart from Roman?' Maria asked.

Roe closed her eyes as she tried to remember. 'No one.' She put her face in her hands. This couldn't be happening. Someone must have given Duke a poisonous drink, but who?

'Was there anything else weird that happened today?' Justin asked.

Roe shook her head but then she remembered. 'I saw someone in the corridor wearing a hoodie but I didn't see their face.'

August gasped. 'Where you found the *A* necklace! Do you still have it?'

Roe took the necklace out of her pocket.

David frowned. 'What's going on?'

Roe explained about the dark figure running in the corridor and seeing Duke earlier complain that he didn't feel well. 'I think it connects somehow.'

'I'm telling you – it's Aaliyah,' Justin said. 'Remember when we were at the rides, she said someone was going to pay for their mistake.'

'She said that?' David asked, surprised. 'Well, there we go. We need to tell Jada. The *A* necklace is Aaliyah's.'

'And we found that curly hair in the necklace chain,' Maria reminded them. 'It was probably Aaliyah's hair.'

'But it's not just Aaliyah here with curly hair and a name beginning with *A*,' Roe pointed out. 'Asia, Annie, even you, August.'

'It wasn't *me*!' August protested.

Roe sighed. 'Of course it's not! And why would Annie poison her own client? What I'm saying is we don't have any proof it's anyone.'

'Maybe we should sneak into Duke's room and see if we can find something?' Maria suggested and Roe stared at her surprised. Maria was always against doing anything that could get them in trouble. She looked down sadly. 'I don't want Roman to go to jail.'

'Nobody's going to jail,' Roe said fiercely, even though her heart was hammering. 'But I think that's a good idea, Maria.'

'I'll come with you,' Maria said, surprising Roe for the

second time that day. 'Guys, if Jada comes, cover for us.'

Roe and Maria walked the short walk up the corridor, and froze when they saw Asia walking slowly towards them, searching the floor. There was no way they could sneak into Duke's room now. Asia looked up when she saw them with worry in her eyes.

'Sorry, girls, but have either of you seen a gold *A* necklace? It's my sister's and she'll kill me if I've lost it.'

6.50 P.M.

'GUYS, YOU WILL NOT BELIEVE THIS!' Roe said as soon as they returned to the room, and then she explained what had happened. All of Masquerade's mouths dropped open.

'So it is Aaliyah,' Maria said. 'Thank God Asia believed us when we said we didn't have the necklace.'

Everyone began to talk at once. Roe's phone rang and *Mum* flashed up on her screen.

'One sec, guys.' Roe hurried to the bathroom and shut the door. 'Hi, Mum.'

'Roe! Jada called us. We're heading over now. Are you OK?'

Roe wanted to cry just hearing her mum's voice, but she knew that would only make her mum feel more scared. 'I'm just worried, but we all know Roman didn't do it and everyone will realise that as well.'

'Of course they will, baby. Just stay strong and me and Dad will be there soon. I love you.'

'Love you too, Mum. Bye.'

Roe hung up and when she went back into the room, only August was there waving at someone on her phone.

'Ciao, Nonna,' she said before she looked up at Roe. 'My grandma called so everyone stood outside so I could talk to her. Everything OK?'

'Yeah, my mum and dad are on the way.' Roe sat next to August and instantly rested her head on her shoulder. August's curly hair tickled her nose.

Roe glanced at August's phone and suddenly had an idea. 'Can we look at the Fallon sisters' Instagram? Let's see if we can see the necklace.'

'Good idea.' August pulled up their profile and they looked at picture after picture. 'There it is!'

Roe frowned. It was the *A* necklace but it wasn't on Aaliyah, it was on Asia. 'That's weird. Asia said it was her sister's necklace.'

'Maybe she borrowed it,' August suggested.

'Hmmm, maybe. She said to me and Maria that her sister would kill her if she lost it. I took it like her sister didn't know she had it.' Roe drummed her fingers on the bed. 'Let's see the footage you took of the party earlier? Maybe there's a clue somewhere?'

August pressed play and they watched it together. Most of it was just August grinning as she pointed stuff out.

Roe winced when she saw Duke fall to the floor and the glass smashing. Roe squinted her eyes. *Were those petals landing on the ground? That's odd.* Roe was just about to give up when she saw something in the back of the shot.

'Rewind that, please,' Roe asked and August took the video back several seconds. 'OK, stop there. Can you zoom in?'

Roe stared closely at the table before getting out her phone. She gasped. It all made sense!

She knew who the murderer was! And she wasn't about to let them frame her brother.

7 P.M.

The party lights were turned off and the room was filled with police. Duke was already gone and Jada was sitting in the corner with her arms protectively around Roman whose eyes were red and puffy. Roe just wanted to give him a massive hug.

'Jada!' Justin called as they ran up to her.

Jada's eyes widened and Roman looked at them, confused. His eyes landed on Roe and she gave him a reassuring smile.

'I told you to stay in the bedroom,' Jada hissed.

'What's happened to Duke?' August asked.

'They said they found traces of cyanide in his drink and he was poisoned. He didn't . . .' Jada didn't need to finish the sentence for them to know.

Roe's eyes welled up. Duke was such a talented dancer and didn't deserve to die in such a horrible way. She wiped her eyes with the back of her hand.

'Annie says Roman poured the drink that killed him,' Jada continued.

'Why would she think Roman would do that?' Roe asked.

Roman sighed. 'Because she thinks I wanted to be the headliner at the show tomorrow. Remember when I said I know all of his routines and you said I should headline?'

Roe's mouth dropped open in disbelief. Annie was accusing her twin of murder over a silly JOKE!

'We know who did it,' Justin said loudly and Jada's eyes widened. Everyone in the room went silent and was staring at them. 'It was Aaliyah Fallon that poisoned him.'

'No, it wasn't!' Aaliyah screeched from across the room at the same time Asia screamed, 'That's not true!'

'She's right,' Roe said and her friends exchanged confused glances. 'But you were in the corridor, all dressed in black, by Dukes's room, weren't you, Asia?'

There was a stunned silence in the room.

'What is she talking about?' Aaliyah asked her sister.

'I-I . . .' Asia stammered.

'If she was creeping around outside Duke's room, I would say she was a suspect,' Annie said, crossing her arms.

Asia's mouth fell open.

'We thought it was Aaliyah because she was so angry with Duke, and we found that *A* necklace with a curly hair strand tangled in it,' Roe said. 'Asia said it was her sister's but we saw Asia wearing the necklace on her Instagram, so why would she lie?'

Roe took a deep breath as all eyes stared at her. She took the gold necklace out of her dress pocket and it shone as it caught the light.

'I saw the footage on August's phone and everything finally made sense,' she continued. 'Duke wasn't pointing at Roman. He was pointing at the window where he could see the reflection of his killer. But where did the cyanide come from in the first place . . .? It was both Asia and Annie working together!' Roe said triumphantly. 'Asia delivered the bouquet of hydrangeas and Annie had them in her hair earlier but now they're gone.'

Asia's bottom lip trembled.

Annie patted her hair that still had the plait but no flowers. She laughed. 'I have no idea what you're talking about.'

'Oh yes, you do,' Roe said. 'Duke dropped a glass of drink before he fell. My brother poured all the drinks and you took none of them. But on the video, I saw that you made your own drink. When no one was paying attention you took the flowers out of your hair and put them in a glass. Then you took a small bottle out of your pocket and mixed the liquid with the flowers like some weird potion. You handed the drink to Duke. Funny how petals fell out of the glass once it smashed.'

Annie rolled her eyes. 'That's the dumbest thing I've ever heard. So what if flowers were in his drink. How could they poison him?"

'Because hydrangeas are toxic and release cyanide when digested! You gave him hydrangea juice!'

A collective gasp echoed around the room.

'Asia was the person in a black hoodie in the corridor, and she gave you the bouquet of flowers to finish off Duke. Problem was, she dropped her necklace and had to go back for it, but then tried to take the scent off herself by lying and saying it was her sister's necklace,' Roe finished.

'Asia! Tell me that's not true,' Aaliyah cried.

Roe expected Asia to deny it but instead she burst out crying.

'I'm sorry, Aaliyah. I panicked and said it was your necklace but everything was her idea!' Asia pointed at

Annie, who went to lunge for her but was held back by the police. 'She told me Duke would be too sick to dance so you could have his place. All she asked me to do was buy the flowers and said she would take care of the rest. I didn't know he would die! I would never have agreed to that.'

'Liar!' Annie screamed, her perfect bun unravelling around her raging face.

'Annie Matthews, you're under arrest for the murder of Duke Collins,' the female police officer said, putting Annie in handcuffs. 'You do not have to say anything but anything –'

'He took everything from me!' Annie yelled. 'This was my dream and because I covered for Duke at that dance workshop I fell and injured my back. Now I can't dance anymore. If that hadn't happened, I would have won *Britain's Got Talent* and my whole life would have changed. He deserved to die! And I wish –' But whatever else Annie was saying got lost as she was dragged out of the room.

'Asia Fallon, you're under arrest for the attempted murder of Duke Collins . . .'

Unlike Annie, Asia hung her head and offered her wrists without a fight.

Aaliyah was frozen to the spot and Roe felt sorry for her. It was clear she had no idea what her sister was up to.

Once Asia was led out of the room, Aaliyah glanced over at Masquerade. She took a deep breath before coming over.

'I'm so sorry. Roman, I didn't . . .'

'It's OK,' Roman said kindly.

'I don't know why Asia did this. Is this my fault? Did she think I wanted him dead, because I didn't.'

'Aaliyah, go be with your sister,' Jada said firmly. 'She needs you.'

Asia nodded and wiped her wet eyes. 'I really am sorry,' she said before she left the room.

Jada looked at Roe in amazement. 'Roe, that was brilliant.'

'More than brilliant.' Roman grabbed Roe in a massive hug. 'You're an absolute mega genius!'

Roe squeezed him back, grateful that her brother's name was cleared.

THREE DAYS LATER
4 P.M.

Annie was in jail awaiting trial, and every news outlet across the world was discussing the murder of Duke Collins. The autopsy had revealed that there was a significant amount of cyanide in his system. Duke was already dying and nobody but Annie knew. She had been poisoning him for months with her hydrangea juice concoctions, which explained his light-headedness and confusion, and traces of cyanide were even found in his water bottle. Asia was released and not charged, as she had no idea about Annie's plan to kill Duke. Aaliyah had deleted all of their social media and their upcoming performances were cancelled. The Fallon sisters completely disappeared.

The dance community was in mourning for Duke and there was an outpouring on social media from all the dancers that had loved him. Roe couldn't see anything on her feed apart from Duke's face and every time she did her heart broke.

Roe's name had been mentioned in the story a great deal for solving the crime. She had even got a special shout-out from the prime minister for her 'bravery' and 'brilliant instinct'.

Even though the 20th Anniversary Showcase was postponed out of respect for Duke, Masquerade were given a lifetime membership to Astro Towers, although they had no plans to ever return! Roe's favourite theme park now held horrible memories and she didn't want to set foot there again.

As Roe and Roman were walking to dance rehearsals, their phone beeped at the same time with a message from Jada in the Masquerade WhatsApp chat.

Hey guys! Once again I'm so proud of you all and how lucky am I to be the choreographer of the smartest bunch of kids? We've been asked to headline at the tribute show that Duke's family is putting together next month. I think we should find all the best videos of Duke and recreate them. What do you think?'

'I wish we were dancing with Duke,' Roman said sadly. 'Now we'll never get the chance.'

Roe suddenly had an idea. 'Maybe we can!' She quickly began to text back.

This is great. Maybe we can have Duke in the original videos shown onscreen behind us, so it looks like we're dancing together?

It only took a few seconds for everyone to message back that it was a brilliant idea and Jada said she would ask his family.

'You really are clever, you know that, Roe?' Roman said, wrapping his arm around her shoulders. 'What would I do without you?'

Roe grinned. 'What would I do without you?'

She put her arms around him so they walked down the road, joined at the hip.

MAISIE CHAN

THE
TREETOP
TRIALS

TOP SECRET

PROPERTY OF THE SUPER SUNNY MURDER CLUB

THE TREETOP
TRIALS

By Maisie Chan

As we drove past the sign for Yarrow Falls Holiday Park, Dad was trying to grab my attention in the rear-view mirror. I took out my earbuds.

'Earth to Xavier! Did you hear what I said about the Death Drop?' he asked.

'Uh . . .?' I replied. *Death Drop?*

'He didn't hear you,' snarked Paisley from behind her latest read. 'He's listening to gaming music. It all sounds the same,' she added.

Could it be helped that the soundtrack to *Zelda: Breath of the Wild* was amazing? I think not.

'What's the Death Drop?' I asked.

'They've got the new Treetop Trials opening today,' Dad said.

'What's that? A courtroom trial where an oak tree accuses a beech tree of stealing their acorns?' Paisley asked, laughing at her own joke.

'Nope, it's one of those harnessed rope courses. At the end, there's a massive drop of eighteen metres – you literally step off the platform into thin air! That's the Death Drop. The mayoress is going to be the first person to try it out after the opening ceremony! It's why I booked this place.'

'Sounds all right,' I said.

'The website said it's five double-decker buses high!' Dad said.

'Is there a mat or netting to catch people?' I asked.

'They're in a harness, remember, and they're lowered to the ground by a different rope,' said Paisley. 'I've seen it on the telly.'

I put my earbuds back in.

The truth was the whole holiday sounded a bit boring. Mum was away in Crete with her new boyfriend Pablo. The divorce had been hard on Dad and this was the only holiday he could afford.

We were staying in caravan thirteen. It was right at the back of the holiday park next to a tall fence. I could see the ledge of the Death Drop if I craned my neck towards the top of the trees.

The caravan itself was small and very beige. Beige sofa, beige carpet, beige kitchen cabinets. The bedroom I had to share with Paisley was the size of our bathroom at home. And my BookTuber sister had already taken it over, putting her ring light on the bedside table. She plonked down a stack of books. All whodunnits, her favourite genre.

'Xav, the bedroom is out of bounds when I'm recording. I'll put a Post-it note on the outside.' She stuck a pink Post-it on the door.

'Wait . . . is it out of bounds *now*?' I asked.

'You're such a clever cookie, now off you go.' She flicked the back of her hand as if shooing away a fly.

'Go where?' I huffed.

'We could rent bikes?' Dad suggested as he lugged the shopping bags into the kitchen.

'Er, maybe later?' I sneakily scanned the room for a Wi-Fi code so I could play Switch online. Dad wanted me to be 'active' and 'touch grass' not be on my 'technology' but he didn't say anything about Paisley making her videos with her mobile.

'Open the window, let some fresh air in,' said Dad.

I wandered over and opened the window. By the side of next door's caravan sat an old lady in a deckchair. She was surrounded by gnomes. A little white dog sat by her feet. The dog sprang up and charged towards the fence near the Death Drop. It started barking.

'Be quiet! Pookie! Come back here!' the old woman said, flustered. She saw me watching her. 'It's all right, love, he's very friendly. He only barks at squirrels. He hates them.'

I closed the window. Fresh air would have to wait. Dad sidled up next to me with a bunch of leaflets.

'This is a great location, it's less noisy than being by the kid's club or the bar. We can cycle over to Wainwright's Farm. We might see horses and cows,' said Dad.

'Is it all right if I go and have a look around by myself?' I asked. 'Paisley is filming.'

'Sure! Go and get some fresh air!'

Dad was obsessed with fresh air. I didn't tell him I was going to look for a Wi-Fi signal.

As I left the caravan, I saw the dog was still barking near the trees. I hoped it would be quiet at night. I didn't fancy trying to plug my ears with toilet tissue. I walked down a wide road with caravans on either side.

As I turned towards the reception area, I saw balloons and a crowd of people to the right of it. The entrance to the Treetop Trials had a huge red bow across it. Next to that was a wooden hut for putting on the harnesses and helmets.

A marble plinth was set up and a few people stood next to it. There was on older teenager in a green polo shirt – her badge said *Jenny* and she was biting her nails.

Next to her was a middle-aged man in a dark grey suit. He put a large black box down on a table. The crowd was made up of a lot of families and old people. Probably holidaymakers and locals who had come for the free biscuits. The man stepped up to the microphone.

'Thank you all for coming here today! I'm Gerald Oliver, the manager. I'm excited to be launching a brand-new, thrilling activity – the Treetop Trials – which will be open to the public and those staying at the holiday park.

'We've got lots of fun things happening,' the manager continued. 'Face painting, archery, and for our younger guests I'd like to introduce a new character – Stevie the Squirrel!' Gerald Oliver held out his hands. He looked expectantly at green polo shirt girl, who shrugged her shoulders. 'Stevie? Where's Stevie?' he hissed.

There were murmurs and people looked around.

Suddenly, a giant red squirrel in a yellow T-shirt bounded through the crowd. He stopped next to the manager and began waving his big, furry paws in the air.

'Our next special guest is Mayoress Julia Cressy!' Gerald Oliver said. The crowd clapped their hands. I had thought mayors were old people who wore gold chains. This one had straight blonde hair, and was wearing jeans, hiking boots and a purple raincoat. She didn't look that old either, maybe Dad's age. She stepped up to the microphone.

'Thank you for inviting me here today. I've been

mayoress for eight years, but I've lived around here all my life. I have always wanted what is best for the area and its people. This exciting new venture was an idea I mentioned to Gerald a few years ago, I think he's forgotten about that. I'm so glad my efforts at finding investors made this possible.'

She glanced at Gerald Oliver who looked down at the ground.

'I've climbed in the Himalayas and trekked in Bolivia. And today I am looking forward to a new challenge – the Treetop Trials! I can't wait to step over the infamous Death Drop!'

The crowd cheered. The giant squirrel shook its butt. It started high-fiving kids at the front of the crowd.

'I'm delighted to open the new Treetop Trials, which I am sure will attract more families to the area. Tourists are the lifeblood of this community!'

I heard a grunt from the back of the crowd.

'What about folk who don't want tourists coming here? They're ruining the lane, leaving a mess, and now we've got to listen to people scream on this abomination!' a voice boomed.

It was a man wearing a flat cap. He wore a dirty waxed green jacket. His face was gaunt. 'This place just keeps expanding, spreading like poison ivy. It's going to ruin this village and YOU . . .' he pointed to the mayoress,

'YOU are the one letting this happen!'

'I think you're being a little harsh,' said the mayoress. The giant squirrel put its hands on its hips and shook its head.

Gerald Oliver moved to the microphone. 'Everyone, this is Sam Wainwright from Wainwright's Farm next door,' he said. 'Sam, we had the appropriate planning permissions, plus we've created lots of new jobs. Isn't that right, Jenny? Jenny here is our latest hire.' He looked wide-eyed to the girl in the polo shirt.

'Er, yes . . . that's right,' said Jenny awkwardly. She looked at Mayoress Cressy who edged her way to the microphone once more. Gerald Oliver moved to the side.

'Sam, let's talk afterwards at the drinks reception. I'm sure Gerald could sort out free passes for your family to use the facilities here,' said the mayoress.

'That would be no problem,' said Gerald. 'Now, to the main event.' He opened the large black box and took out a pair of shiny silver scissors as long as gardening shears. 'Remember, kids, scissors are sharp! You don't want to get impaled on these things!' He laughed and quickly passed them to Mayoress Cressy, but the sharp tip snagged her jacket.

'Be careful, Gerald!' she said.

He muttered something under the breath. I only caught one word – '*die!*'

'I hereby open the Treetop Trials!' The mayoress cut the ribbon with a snip.

Most people cheered. Sam the farmer huffed away. Once the photographer had taken photos, the mayoress turned to Jenny and said something, holding her hand over her mouth. I watched as they went into the area where you put on the harnesses and helmets. The giant squirrel jumped up and down and threw paper confetti in the air.

I headed back towards our caravan, hoping that I would be able to see the Death Drop from where we were staying. A lot of the course was hidden from view because of the tall fence but as the Death Drop was so high up, maybe I'd be able to see the mayoress take the leap. As I got closer, plumes of white smoke snaked through the air. It was Dad. He wasn't on fire, he'd started the barbecue.

The white dog from next door was growling at a squirrel clambering up a tree next to its caravan. The old woman was nowhere to be seen.

Dad waved at me and flipped over a veggie burger. It looked a bit burnt. I was starving. I jogged over.

'How was it, Xav?' Dad asked. 'Did you see the Treetop Trials?'

'Yeah, it looks OK. It's higher than I thought, and that Death Drop looks well scary! The mayoress is on it now, but she should be finished soon.'

Paisley came out of the caravan holding her phone in the air. 'Like and subscribe!' She tapped a button and then put her phone in her pocket.

'Who wants a veggie burger?' Dad asked, putting a charcoaled disc in a floury bun.

'Me!' shouted Paisley, grabbing the paper plate Dad was holding.

'Hey! I was here first,' I said. I was about to take the plate from Paisley when a shrill scream sounded through the air. Paisley dropped the veggie burger on the floor.

'What was that?' she asked looking towards the Death Drop.

Dad bent down to pick up the fallen veggie burger. He blew on it. He had a five-second rule about food that had fallen on to the floor.

'It's probably the mayoress having a whale of a time,' he said. He held the contorted veggie burger out to Paisley who scrunched up her nose. Then he offered it to me. I was too hungry to refuse it. I bit into it. It had bits of grass on it. I put it down on the wooden picnic table.

'Let's go see what happened,' said Paisley.

I followed Paisley and Dad over to where we'd heard the scream. It was hard to see through the cracks in the fence. We heard someone running towards the scene. Then we heard a voice.

'Call an ambulance! Now!' I saw Jenny, the girl in the polo shirt, on her knees. She held a walkie-talkie. Static crackled across the airwaves distorting a muffled voice. 'I can't hear you – can you repeat?' Jenny asked into a black device.

'I said: IS – SHE – DEAD?' the voice boomed. I recognised it as Gerald Oliver. Paisley's eyes were wide as saucers.

'She might be!' whispered Paisley to me, a little too excitedly. I could tell she was hoping for foul play because then she would have a true crime to solve. She crossed her fingers. I nudged her.

'Inappropriate times a hundred,' I told her.

'What?' She shrugged. We all turned back to the crack in the fence and held our breath waiting for the answer.

'She . . . she's . . . I think . . . She's . . . alive!'

I let out a sigh of relief.

'An ambulance is on its way,' Gerald Oliver's voice said. 'I'll cordon off the entrance and tell people it's closed. Keep everyone away from the area, Jenny. Don't move her! Wait for the paramedics!'

I looked at Dad. He looked relieved and smiled.

'I'm glad she's alive,' he said. 'Maybe it's best if we stay on the ground this holiday, eh?'

I nodded, but felt disappointed that the best thing about this place was now out of bounds. Paisley walked away from the fence and looked up at the Death Drop ledge and took a photo of it.

'My followers are going to eat this up!' she said. She took a selfie by the fence. 'Deathly Death Drop Does Damage! Is that too much alliteration?' she asked.

'You're too much!' I said, rolling my eyes.

Dad sprinted back to the barbecue, which was on fire, its smoke billowing all over the place.

'It could have been an accident,' I asserted.

'No, I smell foul play,' Paisley said.

'I only smell burnt burgers,' I said. What was Paisley going on about?

'I think someone was trying to kill the mayoress,' Paisley urged. 'Look up there.'

I peered to where she was pointing but wasn't sure what I was looking for. *What did she see?*

Paisley shook her head. 'At first, I thought maybe she was pushed off the ledge, but that wouldn't make sense as there's only one set of ladders and we would have seen someone trying to get down. There are no ropes on that pulley. So the rope or harness had to be tampered with.' I was quite impressed with my sister's deductions, but I didn't want to tell her that.

Her suspicious nature was rubbing off on me. 'Yeah, this is a new course; all the equipment is new so it's not going to be *wear and tear*. What should we do?'

'We investigate!' grinned Paisley. 'I can finally be like Enola Holmes! I will need a sidekick, Xav – you can be Doctor Watson if you want.'

'I'm no sidekick!' I protested.

We heard the ambulance heading to the park. Maybe this holiday was going to be more exciting than I'd first imagined.

Dad wouldn't let us get sleuthing until we'd had something to eat. The barbecue was a charred mess. So instead, he made some sesame oil ramen with a fried egg and green beans.

There was a knock at the door. Dad opened it. It was Gerald Oliver. I watched him from the sofa, Paisley huddled up next to me with her notebook and pen.

I whispered to Paisley, 'He was acting weird at the ceremony and made a comment about the mayoress being stabbed by the giant scissors. Then he uttered the word "die". The mayoress said it was her idea to install the Treetop Trials here and not his. He looked quite put out about it. I think it's him!' Paisley wrote out a suspect list in her notebook. So far it only had one name on it.

SUSPECT NUMBER ONE – GERALD OLIVER (manager with bruised ego)

We strained to hear what he was saying to Dad.

'Hello, I'm the manager. There's been an incident and unfortunately the Treetop Trials will remain closed for the duration of your stay.'

Dad asked about a partial refund or a discount on a future stay, but the manager said he wasn't sure the holiday park would survive this episode, he sounded upset. Then he rushed over to our neighbour, the lady with the gnomes and the yappy dog.

'It's not him,' Paisley said.

'But he was acting suss at the ceremony.'

'Yeah, but you heard him. He wanted the park to succeed, and this attempted murder will drive business away, which means less money. He might lose his job. It's not him.'

'Who else can it be?' I asked eagerly. I'd wanted to help Paisley with her videos for ages. We used to hang out loads when we were younger. But since she's started secondary school, we don't do much together any more. This was a chance to work with my sister AND have a bit of fun in the process.

'Xav, tell me everything you saw at the opening ceremony. The suspect might be someone who was there.'

'There's Jenny, who found the mayoress after the fall. She had access to the harnesses and ropes. Plus, she looked nervous at the ceremony.'

'Great observations, detective! She had the means and opportunity, but does she have a motive?' asked Paisley.

'Let's try to find her.'

SUSPECT NUMBER TWO – JENNY (jittery Treetop Trials worker)

We ran over to the entrance to the Treetop Trials. The ambulance was driving away.

Jenny was sat on a bench near the kids' playground. She was dabbing her eyes with a tissue. Next to her was Stevie the Squirrel. We watched as he took off the squirrel head. A sweaty blond-haired guy appeared; he was around the same age as her. I pretended to play a game on the top of the slide. Paisley sat on the swings.

'It's not your fault. You did all the checks; the harness was fitted properly, and you double-checked the ropes the day before. Gerald can't blame you.'

'But he does! He said the park is ruined now. He said the police are coming to investigate. I would never hurt her, even though . . .' she paused, 'she wasn't the easiest of people to live with.'

I felt my insides bubble with excitement.

'I didn't know you lived with her,' said Stevie the Squirrel.

'She was my great-aunt. She got me this job – we didn't want anyone to know because, well . . . nepotism. She didn't think I could get a job on my own.'

'That's what family does – looks out for each other,' Stevie said.

'I know we haven't known each other long, but I feel like I can trust you,' said Jenny. 'Great-Aunt Julia wasn't that *great*. She was controlling. My parents passed away in a car accident when I was a baby. She shipped me off to boarding school when I was four. Since I moved back, she's the one making all the decisions. She's always threatening to write me out of her will. I actually hate her.'

'Sounds complicated.' Stevie patted Jenny's hand with his big, padded squirrel paws.

'I found this locket on the ground next to her, the chain has snapped.' Jenny held up a gold oval locket and opened it to show Stevie. I couldn't see it very well. 'I didn't know she cared enough to carry pictures of me as a baby around with her – look, she even had Jenny and Julia engraved on it: *J & J*.'

I lifted my eyebrows at Paisley, and she nodded slightly. Motive times a hundred! Jenny had moved to the top of the suspect list.

'You're not a bad person,' Stevie said. 'And I don't think you had anything to do with the fall. Actually . . . I overheard Sam Wainwright on the phone before the ceremony, when I was doing meet and greets. He said something about "cutting" and "running" – it sounded weird at the time.'

Aha! Another clue! I tiptoed over to Paisley and sat on the other swing. I started pumping my legs back and forth. I tried to lean over to tell her what I'd just heard.

'We've got to check out Sam Wainwright . . . he could have cut the rope on the Death Drop . . . way before the ceremony began.' We were out of sync on the swings.

'I can't hear you!' Paisley said. 'We need to swing at the same time!'

Once we'd got into a rhythm, I repeated what I had heard Stevie the Squirrel say about Sam. Paisley stopped swinging. Then I did the same.

'Interesting! *Shush* . . . he's saying something else.' Paisley got up and urged me to follow her to the roundabout. Jenny was standing up. Stevie was giving her a hug.

'Thanks for listening, Josh,' Jenny said. 'You're the only person I can really talk to around here.'

'No problem' he replied. 'OK, I've got to go to the kids' club, but let's catch up later.' We watched as they both left and headed in different directions, Stevie the Squirrel to the kids' club in the main building, and Jenny headed towards the entrance to the Treetop Trials.

There, she bumped into Gerald Oliver who was carrying a box of harnesses and a rope. He stopped and scowled at her. 'That's it. We're officially ruined. This rope was cut. Look at that edge?' Jenny looked like she might burst out crying again.

'Someone did cut it! We were right!' I felt all bubbly inside. No wonder Paisley liked reading whodunits; it was so exciting trying to work out who the culprit was. I decided I would read some of the books Paisley had brought with her.

'Does that mean the police will get involved?' Jenny asked. Gerald Oliver nodded. 'They're on their way now. The news is already out about what happened. People on social media are posting about the accident. I've just had twenty families cancel their holidays with us next week. It's sabotage, that's what it is!'

Sabotage.

It all pointed to Sam.

SUSPECT NUMBER THREE – SAM WAINWRIGHT (disgruntled farmer next door)

Paisley and I walked down to Wainwright's Farm.

We found Sam Wainwright in a barn, milking a cow. I didn't want to go too close to him. He might kill us using the cow or something.

'What are you kids doing on my land?' he asked, without turning his head.

'Er, hi . . . we're here to find out who tried to kill the mayoress,' I said.

Paisley rolled her eyes and elbowed me. 'You're not supposed to tell him that!'

He turned and sighed. 'I've heard all about the accident. It's awful and I hope Julia pulls through.'

'You knew her well?' Paisley asked.

'Yes, we were sweethearts in school. I'd never want to hurt her.'

'But you shouted . . . at the opening ceremony,' I said. 'You hate the holiday park.'

'I do. Julia had promised me the park wouldn't be anywhere near my farm. But she went back on her word, like she always did.'

'Like she always did?' Paisley asked. 'You mean, she had hurt you before?'

'Yes, we were engaged many moons ago. But she broke it off.' Sam pulled on an udder and milk squirted into a bucket. It was kind of cool to see milk squirting out of an animal.

Jilted boyfriend – *interesting*!

'She said a personal matter had to be taken care of and she wouldn't have time for me.' He stopped milking and turned to look at us. He had bags under his eyes. But I think she used it as an excuse. She didn't want to settle down and live on a farm, she didn't want a quiet life, she wanted power. She was ambitious and after the next big adrenaline rush.' He stood up and sighed.

'You must have felt angry about that,' Paisley asserted.

'I was angry about bored holidaymakers traipsing all over my land. A bunch of lads tried to push Daisy over last month. Someone started a campfire in my woods, and it burnt one of the birches. I'm sick of it. However, when

I got back from the ceremony I was here with Daisy.' Sam looked off at the holiday park in the distance.

A cow was hardly a good alibi.

'And before the ceremony, where were you?' I asked. 'You were overheard saying something about cutting and running.' The farmer looked at me intensely. Then wiped his hands on his trousers and put his hand inside his jacket pocket.

Paisley jumped forward and put her arms out, as if trying to protect me.

'He might have a gun!' she exclaimed.

'You've got an overactive imagination, haven't you!' He laughed. 'I'm just getting out my mobile.' He took out a small Swiss Army knife, a packet of Tic Tacs and his mobile.

'I was on a video call with the vet. Sharmila, my sheep, was stuck to some barbed wire. I wanted advice about cutting her free. You can check yourself. Look.'

He got out his mobile and showed us his call log. He was right. He was on a video call before the ceremony.

'Do you always carry a knife?' Paisley asked. I could see the cogs of her brain twirling.

'This is a new one. I misplaced my other. I think I lost it around the holiday park. I was working on mending a fence post and I left my jacket there overnight. When I collected it the following morning, my mobile was still there but the knife was gone.'

'Interesting,' said Paisley, making notes.

'Thanks for co-operating. I think you're innocent, but my sister probably still thinks you could have done it.' Paisley glared at me. I probably wasn't supposed to tell suspects that, was I?

'Well, all it takes is one person to believe you. I hope Julia makes a full recovery. I'll try to go and see her later if she's well enough. I do miss her.' It was the first time I'd seen him smile. We walked back to the holiday park.

'Who next?' I asked Paisley as we entered the caravan and sat down in our bedroom. Dad had left a note saying he'd gone cycling.

'Sam lost his knife – maybe the wannabe killer used it to tamper with the rope?' she said.

I scanned her notebook to see if I could fathom out what was missing.

SUSPECT LIST

JENNY - had motive - to inherit her great-aunt's wealth. Means - yes, she could have done something to the rope. She knew the trials better than anyone else. We don't know where she was before the ceremony.

SAM WAINWRIGHT - disgruntled farmer who

didn't like the holiday park expanding. Didn't have a solid alibi. He had been dumped by Mayoress Cressy as a young man. Lost his knife (was it stolen by the rope cutter?).

GERALD OLIVER - annoyed that Julia Cressy had taken credit for the idea of having the rope course. But not enough to try to kill her, and he's upset that the park is in jeopardy.

'That dog is so annoying! It's barking again,' I said.

'Yeah, it wouldn't shut up earlier. It was barking all through my recording. Then it was quiet for a bit. Then Dad called me for food.'

I noticed the ring light was set up opposite the window where you could see part of the Death Drop ledge. I had an idea.

'Can we watch that video back?' I asked.

'I've not edited it yet, I need to adjust the light and cut out the barking.'

'It doesn't matter about all that right now, we've got a killer to catch,' I said.

'Attempted killer,' Paisley added. She got out her mobile and tapped on the screen.

We sat on the bed and watched the video of Paisley talking about her latest read.

'Pause it!' I spoke. She tapped the screen.

'There!' I pointed at something moving on the screen. 'I know who did it!' I said, butterflies fluttered about in my belly. 'I just don't know why.'

'Columbo,' said Paisley.

'Eh? Did he do it?' I said, confused.

'No! He's a TV detective. We need to be *like* Columbo. He knows who has committed the murder at the beginning of the episode. He often doesn't know the motive but begins to work it out and gets a confession by the end of the episode.'

I told Paisley my theory about who had tried to kill the mayoress and what I had seen on the footage. It was all starting to make sense.

'If what you're thinking is right then we'll need more evidence. I'll contact one of my subscribers. Her mum's a private detective. I need her to look up some birth records for me. You go and tell everyone that there's going to be a gathering at the entrance of the Treetop Trials in half an hour. The police are coming so we can tell them who they need to arrest!'

I ran around the holiday park telling everyone to gather for a very important meeting. We arrived at the entrance of the Treetop Trials, which was now cordoned off with police tape. Paisley stood on a chair and waved her hands

in the air to get everyone's attention. She was also live-streaming to her thousands of followers on YouTube.

'Everyone! Gather around!' Paisley shouted. The main people from the opening ceremony were back – Gerald, Jenny, Farmer Sam, the holidaymakers and Stevie the Squirrel.

'We have gathered here to let you know who tried to kill Mayoress Cressy!' There was a collective gasp. 'Go on, Xavier, you cracked it. You tell them what happened,' Paisley said.

'There is a wannabe murderer AMONG US!' I said, cracking up inside. I'd managed to get my favourite game into my speech.

'Be serious, please,' Paisley said through gritted teeth. 'My followers are watching.'

'The rope to the Death Drop was cut on purpose. Someone wanted Mayoress Julia Cressy to die a gruesome death. At first, we thought it was the manager here. The mayoress took the credit for the new attraction, and I overheard him say the word "die" at the ceremony,' I said.

'It was an expression of anger. I didn't mean it, officers,' whimpered Gerald to the police who were listening to the side of us.

'We know it wasn't you,' Paisley said. 'Then next, we turned our attention to Sam, the farmer next door. He hates this place, but it seemed a bit far-fetched that he would kill the mayoress to sabotage the holiday park. He has feelings for her as they used to be sweethearts.' I was feeling quite confident now as I continued. 'There was another person who would directly gain from the mayoress dying – Jenny. She is Mayoress Cressy's great-niece! They were keeping that information a secret. She would have inherited all of Julia's fortune.'

Jenny looked like she was going to throw up and her hands were shaking.

'It wasn't Jenny. She said she found a locket where Julia fell that was inscribed with *J & J*. She thought it was Julia and Jenny. But she hadn't seen the locket before which made us think it wasn't actually the mayoress's. What if it belonged to someone else?' I said. 'And she mentioned "pictures" – plural. There was more than one picture in the locket. Could it be two babies that looked the same? Twins?'

'Twin? I've got a twin?' Jenny muttered. She stood up, confused.

'Yes, you do. I've had it checked out. But it wasn't just that. The dog next door was a big clue,' added Paisley.

'It was barking a lot before the ceremony began,' I said. 'And its owner said it ONLY barks at one thing – squirrels!' This was so exciting!

'I was recording a BookTuber video at the time and a bit of the window was behind me. You can see the Death

Drop ledge. Xavier said we should watch it and he was right. Because what did we see in the background?'

'A giant squirrel tail!' There were gasps. Everyone turned to look at Stevie the Squirrel who was shaking his head and holding up his big, furry hands in protest.

'His name is Josh! He's the other J on the locket. He's the one that dropped it, not Julia! He tried to kill the mayoress!' I told them.

Paisley and I pointed to Stevie the Squirrel.

The giant rodent turned and started to push through the crowd to escape the police men and women who were trying to grab him. Just then Dad arrived on a bicycle, confused by the crowd.

'Dad! STOP THAT SQUIRREL!' I yelled. Dad hopped off his bike, opened his arms and tackled the giant squirrel to the floor. Paisley and I ran over and sat on top of the big, bouncy squirrel costume. We pulled off the furry head.

Josh was sweating and angry. 'You pesky kids! You're only half right – it was revenge, but my plan was bigger than that. Julia left me to rot in an orphanage. She let Jenny have an education and I got nothing. I was planning to bump off Jenny too and then declare I was her long-lost brother. I would have inherited everything if it hadn't been for you two!'

The police took Stevie the Squirrel away. Paisley took

some photos of him in handcuffs for her socials.

Dad put his arm around Paisely and me.

'You two all right?' he asked. 'You make quite the team. Sherlock and Watson.'

'Columbo and Enola Holmes,' I said, smiling at my sister who nodded.

'We worked quite well as a team,' I said to Paisley.

'We did, little brother, we did.'

'I'm sorry the Death Drop was closed and there was a murderer on the loose,' Dad said. 'We can try somewhere else next time.'

'No!' Paisley and I said together.

'Let's come back every year,' I said.

'I'd like that,' said Dad, 'I'd like that a lot.'

BENJAMIN DEAN

THE
THIEF WHO
STOLE
SUMMER

TOP SECRET

PROPERTY OF THE SUPER SUNNY MURDER CLUB

THE THIEF WHO STOLE SUMMER

By Benjamin Dean

On the first day of summer, I saw the thief steal a sunflower in the middle of the night. I admit, I should have been asleep. If Mum knew I was awake past midnight playing on my Switch, I would've been grounded quicker than you can say 'Mario Kart' and that would have been the worst start to the summer holidays on record. But let's ignore the fact I was breaking house rules and concentrate on the important matter here – the thief stealing the sunflower.

I was sneaking across my bedroom to put my Switch back in its dock when I thought I saw a shadow move in the garden out of the corner of my eye. I frowned. A fox, maybe? Or perhaps it was my mind playing tricks on me. All I could see in the window when I looked properly was my own reflection staring back in the golden glow of the lamplight. Nothing strange about that, so I went on about my business.

My Switch safely charging, I crept back to bed, nestling down and thinking about how much fun this summer was going to be. It was going to be a scorching-hot one, the weatherman said. Molly Brown was throwing a birthday party next week and had handed out the invites yesterday on the last day of school. Rumour had it there would be a bouncy castle and Slush Puppies and a four-tiered cake that revealed rainbow layers when you cut into it. Someone even said there would be a DJ, as if a Spotify playlist wasn't good enough for Molly Brown. Either way, I was excited, and that was what I was thinking about as I turned off the lamp and lay there in the dark, already dreaming about blueberry and raspberry mixed slushies.

And then I heard a noise.

I'm sure I don't need to tell you that a noise in the middle of the night is a cause for concern. You (yes *you*, reader, I see you) seem like a pretty decent person – of course, I'm making assumptions here, but I do hope I'm right – so therefore I'm assuming you know it's kind of rude to go around making noises in the middle of the night when people are trying to sleep. Not to mention it's . . . well, sort of terrifying when everything is supposed to be all quiet and still. It's just not on.

I told myself it was a figment of my imagination, or maybe it was just the cat from number eight being a nuisance as usual. But just when I had planned to ignore it, there it was again! The sound was a quiet clang, like metal on metal, and it was coming from the garden. I immediately started to think the worst. Aliens! Shadow beasts who ate little people like me for snacks! Mrs Vole from down the street coming to offer one of her god-awful attempts at baking! If it was none of those things, then it had to be something equally as terrible. Nothing good comes in the middle of the night.

I lay still for as long as I possibly could, as if simply not moving would be enough to protect me from fearsome creatures and bogeymen who prowled in the dark. But curiosity has always gotten the better of me, and when I thought I'd heard another noise, I decided to investigate. And by investigate, I mean creep up to my window and look outside. I wasn't planning on doing something stupid like follow the noise out into the dark. I am many things, but I'd like to think I'm not a complete and utter fool.

And so there I was, army-crawling across the floor, risking carpet burn on my elbows and knees, until I reached the window. I took a few steadying breaths, then slowly lifted my head until it was level with the sill and I could peep out into the night. As before, I couldn't really see anything for a moment or two. But since I'd turned my lamp off, my eyes finally adjusted and I could begin to make out the familiar landmarks of my back garden under the snow-white glow of the moonlight.

There was the table and chairs, with the large umbrella that Mum had bought especially for this summer, and the fancy BBQ that was Dad's pride and joy every time we were blessed with a hint of sunshine and warm weather. Further down, I could see the spindly arms of the apple tree and the shrubs Mum and Dad took turns in pretending they would eventually try to tame. At the end of the stretch of grass was the shed, a crooked shack that housed some rusty bikes and various other knick-knacks that nobody wanted. And, of course, there was the sunflower patch beyond.

Technically, it wasn't a part of our garden. The houses on our side of the street backed on to a sprawling field that was mostly grass and gently rolling hills. But just beyond the perimeter of our fences was the sunflower patch. There were dozens of them in neat rows, their yellow-petalled faces like miniature suns that had fallen to earth.

And that was where I could see the shadow.

It was a shade of darkness with no distinguishable features. Even under the glow of moonlight, I couldn't tell if it was big or small, short or tall, human or creature. It was just a *thing* moving among the flowers.

My heart was still in my chest for a moment, then began to patter against my ribcage as the shadow slithered through the night. But it wasn't moving further away. It was coming right for me.

Closer.

And closer ...

I immediately ducked, throwing myself to the floor and accidentally banged my head on the carpet with a dull thud. I counted to ten before I moved again, rising slowly once more to peek over the sill. It took me a second, but my eyes finally found the shadow. It had slipped over the fence ... right into our garden! I stopped breathing, completely frozen in place. I couldn't even move to hide. But if the shadow noticed me, it didn't pay me any attention. Instead of coming closer to the house, it veered off towards the garden shed and vanished inside.

I watched the shed for a minute. Then another. Five more. Then ten. But the shadow didn't reappear. It had simply disappeared, which terrified me more than anything.

I didn't sleep a wink for the rest of the night. I wasn't sure if I should wake up Mum and Dad to tell them somebody had broken into our shed, but the thought of calling out to them made me wonder if the *thing* would hear me too. What if it broke into our house and came for *us*? I briefly thought about creeping to my parents' bedroom to tell them instead, but sneaking through the house in the dark was also not appealing.

So, instead, I stayed put. Every tiny sound made me jump in my bed, diving under the duvet as if being invisible might keep me safe. However, in the morning, when I woke from a light and fitful sleep, everything seemed completely normal. No strange sounds, save for Mrs Vole's singing a few doors down.

But as I raced to my bedroom window to look outside, two things struck me as odd. First was the most obvious – the blue skies that we'd been having were nowhere to be seen, replaced instead with dark grey clouds that hung low and close, bursting at the seams with drizzly rain. My heart sank. So much for the searing-hot summer the weatherman had promised. I hoped Molly's birthday party would still be able to go ahead next week.

I looked through the rain, thoroughly miserable and certain things couldn't get any worse. You should never think that, by the way. The moment you do, you're certain to jinx something in the cosmos and be proved wrong. As you can probably guess, that is exactly what happened next.

My eyes found the sunflower patch and I spotted it straight away. One of them was missing, cut away like it had never existed at all. The only evidence of it was a trail of petals that were scattered around the patch. But what alarmed me most of all was that these petals were no longer yellow like the sunflowers I assumed they belonged to. Oh no – these petals had turned black, and they led right up to our shed door.

'Somebody broke into our shed last night,' I said, tearing into the kitchen, a little breathless. It was a Saturday, but Mum was getting ready for work and Dad was busy fussing over his fishing gear to take with him out to the lakes.

'What was that, sweetheart?' Mum said in a tone that made it quite clear she hadn't been listening and wasn't about to start any time soon. Without waiting for an answer, she huffed to herself and slammed the kitchen drawer that she'd been rooting through shut. 'Has *anybody* seen the car keys?'

'In the drawer,' Dad said without looking up from the fishing rod he was zipping into a bag.

'I've just looked in the drawer, Michael,' Mum snapped.

'Try the other one then.'

Mum's cheeks flushed red with frustration before she rolled her eyes and continued her search. I stood in the doorway, a little stung that nobody was listening to my very important announcement. Not to be deterred, I tried again.

'Someone stole a sunflower and broke into our shed last night,' I said, a little louder this time.

Nobody so much as batted an eyelid. Dave, our golden retriever, came to sit loyally by feet, craning his neck to look up at me, eyes wide as if he was vaguely interested in what I had to say. He probably just wanted breakfast but I gave him a scratch behind the ears to say thank you all the same.

'Got them!' Mum half shouted, even though she was mostly just talking to herself. She stashed the keys in her handbag and swung it up on to her shoulder. 'Right, I'm off to work. There's lunch in the fridge when you're hungry, Izzy.' She came over to squash me into a quick hug, planting a kiss on the side of my head. 'Stay out of trouble, won't you?'

'What about the person who broke into our shed?' I said, failing to keep the frustration out of my tone, as I extracted myself from the hug and wiped smudged lipstick off my cheek.

'What on earth are you talking about?' Mum and Dad said in unison.

I sighed. Why is it that parents rarely listen to us kids when we're trying to tell them something important?

'The *sunflower thief*,' I said again. 'Someone stole a sunflower last night and then they *broke into our shed*!'

Dad frowned and wandered up to the patio doors overlooking the back garden. Mum checked the time on her watch and tutted quietly. After a moment or two, Dad shook his head.

'Don't be silly, Isiah,' he said, already putting his focus

back on to his fishing bag. 'The shed looks absolutely fine.'

I went to interrupt but Dad anticipated it and raised the volume of his own voice a notch to cut me off.

'And even if someone *did* break into the shed, which I'm sure they haven't, they would find nothing but old bikes and mop buckets. They'd be doing us a favour!' He chuckled as if he'd just told a rather amusing joke.

'It was probably just the wind,' Mum added, checking the contents of her bag one last time and starting for the door. 'And besides, why would anybody want to steal a *sunflower*?'

Why indeed? I thought to myself. *What would anybody want with a sunflower and a shed full of mess?*

Once Dad had left the house to go fishing, I dropped my empty plate in the sink, put on some yellow wellies and plodded out into the garden with Dave gingerly trotting along by my side. He looked far from happy to be out in the rain and kept glancing up at me with something that looked suspiciously like a glare. But nobody else seemed interested in the fact that someone had stolen a sunflower and broken into our shed, so it was down to me – well, *us*, I wasn't about to do this alone – to look into the matter.

'We're just having a quick look,' I assured Dave. I'm

pretty sure the dog scowled back in response but kept pace with me all the same. I decided to start with the sunflower patch, mostly because I was scared the thief might still be inside the shed since I hadn't actually seen them leave it. We reached the back fence and hopped over, Dave making quicker work of it than me, and approached the sunflower patch with more than a hint of hesitation.

I'd already seen the missing sunflower from my bedroom window, but up close there was something . . . *eerie* about it. The flower had been cut down just below its head, leaving a jagged stem behind that looked mournful in its place next to the other flowers. But what creeped me out most was the footprints that'd been left behind in the soil and mud. I measured them with my own foot, figuring out that they were roughly the same size. Surely these prints belonged to the culprit.

Confused and more than a little scared, I shifted my attention to the blackened petals that were scattered all around, now withered and wilting in the grass as if they were dying. They formed a trail back to the fences and into our garden. Taking a deep breath, we followed them until we reached the shed, where we found the final black petal right in front of the door. The grass was slightly flattened, as if somebody had recently been here.

I swallowed and looked at Dave. Dave gulped and

looked up at me. He cocked his head to the side. *Don't even think about it*, he seemed to be saying. *Don't you dare.* I shrugged.

'It's just a sunflower and a . . . I don't know, someone who really likes sunflowers? What's the worst that could happen?'

Dave looked unimpressed. In fact, that was putting it lightly. But since he couldn't talk, I chose to tell myself he was actually supporting my decisions and slowly reached out for the door. My hand was getting closer to the wooden panels, my breath lodged in my throat. It was almost there. I just had to reach a little further and pull the door open. Just a little more and . . .

There was a sound.

It was faint at first, barely a whisper, so quiet that I actually leaned in a little closer, trying to make it out. Against my better judgement, it was drawing me in, like some kind of lullaby. And then, when my ear was almost touching the door, it finally became clear.

It was a laugh.

A coat of fear, cold and chilling, draped itself over me. It was more of a *titter*, laced with a sinister glee, as if it were hiding some terrible secret. It grew and grew until it reached a final, booming crescendo. Me and Dave both jumped into the air: me shrieking, Dave yelping. The little traitor didn't even try to protect me. He turned on his paws and bolted, galloping back to the house. So much for a guard dog.

I legged it after Dave, slipping on the rain-soaked grass and landing in an ungraceful heap. I scrambled to get back up and began running once more, not stopping until I was back in the safety of our kitchen with the patio doors locked, breathing heavily. Dave hadn't deemed this safe enough and had snuck into his den under the stairs, as if he was trying to escape from whatever was in the shed and my own terrible idea to investigate it. He poked his head out, his eyes slightly narrowed. I translated his stare to mean, *Don't go getting any more bright ideas, let's just stay inside where it's safe.* I silently agreed. Well, until my heartbeat had returned to normal anyway. And then I started to wonder what on earth could be hiding out there in our garden shed.

Over the next week, the sinister sunflower stealing continued. Every night, I crept over to my window to spy out into the garden. Sometimes, when the clouds were at their thickest, I couldn't see anything, so absolute was the night. But others, the moon would break free and I'd look down to the patch to find the shadow taking another sunflower. Just like the first night, it would cut the stem and take it back to the shed, where it would disappear, not to be seen again until the following night.

And the rain continued too. It wasn't just a light drizzle either. It was a torrential downpour that wouldn't relent or go away. The clouds above hung over us, dark grey and ominous, threatening to never leave again. There wasn't so much as a single patch of blue sky to be seen, something which baffled the weatherman on TV, who said that it was *supposed* to be hotter than Spain. In fact, the rain got so bad that Molly's birthday party was cancelled too.

In my heart, I knew the sunflower thief and the weather had to be connected. There had been no signs of rain until the first sunflower had gone, but now one was being taken every night, the rain wouldn't go away. It couldn't be a coincidence. The thief was not only stealing our flowers, they were stealing our summer too!

A big part of me wanted to investigate but it didn't exactly go to plan. On one attempt to build the courage to look inside the shed, I donned a bike helmet and armed myself with a lightsabre. Sure, it was fake and made of plastic, but it was better than the kitchen mop, which was my only other option when it came to weapons. I tried to put a smaller helmet on Dave, but his ears kept getting in the way. When we crept up to the shed, however, my bravado evaporated as if it had never existed in the first place, and when we heard that foreboding laughter once more, we both high-tailed it back to the house and locked the door, breathing hard.

So much for courage and bravery, huh?

I tried to tell Mum and Dad but they just waved my words away as if I was talking nonsense. I started to worry that maybe I *was* losing the plot, that I was making up some terrible story in my head that simply wasn't true. That stopped me from recruiting any friends into my mission to investigate – the last thing I wanted was to return to school after the holidays with everybody thinking I had lost my mind.

At one point, irritated with my constant nagging, Dad reluctantly strode out into the garden and threw open the shed door while me and Dave watched from the kitchen. He spread his arms wide and stepped aside so we could see. All I could make out were the bikes and buckets and broken toys that nobody ever bothered with any more. There was no sign of the sunflowers, and certainly no thief.

'See,' Dad said. 'There's nothing here. You've got too much of an active imagination, kid. Now will you stop fussing and let me get back to what I was doing?'

Not to be deterred, I took my *active imagination* elsewhere.

'Aliens?' I suggested.

Dave didn't react to my theory. We were alone in the

nook under the stairs, sitting on his dog bed. Dad was in the garage messing around with an old rusty car that he swore he could *get up and running again like it was brand new.* Mum didn't believe him and I'm not sure I did either.

'Hmm. Demons?' Dave let his tongue loll out of his mouth. 'No? OK, tough crowd.'

We went back and forth – by which I mean I offered various mythological and supernatural creatures out loud while Dave lost interest and tried to nap in my lap instead – but after a short while I knew there was only one thing for it.

'We have to follow the shadow into the shed.'

At this, Dave got up out of my lap in disgust and went to sit in the opposite corner. He took one look at me, yapped his disdain and then turned his back, letting me know in no uncertain terms what he was thinking. Well, I certainly wasn't going to creep around in the dark on my own.

'I'll sneak you doggy treats every day for the rest of the summer?'

Dave *almost* didn't move. But at the sound of treats, he eventually swivelled his head back round to face me. I went in for the kill.

'And walks to the woods every day.'

Dave still didn't look happy about this, but he stood up and padded back over, pushing his snout into me until he'd positioned himself under my arm. I gave him a squeeze.

'You and me together, buddy. What's the worst that can happen?'

At just past midnight, me and Dave were sitting at my bedroom window once more, peering out into the garden. The rain had ceased and the clouds had broken away, as if the spell of bad weather had been briefly broken. Nothing moved in the dark and everything was as it should've been. But I knew it wouldn't last.

As if on cue, the shadow appeared, seemingly out of the very night itself. Using the dark as a cloak, it slipped over to the sunflower patch. By now, the whole first row of sunflowers had been cut down, so it started with the second. A moment was it all took, but then the shadow was on the move again. I could just about make out the sunlight-yellow head of the flower it had stolen. As I held my breath (and Dave held his), the shadow quickly made its way over the fence, into our garden and to the door of the shed.

And just like that, it was gone.

But this time, I stayed at the window, watching carefully, and something different happened that I hadn't noticed before. A light. Well, it was more of a flash, heavenly white, pulsing out through the cracks in the door before disappearing altogether.

'Come on,' I whispered, my voice trembling with fear. I forced myself to stand up on shaky legs that felt like they might give way at any moment. 'Let's go and have a look.'

Dave whined his displeasure but when I stepped out onto the landing and crept down the stairs, he followed on my heels, too scared to be left on his own in the dark.

In the kitchen, I slid the patio door open and, before I could talk myself out of it, I slipped out into the garden. The night was still and silent, pearly moonlight glazing the grass. It crackled slightly underfoot, but in the quiet, it sounded a million times louder, giving me away with every step.

At the shed door, I hesitated. This time, there was no laughter, or any other sound for that matter. Just dead silence. I told myself that Dad had already shown me that nothing was inside the shed. Maybe my eyes were deceiving me. Maybe my imagination was simply making things up that I was starting to believe. There was only one way to find out.

I reached for the door quickly, and before I could take my hand back, grabbed hold of the handle and whipped it wide open. I half expected something terrible to swoop out and attack me, or a ferocious roar to bellow from the shadows. But, again, there was nothing.

Nothing except a sunflower.

It was perfect and pristine, sitting in the middle of the shed among the junk. It quite literally glowed in the dark as if it were a tiny sun. The light stretched its way outwards, reaching for me and inviting me in. I could feel its warmth, even more so when I realised the clouds had gathered above once more and that drops of rain had started falling from the sky. Instinctively, I stepped inside the shed, Dave reluctantly followed my lead as the droplets turned into a downpour.

The sunflower seemed to pulse as we got near. I felt hypnotised by it, like I couldn't help but be drawn in, closer and closer. Dave whined but I could barely hear him. A loud buzz was sounding in my ears. At first, it was indistinguishable, nothing more than white noise. But as I neared the flower, it turned into a lullaby of sorts, soothing music that made me forget my fear. I wasn't scared any more. I reached out for the flower and . . .

As I touched the sunflower's stem, the golden glow quickly vanished, plunging us into darkness. And then I began to fall.

The fall was long. So long I had time to think: *This fall is long.* And *Oh my god I'm going to be in so much trouble when Mum and Dad can't find me in the morning.* But after what felt like an eternity I landed hard. It should've hurt, but a thick tuft of luscious grass broke my fall. It seemed to take hold of me as if it were alive, nestling me in its grasp for a moment, before gently unfurling me so I could stand upright. A panicked bark gave me some relief. Dave was with me, which meant I wasn't quite so alone. I quickly found him, fighting to free himself from his own tuft of grass, and crouched to give him a reassuring hug.

'It's OK, boy. I'm here too.'

But where was *here* exactly? I looked all around me, slowly standing and spinning around on the spot, taking in the landscape that surrounded us. We were outside, seemingly in some kind of small meadow with wildflowers of every colour. A mountain painted the horizon all around us, while the sky above was the pure ocean blue of a midsummer's day without even the faintest hint of a cloud to blemish its beauty. There was the sun we'd been missing for more than a week now, glowing down with a soft warmth that wasn't too hot but instead felt just right.

Before I looked away from the sky, I noticed the smallest pinprick of darkness. It was directly above where we stood, like a hole had been torn into the sheet of blue. I wondered if that was *our* world, back home, dark and gloomy. Because surely the place we'd landed was a different world altogether. There was no other explanation. It was the complete opposite from the place we'd just left.

'I told you this was a bad idea.'

I whirled around on the spot, looking for the owner of the snappy voice that sounded far from happy. But there was nobody there. It was just me and . . .

'Stupid human. Never listens to me. I told him we should've *stayed in bed* but oh no, Mr Super Detective had to go and investigate the shed in the dark. I mean, WHO goes and follows a weird shadow out into the garden in the middle of the night? Stupid, I tell you.'

I was almost too stunned to speak. 'D-D-Dave? Are you . . . are you talking?'

Dave tilted his head up to me, the scowl on his face now blank and confused. His eyes widened and then he suddenly got all excited, his tail wagging a hundred miles an hour. 'Wait, you can HEAR me? You can really hear me?'

I started to feel dizzy. 'This is *not* happening. This is a dream. It has to be.'

'Oh my GOD, you *can* hear me! I have waited for this moment for SO LONG!' Dave started bounding back and forth, grinning from ear to ear. 'All my life I've been ignored and I can *finally* tell you what I've been trying to say all along.'

I put a hand to my forehead, checking for a temperature. 'Which is?'

Dave stopped his pacing and looked me dead in the eye, grimly serious. 'The dog food you've been feeding me lately? It tastes like stale cardboard. I must insist we go back to what you were feeding me before. The chicken and veg? Now *that* was the good stuff.'

I fell back into a sitting position, a tuft of grass catching me once again and forming some kind of seat. I was too distracted to even be impressed. Instead, I was focusing on the dog I'd known for most of my life *actually* talking to me like he was human.

'Oh, and I really do think we should stop walking in the woods,' Dave continued, as if now he'd started talking he simply couldn't stop. 'I get it, nature and all that good stuff. But it's giving me the creeps. I think we should stick to the park. It seems safer.'

'Chicken and vegetable dog food, walks in the park. Got it,' I replied, too bemused and baffled to continue wondering how on earth my dog was now chatting away happily like it was the most normal thing in the world.

'OK, now we've got the important stuff out of the way ... where the hell are we?' Dave surveyed our surroundings, freezing when something caught his eye. 'I believe, dear friend, we have company.'

Delighted to be promoted from 'stupid human' to 'dear friend', I nearly didn't notice the shape coming towards us. It was small, maybe half my size, and seemed to be wearing all black that covered its body and face. But as it got closer, I realised it was not so much walking as it was *floating* and what I had taken to be a person was actually nothing more than darkness that had taken a vague form. It stopped a few metres away as I stood back up. Dave immediately started to growl.

'What are you?' I whispered, trying to stop my legs from shaking.

The thing – there really was no other word for it – started to transform into a shadow, growing taller until we were the same height. It laughed too, a tittering sound like a maniacal clown that gave me the creeps. I immediately recognised it as the laugh we'd been hearing from behind the shed door.

'I was wondering when you'd arrive,' the shadow said. Its voice sounded raspy, gravelly, as if it hadn't been used in far too long.

'W-w-what are you?' I asked again, my own voice quiet and laced with fear. My throat felt dry and I had to ball my hands into fists to stop them from trembling. 'Where are we?'

The shadow seemed to ponder this. If it had a face, I wondered how it would look. 'This is your home!' it said, spreading its arms far and wide as if proud.

'My . . . home?'

The shadow nodded and pointed to my head. 'In here.' His finger moved down a little and came to rest over my heart. 'And in here.'

I frowned. 'You mean, we're in my imagination.'

I'm sure the shadow would've frowned if it could have. 'Not exactly. This is all real, of course. It's just a place deep inside you, where your thoughts begin to brew and your emotions start to boil, where your fears and dreams are born. The darkest things you don't even think about. Down here is everything that makes you ... well, *you*.'

Dave scoffed. 'This thing is a few marbles short of the full set, if you ask me,' he muttered under his breath.

The shadow turned to Dave. 'Then how do you explain the fact that you can talk down here?'

Dave's eyes widened a little and my heart skipped a beat. How *could* Dave suddenly talk like a human? He hadn't presented that skill back in the real world. Why could he do it now? And, more importantly, why was I talking to a shadow as if that was completely normal?

The shadow gestured around at the meadow. 'It took a lot for me to spruce this place up. Before the sun came down here, it was pretty dark and stormy. Gloomy. Not a very nice place to live, let's put it that way.'

I tried not to be offended, but it crept into my retort all the same. 'What are you trying to say about ... the inside of my head or whatever?'

The shadow raised its hands in surrender. 'Only that it was once dark down here, and living in the dark is no way to live at all. I brought the light.'

I narrowed my eyes. 'You mean you stole it. You've been taking the sunflowers and . . . I don't know, doing some kind of dark shadow magic with them to bring the sun down here, into whatever you call this place. You're a thief.'

'A prisoner,' the shadow corrected with contempt. 'Locked away down here, made up of all the things you try to push away.' I felt my eyebrows rise up my face, but the shadow kept on going. 'While you've been living up there in the light, basking in the sun, I've been trapped in your darkness. Do you know what that does to a person?'

I shook my head, more out of confusion than anything else. The shadow barked a bitter laugh, then took a few steps until it was right in front of my face.

'It can drive you quite mad.'

I backed away, suddenly more frightened than I'd been before. The shadow didn't seem to mind. It waved a hand and a perfectly pristine sunflower appeared in it. The shadow plucked the petals one by one, each one turning black. As it did so, the warmth of the sun above started to fade, the blue sky darkening as stormy clouds rolled in. I continued to back away until I tripped and fell hard on the ground. This time, no tuft of grass broke my fall. In fact, the grass was no longer even there. The meadow had vanished entirely, thorny trees sprouting all around us. Dave whined, curling himself next to me. The light disappeared entirely. Only the small glow of the flower remained.

'I think I'll take the light with me when I go,' the shadow said. 'I'm used to it now.'

'W-when you go?' The words felt sour on my tongue.

The shadow offered nothing but a cruel laugh. 'When I go,' it said again. It looked up at the sky. The pinprick of darkness that had been directly above us before was now a faint light. I squinted and could've sworn I could see the sun beginning to rise back in the real world.

When I looked back at the shadow, it grinned. But ... that was impossible. Shadows couldn't grin or smile or even offer any expression at all. They were simply nothing but darkness. Except now the shadow had a mouth. And the rest of it was beginning to take shape too.

Where there had been nothing before, a face began to appear, features I vaguely recognised moulding themselves out of the dark. Two arms, two legs, two ears, eyes, nose, hands, feet, even clothes, until finally the transformation was complete.

I recoiled in horror. The shadow was no more. Now I stood face to face with a boy, holding a glowing sunflower. But I knew this person, better than anybody. The boy I was staring at was ... me, with a wicked expression on his face.

Or a version of me anyway. If I looked closely, the features were distorted slightly, not quite right. But it was unmistakably my clone, born out of darkness. I scrambled backwards.

'Hello,' I heard myself say, but the voice was coming from the shadow instead.

'W-w-what are you?' I asked, my own voice quiet and laced with fear.

'I think you already know the answer to that question,' the shadow said. It looked itself up and down, then swivelled its eyes, a few shades darker than my own, to take me in. The shadow smiled to himself. 'I'm you, of course.' The shadow laughed and began to float away, taking the sunflower and the last remaining light with it.

As the darkness closed in on me from all sides, I began to scream.

Izzy woke up with a shout, jolting upright in his bed. His hands flew up to his face, then patted the rest of his body as if he were checking that he was all there, in one piece. His chest heaved with deep breaths, his heart hammering in its cage.

There was the sound of hurried footsteps, then the bedroom door sprang open. It was his mum, a panicked look on her face. Her eyes darted all around the room, searching for signs of danger. When she couldn't find any obvious threats, she frowned in Izzy's direction.

'What's going on in here?' she asked, confused.

Izzy checked the room for himself, sweeping it with a quick glance. Finally, his eyes settled on the window, where the gap in his bedroom curtains revealed gentle sunlight and a cloudless sky. He breathed a sigh of relief.

'Just a bad dream,' he said. 'That's all.'

Izzy's mum clapped her hand to her chest. 'You had me worried for a minute! Breakfast in ten?'

'Sure,' he said.

His mum gave him a smile and set off for the kitchen, leaving the bedroom door open. In her place, Dave appeared. The dog didn't come into the room. Instead, it watched Izzy carefully, tilting his head as he did so. Izzy looked right back.

'Who's a good boy?' Izzy cooed.

The dog hesitated for a moment, and then it began to growl.

Izzy ignored him and lay back into his pillows with a smile. Outside, the birds were tweeting their pleasant morning call. But inside his head, the shadow could still hear the faint echo of a scream.

ROOPA FAROOKI

POISON PLAYTIME:
A MIDSUMMER NIGHT'S
MURDER MYSTERY

(A DOUBLE DETECTIVES' MINI
MEDICAL MYSTERY)

TOP SECRET

POISON PLAYTIME: A MIDSUMMER NIGHT'S MURDER MYSTERY
(A DOUBLE DETECTIVES' MINI MEDICAL MYSTERY)

By Roopa Farooki

Ali did a fake sleepwalk into the kitchen, still in her PJs, with her arms out in front of her in grabby-zombie style. 'Brains,' she moaned. 'Brains . . .'

Tulip rolled her eyes. She was already sitting at the table, dressed in her uniform, and finishing off her cereal. 'You'd better put an end to that sentence,' she said. 'You're scaring our guests.'

Jay and Zac, the other twins in their class, were sitting at the table too. They were picking at the withered grapes in the fruit bowl. They wouldn't eat the cereal, as they were gluten-free and dairy-free vegetarians.

'Yikes,' whispered Zac to Tulip. 'And you have to share a room with her. I just wouldn't sleep.'

Jay got up and sensibly steered Ali towards the table, sat her down and poured her a glass of juice.

'Think she just needs sugar,' he said.

'Brains,' moaned Ali again. 'My brain's gone to mush! I can't learn the stupid lines for the stupid school play with this pollen count. I was up all night with the sneezles.' She gulped from the glass of juice, and then spat it out. 'Ugh, what's this? You trying to poison me?'

'Mum says juice that comes in boxes IS poison,' agreed Jay. 'She squeezes ours fresh each morning.'

Tulip sniffed the juice. 'Ew, think you left the carton out overnight, Ali,' she said. 'Diagnosis: fermented OJ. It's just too hot in the kitchen.'

'I hate summer,' complained Ali. 'My juice goes off, my eyes are all crusty, I can't sleep.' She sat up and looked properly at Jay and Zac. 'And why are Tweedle-Dumb and Tweedle-Bummer here?'

'Dad dropped us off,' said Zac helpfully. 'Mum's got a hospital appointment, so your mum said we could come here before school, so he could get her there in time.' He fiddled with his blue inhaler. 'Jay's Tweedle-Bummer, right?'

'Seriously?' retorted Jay. 'You'd rather be the dumb one?'

'Nobody's dumb,' said Tulip kindly, before glaring at her sister. 'Ali just has to work on her social skills. What she MEANT to say was "Good morning" or "Nice to see you" or, you know, normal-person words.'

'I know what I meant to say,' yawned Ali. 'And why didn't you put my juice away last night? Thought you were the NICE twin.'

'Being the MEAN twin is so not the flex you think it is,' said Tulip crossly.

They were interrupted by Ali's and Tulip's mum opening the front door and running into the kitchen, her stethoscope dangling around her neck. She was wearing a yellow smiley *Hello! My name is Dr Minnie* badge on her scrubs.

'Hello, sweeties!' she said. 'Girls, be nice to Jay and Zac.'

'Tulip's always nice,' said Zac. Tulip beamed at him, and Ali gave him a withering stare.

Minnie dumped a load of gluten-free and dairy-free treats on the table, having clearly just raided the *Free From* section of their corner shop.

'Here's breakfast for the boys,' she said. 'Thought you might like some gluten-free toast with peanut butter and bananas.'

'Are the bananas fair trade?' asked Zac.

'Is the peanut butter palm-oil free?' asked Jay.

'Umm,' said Minnie. She spotted a beige packet and waved it at them for distraction. 'Look, organic rice cakes! So, um, *bland*-looking.'

'Ooh, awesome,' said Jay, taking it from her. 'Yay, look,

they're made with *brown* rice.' He ripped the packet open with excitement.

'LOVE brown rice cakes,' said Zac. 'They're like my favourite carby comfort food.'

Ali snorted and poured chocolate cereal into her bowl.

'Have a lovely day,' said Minnie, looking relieved. 'Good luck with the show prep today. I never did the school summer performance. I was more into the science fair.'

'Mum won first prize at the science fair,' said Tulip proudly.

'Only after the guy who won first prize got disqualified for cheating,' said Minnie. 'Poor old Evelyn. That was the beginning of the end for him.'

'Don't you DARE feel sorry for Stupid Sprotland,' snapped Ali. Evelyn Sprotland was their evil genius nemesis, who had never got over his school science fair failure after cheating to impress Minnie. They'd managed to put him in jail last winter, for poisoning the Christmas chocolate on the children's ward at Minnie's hospital.

'And don't have that juice,' added Minnie blithely. 'I think it's generating its own life forms! We could maybe use it for an experiment later.'

She gave the girls a big hug, squashing them against her green scrubs top. Then she raced out of the front door, tripping over Witch, their adopted fat black cat, who was stretched on the step in the sun. Witch flung out a clawed paw, as though briefly thinking about vengeance, but then flumped back into her prone position with a yawn.

'Bye, Mum!' called Tulip. 'Have a nice day brain-doctoring! Love you!'

'Bye, Minnie,' called Jay and Zac politely.

'Shut the door, Mum,' screeched Ali. She ran down the corridor and pushed Witch off the step. 'Stupid fat cat is letting all the pollen in.'

She went back to the kitchen, snatched the packet of rice cakes from Jay and stomped back upstairs. 'I don't know why I even sit with you guys,' she complained as she went. 'You ferment my OJ, poison me with it, criticise my social skills and troll me about my allergies!'

'You don't get to own allergies,' Tulip called upstairs after her. 'I've got hayfever too. And Jay has urticaria. And Zac has asthma.'

'I'd really prefer you didn't talk about my urticaria,' said Jay crossly. 'Patient confidentiality.'

On the walk to school, Ali was still munching on the last few rice cakes.

'These actually aren't horrible,' she said happily. 'Like chewing bubble wrap.'

'They were mine,' sighed Jay. 'So are you happy with

your part in the play?' Their form teacher, Mr Ofu, had allocated their parts by email the night before.

'Dunno,' said Ali. It was a sore point that Tulip always got picked for a better part than her, as Tulip was more reliable and less likely to do a diva-type explosion.

'I'm the understudy for girl lead again,' sighed Tulip. 'So I have to learn two sets of lines.'

'I'm a lead,' said Zac unexpectedly. 'Sort of. My character's even on the poster.'

'*You're* a lead?' said Ali doubtfully. 'But that's a *donkey* headshot on the poster.' She pointed to it as they approached the school.

'Duh,' said Tulip. 'We're doing *A Midsummer Night's Dream*. Don't you ever read your emails?'

'*Boooring,*' said Ali. 'Why can't we do *A Midsummer Night's Nightmare*? Or *A Midsummer Night's Murder Mystery*? You know, something fun where we can throw red paint around and scream.'

'Your idea of fun is kind of worrying,' said Jay.

'My character's called Bottom,' said Zac sadly. 'Mum is so proud. When I got the email, she literally messaged the whole extended family group chat: *Zac's playing BOTTOM.*'

'Don't stress,' said Tulip, patting him kindly on the shoulder. 'You'll be great as the donkey-head dude.'

Even Ali looked sorry for him. 'Soz, that sucks,' she

said, then added hopefully, 'We could always go off-script and kill you with red paint in the first act. Then we could make the play about who killed you?'

'No going off-script,' said Jay. 'It would mess with my timings.'

'Timings? What part have you got?' Ali asked him.

'I'm head of tech,' said Jay. 'I asked to do the lighting and the music cues and stuff. I'm basically the chair guy with the laptop.'

'Nice,' said Ali. 'Can I be a tech head too? I don't want to be a stupid spare woodland sprite.'

'I've got an extra spot on the team. But it'll cost you,' said Jay. 'You know what I want.'

Ali grinned, and threw him the packet of rice cakes, and Jay caught them one-handed. 'Yum,' he said, biting into one blissfully. 'So, so bland.'

They passed another poster outside the classroom, and they all stopped and stared. It showed a picture of Tulip, with a leafy, flowery crown photoshopped on her head, against a sparkling woodland background stolen from *The Hobbit* poster from last year.

'It's looking great, isn't it?' said Mr Ofu, giving Tulip a thumbs up as he walked past them. 'There's our leading lady!'

'Leading lady?' sputtered Ali. '*You're* Titania, Queen of the Fairies?' She looked like she was somewhere between angry tears and laughter. 'You're the MAIN CHARACTER?'

'Well, I'd say the play is more of an ensemble piece,' said Jay.

'She's the QUEEN of the freaking fairies,' said Ali. 'And I'm stuck in tech with the chair nerds. It's so unfair.'

'Hey! Don't hate on the tech,' said Jay.

'But, Mr Ofu,' said Tulip, looking shocked. 'You said I'd just UNDERSTUDY Titania. That's Adenike's role.' Adenike was the school superstar. She could sing and dance and took the lead in all the school productions.

'Just in case Adenike can't do it,' said Mr Ofu. 'Her casting agent said show day might clash with her yoghurt ad auditions.'

'Yoghurt ad? Oh, she'll be great at that,' said Zac. 'She loves her fro-yo.'

'Auditions?' asked Tulip. 'Since when did Adenike go to auditions? And when did she get an agent?'

An older lady, with midnight-blue hair cut sharply at her jaw, swept out of the classroom. She was wearing a floppy beret, enormous sunglasses and a long dark coat.

'Mr Ofu,' she greeted in a deep, breathy voice, holding out a large, bony hand covered in lethal-looking rings.

'Madame Ekaterina.' Mr Ofu bowed, looking a bit star-struck. 'I didn't realise you were still here.'

'I am like my artistes,' said Madame Ekaterina. She

leaned forward and whispered conspiratorially, 'I am *everywhere*.' She handed him a card. 'Share this with no one. My agency is exclusive and I do not encourage word of mouth.'

She swept away, down the corridors, her long coat swishing around her.

'So who's the old emo weirdo that you've let into our classroom?' asked Ali reasonably.

'She's kind of fabulous-weird,' said Zac, looking after her in awe. 'She has killer presence. Now THAT's main-character energy. Like your Nan-Nan.'

'Nan-Nan's much cooler than her,' sniffed Tulip. 'And I actually think Ali has a point. You can't let any weird old lady run around the school like that.'

'Stop saying weird,' said Mr Ofu, offended. 'That's Madame Ekaterina! She runs the most exclusive casting agency in London.'

'So exclusive that Google hasn't heard of her,' pointed out Jay, holding up his phone after some rapid thumb work.

'Classic chair-guy move,' said Ali approvingly.

'She's deliberately gone off-grid to avoid unsolicited applications,' said Mr Ofu. 'Look at her business card. It's so classy.'

He held it out to them. It was a white glossy card, silver trimmed, which simply said *Ekaterina Casting*, and on the other side there was a QR code and a line which said *By appointment only*. Adenike came out of the classroom, eating a lemon-coloured yoghurt. 'Did you meet Kitty? She said I might be the next Yoglicious kid.'

'Never heard of Yoglicious,' said Ali.

'That'll change when I'm fronting their ads,' said Adenike smugly. She saw Tulip's face on the show poster. 'What's going on? I'm the star of the show.'

'Totally,' Tulip agreed. 'But Mr Ofu seemed to think you might be doing the yoghurt thing instead.'

'I can do both,' said Adenike firmly. 'Just need to call Kitty to sort this. Sorry, Tulip, I know it's cold in my shadow.'

She snapped her fingers and her entourage came out of the classroom. 'Come on, girls,' she said, pulling out her phone. They all flipped their plaits and strode out after her, walking in sync.

'But class is starting,' said Mr Ofu, watching them leave with bemusement. 'They're all going in the wrong direction.'

'Sorry, sir,' said Jay. 'Guessing Adenike had to make a call.'

During rehearsals, Madame Ekaterina was still hanging around the school, stalking the corridors darkly and snapping on the phone to her assistant.

'I don't want attitude, Jessica, I want gratitude! You're lucky you're *allowed* to be part of this team. Now Uber over the new Yoglicious flavours in twenty minutes or you're fired!'

'Toxic boss, much?' muttered Tulip. 'I hope Jessica dumps her.' She turned to Adenike, who was looking resplendent in her fairy crown, strung with fairy lights, with a pair of enormous wings hooked over her shoulders. 'How did you get involved with her? Did you send her a C.V., or something?'

Adenike laughed. 'No way! You can't just apply to Kitty's agency. She *invites* people.'

'So how'd she find out about you?' persisted Tulip. 'Did your mum post something on social media? Like a video of you performing?'

'Don't think so,' said Adenike. 'Guess she just found out about me from someone at school. Everyone knows that I star in all the school plays. Just like everyone knows you're the permanent understudy.' She handed Tulip her phone. 'Can you take a picture of me eating this yoghurt for my Insta?'

'Sure,' said Tulip, clicking the shot. 'Not sure it's a big moment to commemorate. That's your fifth one today.'

'I'm basically more yoghurt than human at this point,' agreed Adenike. 'Everyone's loving these yoghurts. Kitty's bringing in more sample boxes for the whole school.'

'That's generous,' said Tulip. 'She doesn't look like the sort to give out free snacks.'

'Where's Zac disappeared off to again?' said Adenike, looking distracted. 'I need to rehearse my Bottom lines with him.' She finished her yoghurt, puffed out her wings and flew off.

'Did she eat it?' said Madame Ekaterina, popping her head round the door.

'Yikes,' jumped Tulip. 'You kinda scare me. I don't think you're allowed to be here.'

'I don't follow the rules,' said Madame Ekaterina. 'Rules are for little people. Like you, Tulip.'

'Um, how'd you know my name?' said Tulip.

Madame Ekaterina ignored her. 'Ah, she did eat it all. Excellent. The game's afoot!' And she turned on her heel and swished away, her dark coat flapping behind her.

Ali wandered in, looking pleased with herself, adjusting a belt with phones and remote controls around her waist. 'Being Queen TechHead on the production is the BEST,' she said. 'No stupid costumes, no running around on stage pretending to be a fairy like a loser. No donkey head. No dumb lines to learn. And I can spotlight whoever I like. I'm gonna spotlight Zach's bottom, while he's playing Bottom, geddit?'

She saw that Tulip wasn't paying attention. 'Hey, listen to me when I'm making my hilarious witty comments,' she said, punching Tulip in the shoulder.

Tulip was looking at the empty yoghurt pot that Adenike had left.

'Something's afoot,' she said, picking it up and inspecting it.

'No, something's a POT,' said Ali. 'Duh.'

Tulip put the pot in her bag, being careful not to touch the inside.

'Yuck, why are you collecting Adenike's trash?' said Ali. 'She's got her whole group of hair-flipping, phone-clicking minions to do that for her.'

'Evidence,' said Tulip. 'Something's off about Madame Ekaterina and the Yoglicious thing.'

'Hard agree,' said Ali. 'Google's never heard of her. And we've never heard of Yoglicious. Mr Ofu is way too trusting.'

Tulip jumped again as she heard Jay's voice come out of Ali's belt.

'You sure you're not just missing solving a mystery so much that you're inventing one?' said Jay. 'Sounds like you're trying to live your version of *A Midsummer Night's Murder* instead of working on the real play.'

'Hey, it's not been *that* long,' protested Tulip. 'We solved a medical mystery a few weeks back.'

Zac crawled out from under the table with the donkey head from his costume tucked under his arm. He'd obviously been hiding from Adenike.

'TBH that wasn't the most challenging mystery,' he said. 'Even I could have solved it without any medical knowledge. The kid who wasn't getting any sleep was the one who was stealing Mr Ofu's afternoon caramel iced-latte with double-shot espresso.'

'Poor old Otis,' said Tulip. 'And because he was up all night, he was tired during the day, and needed the latte to stay awake in class. It was a vicious cycle.'

'Yeah, but diagnostically it was about as complicated as who ate all the pies,' said Jay, his disembodied voice echoing on the belt.

'Pie-shaming,' said Tulip, shaking her head. 'N'cool, Jay.'

'Ya know,' said Ali to the mic on her belt, 'you're even MORE annoying when you're not here in person, Jay. Didn't think it was possible to be a noob from two hundred metres away.'

At the end of the day, the girls were walking out of the gate when Adenike strolled over.

'Hey, I've got a medical question for you,' she said.

'Sure,' said Tulip.

'Is there any health problem with eating a lot of this stuff?' She was eating yet another yoghurt. Her minion friends were all eating one too. The backup boxes had arrived, and there was a queue at the free samples table in reception.

'Nah, it's basically thick milk,' said Ali, 'with a bit of bacteria. You can go-yo all day.'

'Why'd you ask?' asked Tulip suspiciously. 'Aren't you feeling well?'

'I'm feeling fine,' said Adenike, tossing her beaded plaits so they clinked dramatically. She finished her yoghurt and threw it to one of her friends, who caught it one-handed and tossed it in the bin without dropping her own blueberry heaven flavour.

'It's weird that you're all eating that much though,' said Tulip, watching the line of Adenike's influencer friends slurping it down. 'It can't taste THAT good.'

'It's not as good as fro-yo or ice cream,' agreed Adenike. 'But there's something about it. Take this salted caramel flavour. Normally I'm not a fan of sweet and salty, but in this yoghurt, it's just sort of gimme-more-ish.'

On cue, they heard Momo's ice-cream van pumping out its cheerful jingle as he pulled up outside the school.

'Yay! Fro-yo! Let's go, girls,' Adenike said to her entourage. She snapped her fingers and they all strode away and through the gates.

'Oh, beans,' said Zac, running up behind Ali and Tulip. 'Adenike's minions take ages picking their flavours. I wanted to get my organic lolly order in before them.' He was still clutching the donkey head.

'What's that doing here?' said Ali, pointing to the head. 'It's kind of gross.'

'Mr Ofu said I have to get used to it for the play,' said Zac. 'Apparently you can hear my vivid terror of dark, enclosed spaces whenever I say my lines.' He pulled it over his head. 'I gotta live in here now,' he said even more sadly.

'Wow, you're like Eeyore from *Winnie-the-Pooh*,' said Ali. 'It's like, uncanny.'

Jay came out of the school. He didn't say a word when he saw Zac with the donkey head, but he looked hard at Ali. 'Have you got anything to say?'

'Always,' said Ali promptly, looking pleased. 'Got some new insults I wanted to try out.'

'Anything else?' Jay said. 'Like, admitting to thieving school property? One of the walkie-talkie sets is missing.'

'Oh, doh,' said Ali, opening her blazer. The walkie-talkie was still hooked into her trouser waistband. 'Soz,' she said, 'I was just having a play with it. Hid the other one in the classroom. I was trying to creep out Mr Ofu by saying that I was a ghost from the past to warn him about a terrible crime.'

'Ali!' said Tulip. 'That's a bit over the line.'

'Not gonna lie, that's borderline genius,' said Zac through the donkey head.

'The walkie-talkie is not a toy,' complained Jay. 'Give it back!'

Ali shrugged and pulled it out. 'Sorry, Mr Ofu. Playtime's over,' she said into the walkie-talkie, and tossed it to Jay.

Jay caught it awkwardly, but almost dropped it again as they heard someone speak back.

'Sorry, Ali, playtime's NOT over yet. I'm having too much fun. But tomorrow it'll ALL be over. Over.'

And then they heard a throaty laugh.

'Who's this, over?' said Jay. But the walkie-talkie had gone dead.

'Well, that was creepy,' said Jay, looking across to Ali. 'Did you set that up to troll me?'

Ali's and Tulip's eyes were shining. 'It's a mystery!' they said at exactly the same time. 'Jinx!' they said together instinctively. Then they repeated, 'Jinx! Jinx!' looking annoyed at each other, and, 'Jinx padlock one-two-three.' They fell into cross silence, with Ali waving a fist at Tulip.

'I'm guessing someone has to break the jinx,' said Jay. 'Not gonna be me.'

'I'm too donkey-headed to break jinxes,' said Zac.

Ali wrote on her phone: *We have to investigate who's got the other walkie-talkie! So break the jinx, noob.*

'Aw, when you ask so nicely,' said Jay. 'C'mon, Zac-Zac, I'll get you one of Momo's organic fruit-juice lollies.'

Just then, a black and silver car screeched up towards the school, emblazoned with a prominent disability sticker. The twins' Nan-Nan wound down her car window. She tossed her silver and black hair in exactly the same way that Adenike had done. The sun glinted on the metal studs on her leather jacket.

'Ooh, main-character energy alert,' said Zac, standing up straighter. He was shorter than Jay, even with the donkey head.

'Hey, Ali and Tulip,' said Nan-Nan. 'I was just passing, in a completely non-suspicious coincidence. I'll give you a ride home.' She nodded at the boys. 'You can come too, Jay-and-or-Zac.'

'Gnarly, Nan-Nan,' said Tulip. 'You broke the jinx.'

'Sure, Ms Ruby,' said Jay, pushing back his glasses. He gave a strained laugh. 'It's really funny, that little joke you make every time, like you don't know which of us is Jay and which of us is Zac.'

'Joke? Sure, let's go with that,' said Nan-Nan. She reached out and flicked the donkey head off Zac. 'Sorry, munchkin, you had something stuck on your face.'

'Thanks,' said Zac gratefully. 'I just can't get used to it.'

'When I was a spy, I had a bag on my head for a week as a hostage in enemy terrain,' said Nan-Nan sympathetically. 'Had to cut it off with one of my metal legs. The right one. It has a serrated edge. I got it put in especially.'

'Yeah, we get it,' shrugged Ali. 'You were a spy, you don't have to keep going on about it.'

Nan-Nan smirked and spun the car around in a U-turn. They all piled in.

She took off and tooted at Momo when she passed his van.

'My queens,' Momo called to the girls, waving and grinning. 'I have given your Nan-Nan some most excellent frozen treats. Look in the back! Please share with your friends.'

'Ooh, awesome,' said Jay, rummaging in the box in the back seat. 'He's given us the organic lollies.'

'*Yeuch*, he's put echinacea and cranberries in them,' said Ali. 'You two can definitely have those.'

'It's antioxidant,' said Zac happily.

'I'm having the purple one with jelly beans and glitter,' said Tulip. 'So why are you really here, Nan-Nan? Were you casing the school?'

Nan-Nan looked impressed. 'You catch on fast these days.' She slowed down precisely for the speed camera, waved at it, and then screeched off again. 'Let's talk at home.'

Back at the twins' house, Nan-Nan showed them a photo on her phone. It was a long-distance shot of a woman in dark glasses with sharply cut blue hair under a floppy hat.

'You've seen this lady lurking around the school?' she asked.

'It's Madame Ekaterina,' said Tulip. 'So-called casting agent. I knew she was super sus.'

'Adenike loves her,' said Jay sadly. 'She's going to be really sad that Madame Ekaterina's one of the bad guys.'

'Why'd you care?' said Ali. 'Think *you're* the one who LOVES Adenike.'

'Shut up, Ali,' said Jay crossly. 'She's a friend. More than you, apparently.'

'She's not a *bad* bad guy,' said Nan-Nan. 'She's one of my old informers. Code name Kitty. NOT the cute kind. She's got claws.'

'If she's not bad,' said Tulip, 'why's she pushing this stuff on Adenike?' She pulled Adenike's empty Yoglicious pot out of her bag.

'Clever girl!' said Nan-Nan. 'I wanted to ask you to get me one of these for my lab ladies to test.'

'It's so cool that you have a lab team,' said Zac.

Nan-Nan bagged the sample efficiently in a ziplock bag. 'Kitty's not a good guy either. She plays both teams, and works for the highest bidder.'

'So what's the deal with the yoghurt?' said Ali.

'We'll find out,' said Nan-Nan. 'Have you observed weird behaviour from anyone eating it?'

'Only that they can't stop?' said Tulip.

'Maybe Kitty's spiking it with something addictive,' said Ali.

'Obviously,' said Nan-Nan. 'What I don't get is, why? And why have they been pushing it in YOUR little school?'

'OMG, I've gotta warn Adenike she's having dodgy yoghurt,' said Tulip.

She messaged Adenike, who messaged back straight away: *Lol, you funny. The lead's MINE loser, give up the mind games,* 😴

'Well, you tried,' said Zac.

Nan-Nan pulled off her leather jacket. 'Enough shop talk,' she said. 'I promised Minnie I'd make dinner for you munchkins. Wash your hands, spit-spot.'

Ali and Tulip froze. Nan-Nan was famous for her weird food experiments from around the world.

'What's it tonight?' sighed Tulip. 'Raw beef? Live squid?'

'Aren't you clever,' said Nan-Nan. 'Marinated raw beef! I hadn't thought to add squid, but I'm sure I can find a TikTok on that.' She grinned at Jay and Zac. 'I could do the same thing for you two, but with fungus and seaweed, if you like?'

The boys were edging to the door. 'Um,' said Zac.

'Well, you see,' said Jay, 'Mum said to . . .'

And then they bolted down the hall together, falling over Witch as they escaped out of the front door. Witch screeched in disgust and then stalked up to the kitchen, to leap on Tulip's lap.

'Yeah, they'd better run,' sniffed Ali.

At school the next day, Mr Ofu was in tears.

'The play's a midsummer night's nightmare!' he squealed to the twins, when they came in.

'Yay!' said Ali. 'Finally taking my ideas on board. Let's put the scary in the fairy, and kill the donkey in a mystery crime.'

'I mean, it's a *real* nightmare,' Mr Ofu persisted. 'Everybody's got sick!'

Adenike walked in, clutching her stomach. 'Do you think you can catch lactose intolerance?' she asked, 'I've literally been on the loo since I got into school.' She pulled out a yoghurt. 'Well, better stay hydrated.'

Tulip slapped the yoghurt out of her hands. 'That stuff's poison!' she said.

'You're just jealous cos you're not the Yoglicious Kid,' muttered Adenike, not too convincingly. 'Well, at least you get to step up from understudy.'

'I don't want to be the lead,' said Tulip crossly. 'I just want all my friends to be well.'

'Aww,' said Adenike. 'That's really sweet. Feel kinda bad for clowning you.'

Jay and Zac walked in. 'Have you seen the queue for the loo?' asked Zac. 'What's going on?'

'That's what I want to know,' said Nan-Nan, rolling into the classroom. She had Witch purring on her lap like a film villain's familiar. Witch had clearly had enough of everyone falling over her. Nan-Nan waved her phone, showing the lab results. 'No one should be eating this yoghurt. It contains an addictive agent that mimics lactose intolerance with increased doses. Where's Kitty?'

'Oh, you know Madame Ekaterina?' said Mr Ofu. 'Maybe she can help me bring in some non-toilet-trapped actors for the play?'

'Stop being so thirsty, sir,' said Ali. 'The play's over. It's been poisoned by Madame Ekaterina's yucky yoghurt.'

'Kitty's there,' said Adenike, pointing across the playground. 'She brought in more yoghurt today. We've all been eating it.'

'What's up with Witch?' asked Tulip as Witch suddenly leaped up from Nan-Nan's jeans with a meercat-like alertness. She streaked across the playground in a smoky-black blur, doing the closest thing to a roar that she could do, with claws out.

Madame Ekaterina looked up, saw Witch screeching towards her, and almost fell over backwards. 'No! Not you, stupid cat!' Her voice was completely different. She sounded like a grumpy guy.

Nan-Nan looked across the playground and slapped her forehead in frustration.

'THAT'S NOT KITTY!' she said. 'That's just someone in a wig!'

She raced across the playground in her wheelchair. The Person Who Wasn't Kitty backed away from the yoghurt table, kicked off their high heels and started running.

'Let's go!' yelled Ali. 'This is a proper medical mystery. A poison plot and a bad guy in disguise! I LOVE this bit!' And she raced after Nan-Nan, who was wheeling after Witch, who was hunting the Kitty impersonator.

'No, stop, don't,' said Jay unconvincingly. Then he shrugged, and ran after Ali. 'She's right,' he said, calling over his shoulder with a grin. 'This version of the play is way more fun!'

Mr Ofu looked baffled. 'Poison plot and bad guy? Guess no one has the time to catch me up?' he said.

'Sorry, sir,' said Tulip. She nodded to Zac. 'To the school gate?' she said calmly, gathering up some bits of the play's set.

'Read my mind. After you,' Zac said, just as calmly. 'Can't do all that running, it makes my asthma play up.'

The wig person had almost made it out of school, with Nan-Nan wheeling after them like the wind. Witch caught up first and leaped on to the back of the impersonator's long coat, ripping it to shreds by dragging her claws down it.

The wig person tried to fight off Witch, but tripped and fell at the entrance, thanks to a string of fairy lights that Tulip and Zac were holding like a trip wire across the gate.

'What?!' the fake Kitty screeched, flying over and then landing flat onto a pile of raked leaves.

'Yeah, that soft landing is more than you deserved,' sniffed Tulip. She quickly wound the fairy lights and cobweb string-wings from the play around the impersonator, trapping their arms against their sides.

'Oh, well done, munchkins,' said Nan-Nan, grinning as she wheeled towards them. 'Who'd have thought you could fight crime with costume design?'

'Nice work, Tulip,' said Jay. '*Though she be but little, she is fierce!*'

'Wow, you really do know the play by heart,' said Tulip.

'Hey, no fair,' said Ali, breathing raggedly with all the effort of running, clutching her tummy and looking crossly towards Tulip and Zac. 'I've got a stitch! How did you get here before us?'

'Easy beans,' said Zac. 'We just came straight to the exit, while you guys were doing the circuit of the playground.'

'Can I do the Scooby-Doo bad guy reveal?' asked Tulip. She stooped down and pulled off the imposter's wig.

And a weird plastic mask came off with it.

'*Evelyn Sprotland?*' Tulip and Ali gasped. Their cheating

nemesis, who'd been in their mum's class! He was meant to be in jail after tampering with chocolate and tying up Nan-Nan in the hospital last Christmas.

'Wow, prison really ages you,' said Ali. 'How'd you get out already?'

'I escaped, you interfering brat,' said Evelyn. 'I paid Madame Ekaterina to swap with me. And I've sabotaged the school with my home science project! I've finally WON!' He gave a maniacal laugh. 'I've invented an addictive additive for yoghurt that's NOT gut-friendly, and all your toilets are blocked and the play is doomed!'

'Oh, well done, Evelyn,' said Nan-Nan. 'Much more inventive than your usual evil schemes.'

'And I would have got away with it too,' spat Evelyn. 'If it wasn't for your stupid cat.'

'Yeah, Witch really hates you,' said Tulip, picking up Witch and hugging her. 'She has great taste.'

'Shame about the play though,' said Jay.

'Whatevs,' said Ali. 'I really don't care that much about the play.'

'I'm kind of relieved,' said Zac. 'I didn't want to be the donkey.'

'What?' said Evelyn. 'But this is my revenge! My ultimate revenge! This will scar you for life! Like losing the science fair prize did for me!'

'You really don't know us very well,' said Tulip kindly.

'He's right about the play,' said Mr Ofu sadly. 'We can't do it now. The only people who didn't eat that foul yoghurty stuff are you four . . .'

He looked hopefully at all of them.

They all looked at each other.

'No,' said Ali. 'NO WAY.'

Tulip shrugged. 'Well, I know all the lines. We could work it with the four of us.'

'I know most of them,' said Zac. 'I was already a lead. As long as I don't have to be the donkey-head dude.'

'I know all the lines too,' said Jay. 'It's just basic knowledge as the tech head.'

Mr Ofu's eyes welled up. 'Hooray! The show will go on!'

Nan-Nan laughed. 'You're hilariously bad at this, Evelyn,' she said. 'You've given everyone diarrhoea, so they'll poop out all your poison anyway, and accidentally made your mortal enemies the stars of the school show.'

Evelyn huffed in fury. Then his eyes widened at the approaching sound of police sirens.

Ali put the donkey head on him and snapped a selfie.

'Never looked better, Evelyn,' she said. 'Think we finally found the perfect donkey-dude poster for the show.'

WINDOW
PAIN

SHARNA JACKSON

PROPERTY OF THE SUPER SUNNY MURDER CLUB

WINDOW PAIN

By Sharna Jackson

It wasn't just the pollen. It wasn't the flying ants either. The fact that the entire city smelled like some sick, twisted person had put piles of poop in the world's largest oven, set it to gas-mark nine and left the dirt cake to bake for three months wasn't the worst of it.

This was personal. Summer was Paul's personal hell.

It was the constant sneezing, his red-rimmed eyes, his nose dripping like the leaking hot tap in the bathroom his mum said she'd fix but never got round to. It was Paul's puffed-rice face, his scratchy throat threatening to close at any moment.

The worst of it was the unbearable clamminess anywhere his body folded. When skin touched skin. It was why Paul stood – or lay down when it was cool enough – in the shape of a starfish. He made sure his head was always straight ahead, never ever daring to rest his chin on his chest between June and September.

His neck would never forgive him if he did.

In term time, Paul's classmates would be positively giddy about not wearing a coat as the days grew warmer, or they'd boast about going to even hotter places like Tenerife to . . . tan?

Paul would wear a tight smile and nod, like he agreed and was excited for them, but inside he shuddered, judged them, and made mental notes not to trust them and their poor choices. There would be no Tenerife for Paul, there wouldn't be a Truro either. Summer was time for a hibernation of sorts, to be spent in his sweltering room.

Paul adjusted his reflective wrap-around sunglasses on his brown face and looked out of his closed window. A black standing fan whirred behind him, doing its best to cool the room, but was about as effective as a baby breathing on a bonfire. His bedroom door opened and a reflection of his mum cradling clean bed sheets in her arms appeared in the glass.

'Are you planning on standing there all summer, Paul?'

'I'm out of options, Mum,' he sighed, looking down into his garden. It was a tale of two yards: the first half concreted with a small round patio table and three chairs; the second, a green lawn with coloured flowers around its borders. Beyond his garden, past the three-metre-high chain-link fence, was a building Paul was very familiar with.

'But Dr Anthony said you could try another antihistamine, use hydrocortisone cream –'

Paul put his hand up to stop her. 'We tried, remember? Nothing worked.'

'So you'll stare at your school – your old school – for the next six weeks?' She stretched the fresh blue bed sheet over his mattress. Her curly black hair hung over her face. 'You don't even go there any more.' She paused. 'Is *that* it, Paul?' she asked quietly. 'Are you nervous about moving on? You want to talk about it?'

Paul pursed his lips but he didn't reply. He did not want to talk about it.

His phone, lying on the windowsill in front of him, beeped and lit up. 'Josh is here – will you let him in? Please?'

His mum sighed. 'You allergic to summer and conversation, Josh allergic to the doorbell. Kids . . .' she muttered as she stepped down the stairs.

Josh ran his fingers through his floppy blonde hair and leaned forward. He glanced at Paul, who was biting at the skin around his thumb while he watched the school through his phone. 'What app's that then? How come you can see everything so close up?'

'It's called Binoculars,' Paul muttered.

'Ah. Cool, cool.' He paused. 'So this is what you've been doing every day?'

'Yep.'

'You ain't bored of it, mate?'

Paul shook his head. 'Not yet. It's like they're putting on a play for me; a play that lasts all day.'

Josh raised an eyebrow and tried again. 'You sure you can't come online? I've got some sick new skins to show you . . .'

'When it cools down – *if* it cools down – maybe.' Paul gasped. 'Look! They're coming back from lunch. Told you it was time!' he said, the excitement rising in his voice. 'Like clockwork.'

Josh stared at his old school through Paul's phone. They'd left Ashcroft Primary on Friday – the last day of term, their last day of year six. Josh was ready to move on, not thinking he'd see the school again, but here he was, looking right at it. Today, the following Wednesday, the boys could see the teachers' cars and a second-floor slice of the crumbling red-brick school; two white-windowed classrooms. Miss Fye's, Paul's old teacher, to the left, and Mr Palmer's, Josh's teacher, on the right. A black drainpipe separated the two spaces. 'Don't teachers get summer hols?' asked Josh. Paul shook his head. 'That ain't right – they need a break too.'

'They're training and tidying for the new year sixes, I

think,' said Paul. 'They've been coming in at nine each day – well, Miss Fye has. Everyone else is late, turning up around nine thirty. She's *always* on time.' Paul smiled. Across the garden, in the school, Miss Fye opened the door to her classroom, her long bright red hair swished and swayed around her shoulders as she shut it behind her. 'See?'

Josh looked at his friend. 'Wait . . . you like Miss Fye or something?'

'Course I do,' said Paul. 'She might've been new, but she was the best teacher I ever had at Ashcroft, hands down. Much better than Mrs Bryant.'

Josh bit his bottom lip to stop himself, smiling. 'Is that so? I think you like *like* Miss Fye.'

Paul's head spun at Josh. 'Ew, don't be weird,' he said, irritated, annoyed, trying not to scratch at his neck. 'She's just awesome, all right? She made learning fun; she gave me a nice card when I left with her funny little loopy-lettered signature in it *and* I like her bike.' Paul pointed down to her paint-spattered, flower-adorned bike with its white wicker basket. It leaned against the school's wall in the car park. 'Everyone should cycle –the planet would cool down if they did, then I could go outside.'

'Hmm, yeah, I agree with that,' said Josh. A smile began to form on his face. 'But she wasn't the best teacher, though – not by a long shot. Mr Palmer remains elite –

Six P outranked Six F on every level, no cap.'

Paul snorted. 'If you say so. Mr Palmer was way too prickly for me. Too grumpy, snappy, rude for no reason.'

'Yeah, well, he was annoyed that your *wonderful* Miss Fye snatched his classroom when she rocked up out of nowhere, wasn't he? I would be too – getting turfed out of his space like that after so many years. He had to move all his stuff – his books, that old telescope he loves. He –'

'He should get over it and move on,' said Paul with a shrug.

'Yeah. Good advice,' said Josh. He made his voice low, so low he possibly said this next bit to himself. 'Maybe you should take it yourself.'

'Oh!' Paul shouted over Josh. 'Speak of the devil – here comes your hero now!'

The boys watched Mr Palmer walk into Miss Fye's classroom.

Paul tutted. 'He didn't even knock.'

Miss Fye looked up from the computer on her desk. She ran her fingers through her hair, flipped it to one side, then fiddled with one of her large bright-green triangle-shaped earrings. She did that when she was stressed. Those earrings were her favourites. A present from her parents, Paul remembered her telling the class once. Mr Palmer towered over her, talking quickly in his blue trousers and white shirt. His face flashed with anger.

A large beige envelope was tucked underneath his arm. Miss Fye shook her head repeatedly. He leaned forward, spreading his fingers out on her desk.

Paul drew a sharp breath through his teeth. 'I don't like this. It does *not* seem friendly.'

'Nah, that's just his way,' said Josh. 'He's intense, innit.'

Miss Fye had stood up from her desk and was now in front of Mr Palmer. They were talking intensely, their faces close to each other.

'They're not going to, like, kiss or something, are they?' said Josh. 'Gross.'

As those words left his lips, Miss Fye used both hands to push at Mr Palmer towards the classroom door and wagged her finger firmly in his direction.

'Doesn't look like it,' Paul said, trying to keep his phone steady, but mostly failing.

Mr Palmer threw his hands up in some kind of defeat, then launched his letter at her desk. He stared at her as he walked backwards out of her classroom, shaking his head. He threw open his classroom door and stomped towards to the window. He stood next to his telescope and stared down over the car park below.

'Wow,' Paul whispered as they watched Miss Fye return to her desk. She sat and lay her head down in front of her. Paul's heart lurched, then rattled around his chest. 'You think we should do something? We have to do something.'

'Like what, though?' said Josh. 'We don't know anything.'

'We know she's upset!' said Paul. 'We can both see that!'

That was true. They could.

Miss Fye looked up, her face puffy and her eyes red, much like Paul's. She reached for the letter Mr Palmer had . . . delivered, and tucked it away in her desk drawer. She took a deep breath and stared at the classroom ceiling. She sighed and began to lower her head. As she did, she looked directly into Paul's room. The boys gasped and ducked. Well, Josh did. Paul did a slow squat with his hands out, sliding his phone down against the glass.

Josh's eyes were wide. 'Yo, is it like this every day? Cos if so, I kinda get what you're doing now.'

'It's *never* been like that,' said Paul. He removed the sunglasses from his face and looked directly at his friend. 'What was *that* about?'

'Well, first I thought it was some romance business, but now I don't think so.' Josh shook his head. 'Maybe Miss Fye's done something to Mr Palmer to make him upset – he's probably still salty about his classroom.'

Paul stared at Josh. 'Seriously? She didn't *do* anything! Mr Palmer came in, started shouting and throwing things. There's no reason to do anything like that to her – to anyone!'

'Nah, yeah. You're right,' said Josh with a nod. 'I'm just shocked – but at the same time totally not shocked about the way he acted. I've seen it before.' His phone vibrated in his pocket. 'Ah, I have to go up Central with my dad. New school uniform shopping.' He scrambled to his feet. 'You gonna keep looking?'

Paul nodded at the stupid question. He made a mental note to make sure he made smarter friends at his new school.

Paul starfished by his window for the rest of the day, only breaking for dinner, which his mother demanded he ate with her downstairs. He couldn't concentrate on his fish or his chips, he could only think about what he had seen at the school, replaying the scene over and over. As he pushed his mushy peas around his plate, he wondered how Miss Fye was, hoping she was safe. Hoping she was as far away from Mr Palmer as possible.

That night, he stretched out on his bed, unable and unwilling to sleep. He sighed, stood up and, using the moonlight to guide him, turned his fan on low. He looked down at his phone charging on the windowsill. Josh had messaged.

Anything?

There was nothing to report. Nothing yet.

He placed his phone against the glass and looked over his garden and into his school. In the car park, just one vehicle: Mr Palmer's. Paul stared into his classroom, then scanned the building looking for any sign of the teacher, but nothing. As he held his phone close to him, to reply to Josh, a flash of light caught his eye.

Something was happening. Someone was there.

Mr Palmer, in the car park, his phone torch on, the phone in his mouth.

An anxious breath caught in Paul's throat.

Mr Palmer was walking slowly, awkwardly, but Paul couldn't quite make out why. He zoomed in as closely as he could.

Josh's favourite teacher was pulling a large, heavy crate behind him.

A crate big enough for a body.

Possibly.

His hands trembled around his phone as he squeezed it to take screenshots.

Mr Palmer leaned against his car to pause for breath, while Paul's heart beat as fast as it ever had in his whole eleven years. Mr Palmer wiped his brow, then opened his car's boot. He crouched down and struggled, going toe to toe with gravity to lift his crate up.

Paul bit at his lips, wondering just what – or who – was inside.

He had a feeling. A very, very bad one.

Mr Palmer looked around the car park with his torch. Its beam shone upon Miss Fye's bike.

Paul's stomach lurched.

Don't touch it. Please don't touch it.

But touch it he did. Mr Palmer strode towards the bike, grabbed it by its frame and marched it to his car. He removed the front wheel, then threw both parts of it on top of the crate. He slammed his boot shut then drove away.

Paul's knuckles were paler than the moon.

He didn't sleep. Paul made sure he stayed awake, all night, to make sure he was by his window for eight forty-five. Surely the dread he was feeling was just that – a feeling? A childish, dramatic feeling. Miss Fye would float into her classroom at nine sharp, then he and Josh would laugh about the big misunderstanding later. Maybe he'd make an anonymous call to Ms Roberts, the head teacher, and get Mr Palmer fired. Miss Fye would then send him a thank-you note, which he'd pin next to her card.

At eight fifty-five there was no sign of her or her paint-spattered bike.

Paul looked down at his phone at eight fifty-nine.

Miss Fye, please. Please come to school!

She didn't come. Miss Fye wasn't there by nine, nine fifteen or nine thirty. But Mr Palmer was. Paul watched him, whistling cheerfully as he slammed his car door shut and strode proudly into school.

Paul trembled and his breath quickened. His phone vibrated in his hand. Josh.

What's this photo about? I don't get it . . .

Paul steadied his hand as he typed.

I think Mr Palmer has done something to Miss Fye. Something serious.

Josh walked the length of Paul's bedroom, back and forth. He held his face and pulled it down. 'What are you *actually* saying, mate? You think she's been murdered?'

Paul turned from the window. 'I never said the M word.'

'But you think her body's in the box?'

Paul took a deep breath. 'Well, she's not at school. I saw him lug that crate across the car park. He took her bike, Josh. Chucked it in his car, like he chucked that letter at her! She . . . she never rode home.' His voice began to waver. He looked up at the ceiling to stop tears rolling down his face. 'There's something in that envelope, I just know it.'

Josh sighed. 'I don't get it. Like, I do – I know what you

mean – but *why*? All of this because Mr Palmer wanted his classroom back? It's all a bit much, no? He's grumpy, sure – but this? Kill someone? At Ashcroft?' Josh shook his head. 'I just don't see it. Palmer's a good teacher, a good man.'

'*A good man?* So why is he doing *that*?' Paul asked, pointing at his phone. Mr Palmer was in Miss Fye's classroom, whistling, while he took down her displays.

Paul wanted to say, 'I told you so,' but thought against it. It wasn't the time or the place. Josh paced around the room. 'Nah, OK. That's sus. Right, what are we gonna do? Tell your mum?'

'No way! She'll call the police.'

'That's not a good thing?'

'It is, but not yet.' Paul pushed his sunglasses up on to his wavy hair. 'We need to know more first – we need that letter.' He looked down at his garden, across the car park, then up at the black drainpipe between the two classrooms. He turned to face Josh. 'The teachers will be going to lunch soon. You could go and investigate?'

'Me? By myself? You're not coming?'

As if on cue, Paul sneezed. 'I can't.'

Paul looked between the window and his phone as he watched Josh scale the wire fence and jump down into the school's car park.

'Mate! Can you hear me?' Josh hissed.

'Yes,' Paul replied. 'Flip your camera so I can see the school and not your chin.'

'Oh, right, OK. Better now?'

Paul could see the red bricks and the black drainpipe growing larger, getting closer as Josh quickly stepped forward. 'Perfect.'

Josh sighed. 'I'm going to have to put the phone in my mouth while I climb the pipe, yeah?' He didn't wait for Paul's reply. He stepped back, sized up the pipe and jumped towards it. Back in his room, Paul was impressed and slightly jealous that Josh could do that. Paul watched him reach the classrooms. Josh hugged the pipe with one arm and held his phone out with the other. He leaned to look into Miss Fye's room. 'Can you make out anything?' he asked.

Back in his room, Paul squinted at his phone. 'Hold still if you can, and aim it a bit higher – I want a good look at the desk.'

'Got it,' Josh said as he adjusted his body. 'Anything now?'

A breath caught in Paul's throat. There was something – one of Miss Fye's favourite green triangle earrings, next to her mouse mat. A souvenir for Mr Palmer. 'Yes, something,' Paul whispered sadly. 'But it's not enough.' He thought for a moment. 'Wait, is the window open?'

Josh tucked his phone under his chin and tried to pull the window open with his free hand. Paul heard a muffled yes.

'Do you . . . do you think you can fit through it?' Paul asked. He winced as he said that, knowing it was a big ask.

At the other end of the phone, Josh sighed. 'I'll try . . . but I'm not sure if I'll fit – and hold the phone.'

Paul punched the air, but he absolutely celebrated too soon. As he lowered his triumphant fist, he saw Mr Palmer opening Miss Fye's door. 'Abort, Josh! Abort!' Paul screamed. 'He's right there!' He quickly switched apps and watched as his friend froze in terror. Staying still was actually the best thing Josh could have done in that moment. 'Don't move, don't say anything!' He hissed at his friend as he watched Mr Palmer lean forward and peer into the classroom. Paul could taste guilt and his heart was in his mouth. He could only imagine what Josh was feeling right now, stuck on that pipe, seven metres in the air. When Mr Palmer stepped into the room, Paul thought he might faint or die on the spot. He pressed his lips together and prayed for a miracle.

He got one quickly. Praise the lord.

Mr Palmer began to dig into the pocket of his trousers. He answered his phone with a smile and turned. He left the classroom, closing the door behind him.

'The coast is clear! I repeat, the coast is clear!' Paul shouted down the phone. In response, Josh shimmied down the pipe and bolted across the car park, towards Paul's fence, with the wildest, widest smile across his face.

'You want to go back?' Are you sure? You nearly got caught, Josh!'

'I know. I loved it!'

'Are you insane? I –'

'I don't care! We're getting that letter, mate. The earring's not enough evidence. We'll go tonight – together – when it's dark and cool.'

The sky darkened just after nine that night, but it didn't get much cooler. Paul scratched at the side of his face and turned to his friend. 'I'm sorry, Josh, I just can't do it. I'll only hold you back.'

'Yeah, fine,' said Josh. 'But if I'm going, I'm going soon.' He looked down at his watch. 'It's ten-past nine, and I have to be home by ten.' He put his face against the window and groaned. 'Why is Mr Palmer *still* there?'

'Guilt,' said Paul, staring at the teacher sitting at his desk. 'He probably didn't get much done yesterday.'

'Oh yeah – murder's a real big distraction, I guess.'

Josh smiled at his friend.

'You're not funny.' Paul took a deep breath. 'OK. The plan, up the pipe, through the window, look for the letter and bring it back. Then we'll decide what to do next.'

Josh nodded.

'No video call and no torchlight. Put your phone on silent.'

Paul could just make out Josh's grin and two excited thumbs up before he scaled the fence for the second time that day. He held his breath and nodded encouragingly when he saw Josh's shadow cast across the car park. Paul hissed, 'Yes!' and punched the air when Josh gripped the drainpipe and started climbing. He jumped in the air when Josh leaned over, pulled open Miss Fye's window and swung himself into the classroom. When Josh waved the letter by the window, Paul allowed himself to dance on the spot for a second. They were so close, mere minutes away from figuring this out and getting justice for Miss Fye. When Paul stopped spinning, he glanced over at Mr Palmer's classroom. Mr Palmer was at his window, looking through his telescope – directly at him. Paul gasped. Mr Palmer's head shot up and he stepped away from the telescope.

This was bad.

Time slowed down as the blood in Paul's body puddled around his feet. He felt faint and sick, but he had to warn Josh. He couldn't leave him in the danger zone alone. He switched apps with slippery fingers and quickly typed out a message.

He knows! Get out!

Paul flicked back to Binoculars and stared at the window, waiting for the message to reach his friend. As it did, Mr Palmer's head swung quickly to the left and he stomped to his classroom door.

He'd heard Paul's message. Josh never put his phone on silent.

Josh ran at the glass, his wide eyes white in the night. He bit down on the envelope and lurched for the drainpipe. As his trainer left the window, he seemed to get stuck, and suddenly Mr Palmer was right behind him, grabbing his leg, his white face now red. Josh looked back and screamed. He kicked back at his favourite teacher and slid down the pipe. Paul tore down the stairs with his phone in his clammy palm.

Paul threw open the kitchen door and sprinted down the garden path. It was still hot and skin touched skin. He knew he would suffer for it later, but Miss Fye – and Josh – were the priority now. On the other side of the chain-link fence, Josh was screaming every bad word ever invented as he attempted to escape. Mr Palmer appeared in the car park and rushed towards him. 'Joshua Brody! Is that you?'

'No, Sir!' Josh shouted back. He launched himself at the fence and tried to climb it, but Mr Palmer, once again, had a hold of his foot. Paul glanced down at his phone screen. The keypad shone up at him. He pushed nine three times, then the green phone icon.

'What in god's name are you *doing*?' Mr Palmer shouted, trying to peel Josh from the fence. He glared at Paul. 'And you, Mr Johnson? What's going on?'

'Don't say anything, Josh!' Paul panted cautiously. He stepped on to the fence. 'Just drop the evidence!'

'*Evidence?*' Mr Palmer seemed confused. A good liar, Paul thought.

'OK, but what about me?!' Josh wailed as he let the letter fall.

'Oh, you're in *big* trouble, Joshua,' said Mr Palmer. 'I'm calling the police.'

Paul reached down and snatched the envelope from the ground. He clutched it to his chest. 'Not if we call them first,' he said calmly, and a little bit smugly. 'We know what you did, Mr Liam Palmer.' He glanced down at his phone's screen. He was connected.

Mr Palmer instantly let go of Josh, who scrambled up

the fence and jumped, both feet first, into Paul's garden. 'What *I* did?'

Josh leaned forward, put his hands on his knees and gulped down breaths. 'Yeah. What you did. To Miss Fye.'

Mr Palmer opened his mouth to speak, but Paul shook his head. 'Don't act shocked, Sir. We know you killed Miss Clementine Fye.' He brought his phone, casually he thought, closer to his mouth. 'At Ashcroft Primary School.'

'*What?*'

'We didn't want to believe it either.' Paul shrugged. 'But we saw you arguing in her classroom yesterday lunchtime and she was very upset.'

Mr Palmer's blue eyes narrowed. 'You saw that?'

Josh nodded. 'We did. Then Paul clocked you dragging something heavy across the car park in the dark last night.'

Paul's bottom lip began to tremble. 'And you took her bike. You just . . . chucked it in your boot.'

'Then today,' said Josh standing up straight. 'One of her favourite earrings was on her desk, and *not* with her.'

'She's nowhere to be seen,' said Paul. A tear rolled down his face. 'And she's always, always been on time. At school by nine. Miss Fye has gone – and it's your fault.'

Mr Palmer smiled as he leaned against the fence, the moonlight casting shadows from it onto his face. 'Well,' he said, raising his hands. 'You've got me!'

The boys gasped in unison.

'Miss Fye has gone . . . and it *is* my fault.'

'Because you murdered her!' Paul shouted.

Mr Palmer shook his head and laughed. 'No. Because I married her.'

Paul stepped backwards in shock. Murder would be worse, but marriage was a close second. He looked between his phone and the teacher, unsure of his next move.

'You what, Sir?' asked Josh. He turned to Paul and laughed. 'See? I told you it looked a bit kissy in the classroom, didn't I? Congrats, Mr Palmer!'

'Don't celebrate, Josh!' Paul snapped. He narrowed his eyes at Mr Palmer. 'I don't believe you. Why should I?'

'I can explain,' he said. 'I shouldn't need to, not to you two, but here we are.' He took a deep breath. 'We wanted to keep it a secret. For us, from you lot. We didn't want Ms Roberts to know either. We didn't want to get fired. It's not . . . very professional to be in love at school.'

Paul shuddered when Mr Palmer said the L word. 'Say I believe you – which I don't.' He raised his phone towards his mouth as Josh looked on, confused. 'What about her earring? What about her bike?'

Mr Palmer crossed his arms. 'She likes to cycle – plus it's better if we don't travel together. She got a puncture on her way in yesterday. It stressed her out so much, she fiddled with her earing until it broke.'

That made sense to Paul. He'd seen her do that. He desperately thought of something else. 'So what were you dragging out of school in the crate, then? In the dark?'

'Her personal books and other bits she brought into the classroom.' Mr Palmer shrugged. 'She didn't need them here any more.'

'Because she's really dead, isn't she?' Paul whispered.

'No, stop. Because she's left the school. She resigned because she's got another job. I didn't want her to leave, but there we are.' He pointed to the letter Paul gripped in his hands. 'There's her letter. Read it if you want. It doesn't matter now – she's gone.'

Paul tucked his phone under his chin and opened the letter. Josh shone his phone's torch on top of it. It was indeed a letter, addressed to Ms Roberts from Miss Fye. It was short and said while she liked the school, she was leaving for personal reasons and stress. At the bottom her name was signed in thin, tall, scratchy letters. It was nothing like the looping letters she used to sign Paul's leaving card, his merits, or any of his reports.

It was not her signature, not even close.

Paul gulped, breathed heavily through his nose as he clamped his mouth shut, afraid of what to do or say next, praying the police were still listening, if they were ever listening at all.

Josh laughed and nudged Paul in the ribs. 'What if he

made this himself, eh, Sherlock?' Paul smiled weakly in response, it's all he could do.

Josh continued. 'I mean, I believe you, Sir, but if she *is* your wife, call her. Let's hear it from her. Right, Paul? Then we can all laugh about it and I'll go before I get grounded.'

Paul nodded. Josh *thought* he was joking, but he was absolutely right. Somewhere, in the distance, sirens sounded. Paul's ears pricked up; he could swear they were getting louder.

Mr Palmer chuckled. 'As you wish.' He patted himself down. 'Oh, wait, my phone's upstairs, I'll get it. We can end this tonight.'

The boys watched Mr Palmer walk towards the school. Instead of heading for the main entrance, he stopped at his car. He looked back at Paul and Josh, grinned and pulled the driver's door open.

'She should have stayed at her old school, boys!' he shouted back at them with a cold chuckle. 'And minded her own business!' As he slammed his door shut, his engine roared into life. His tail lights flashed bright red over the boys' contorted faces.

Mr Palmer's car screeched as it tried to swerve out of the car park, but they could barely hear it – the sirens Paul had heard before were now deafening. Mr Palmer tried to inch his car forward but he couldn't – he was blocked in. His red tail lights were swamped, drowned out by a sea of blue. The police were here.

Paul glanced over at a ghost-white Josh and ended his call.

Mr Palmer wasn't at school the next morning. Miss Fye wasn't either.

Miss Fye wouldn't be going anywhere, ever again.

Of all the teachers at Ashcroft, only Ms Roberts was there to show the police around, like the school was having a sad, twisted, tragic open evening. The police had wrapped their blue-and-white tape around the building as they searched the classrooms in question and combed through the gravel in the car park on bended knees.

Paul's mother and Josh stood silently at Paul's bedroom window, Paul in the middle, all three staring at the scene through his phone. His black fan made nothing but sad squeaky noises behind them. A policewoman, searching for clues close to the chain-link fence, clearly felt their gaze. She looked up and caught six eyes. She nodded silently, gratefully, then returned to her urgent work.

Paul nodded back. Tears rolled down his face and hit his windowsill. His mother reached for his hand and Josh patted his bare back. Skin touched skin, but this time it didn't hurt, and Paul didn't mind.

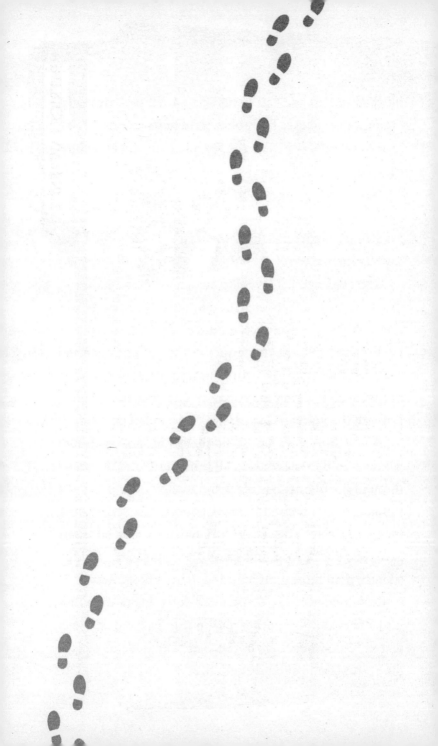

PATRICE LAWRENCE

BEHIND THE SCREAMS IN THE MUSEUM

TOP SECRET

BEHIND THE SCREAMS
IN THE MUSEUM

By Patrice Lawrence

ULRIC

My sister Evie's changed, man. She's like Melody, our older sister, who pretends that we're a ghost family that everyone else can see 'cept her. Now I've become Evie's ghost.

You want to know the reason why? Evie and her friends have got into some boy band called DBS. That's supposed to stand for Don't Be Sad, but I *am* sad because my sister doesn't want to know me no more. They all hang out in her room watching videos of DBS – and man, there are hundreds and hundreds of them videos. DBS singing and dancing, and practising singing and dancing, and talking about singing and dancing . . . I thought she might get bored and remember I exist, but she doesn't.

At the start of the summer, DBS brought out a song

called 'Explosive'. That song follows me around like I've got a spare butt. It's advertised on a massive billboard near the station. Then I see DBS smiling out of the screen in the adverts in the *Young Hulk* show. And every time Mum turns on the radio, it's playing.

My hea-ar-art is beating hard,
Shatters like a mighty shard . . .

I'm so, so bored. My best friend Levon's gone to see his family in America. Alexa, my other best friend, has signed up to a summer football academy and she's away all week. D'you know what I did? I was so bored I learned the words and dance to 'Explosive', even though I hate that song, and knocked on Evie's bedroom door to show her. She just opened it a crack and told me to go about my business.

Then yesterday, a flyer was pushed through our letter box. It wasn't even for pizza. It was for our local museum. We've been going there for as long as I can remember. It's a museum of everything! There's a room about astronomy and a room full of weird stuff in jars and a room with flying things and some boring rooms crammed with bits of broken pots. Evie used to love the room of warrior queens, especially Queen Nzinga's bangles.

But now – NOW – the museum's been loaned a very special item. It's a golden flute! And not any old golden flute. It's called the Child Whisperer. There's a story that it's the one the Pied Piper of Hamelin used to magic away the rats and then the children. Of course, I'm not little no more. I don't really believe in magic. Or fairy tales. But what if . . . I mean, imagine if something like that was real? An instrument that makes music only children can hear? It must do something or the museum wouldn't be bigging it up. They had to get special guards because it's so valuable.

I show the flyer to Mum.

'We have to go and see it! It's the last day today and they might show us how the flute works!'

Mum flips her eggy bread over and won't meet my eye. 'Ulric, my gorgeous one, you know I don't have time this week. Next week, though . . .'

'It's not on next week!'

'I'm sure Evie will take you.'

Even Mum doesn't sound convinced. Evie's sitting at the breakfast table with her DBS-branded earbuds jammed in. Man, I even recognise the beat her feet are tapping. My world's so bad now that I know 'Explosive' from jiggling toes.

I want to see the flute. I'm gonna have to ask her. I wave the flyer in front of her eyes. She taps her phone to pause the song, pops out one earbud and glares at me.

'What?' she demands.

I try to stop my voice sounding whiny. 'Can you take me to this, please?'

She glares harder at me and then flicks the flyer away. 'No.'

'Why not? You used to love the museum.'

'Exactly,' she says. '*Used* to. It's boring now. I know every single thing in every single room. Why would I want to see them again?'

'Because there's a magic golden flute.'

Evie rolls her eyes. Now Melody's stopped doing that, Evie's started.

'There's no such thing as magic,' Evie says and pushes her earbud back in.

Mum slumps down at the table with her breakfast. She opens a book and starts reading. She's not gonna take sides. I have to take direct action and do a very bad thing. I've saved this for a special occasion. *This* is a special occasion. I head to the family computer in the sitting room and tap on Mum's profile.

EVIE

Ulric is no longer my brother. I reckon someone changed him for a demon that's identical to him. Only a demon would do what he did. He went into Mum's Wi-Fi account, guessed the password, then changed it. He refused to tell us the new Wi-Fi password until someone agreed to take him to see that stupid flute. And guess who that someone is?

He doesn't care that I'm vexed as hell.

He doesn't care that I'm not talking to him.

He's striding beside me with a big smile on his face. And, OK, he's not smiling because he's made me do something that I don't want to do; he's smiling because he's actually really happy about going to see this fake flute thing. A tiny bit of my heart feels pleased for him; it's cute that simple things like this still make him cheerful.

The pavement gets busier and busier as we head towards the museum. It's like every kid in our area wants to see that flute. There are big posters about it on the billboard opposite the museum and volunteers handing out more flyers. One of them's even dressed like the Pied Piper in a red and yellow cloak and a red floppy hat with a feather in it. Ulric takes another flyer even though he's already got one.

'It's got a map of the museum on it,' he says.

I don't need a map. Like I said, I know every centimetre of this museum already.

I say, 'Don't forget that the deal is two hours max!'

My new DBS merch arrived yesterday – stickers and stationery. I've got it with me because I promised to meet Lola later to compare and swap.

'I need to go to the toilet,' Ulric says.

Of course he does. He always does! We head to the nearest loos – well, not the nearest. We know the museum so well we automatically go to the quieter ones, tucked under a staircase.

'Meet you by this pillar,' I say.

I see there's no queue for the cubicles, so I might as well go too. Just as I'm about to flush, there's a sound – high and loud. I clutch my ears almost expecting to see some scrambled brains leaking out, or my eyeballs plop out of their sockets. I just want to find where it's coming from and stop it. Then it does stop.

What. Was. That?

I hear laughing from the other side of the door.

A woman's voice says, 'Do you think it worked?'

Another woman says, 'I know it works! I tried it in the garden last night and the kid next door started yelling at his brother to stop making that noise. Though maybe you shouldn't blast it too hard.' She chuckles. 'We want a distraction, not ambulances.'

The door bangs shut. I wait a moment then open the cubicle door a crack. There's no one around.

What's just happened here? What happened to my head?

I come right out of the cubicle and stand there, a bit stunned. My face feels hot, like I danced the full 'Explosive' choreo workout without stopping. I wave my hands under the tap, then study the sink closer. There's a smear of gold; it looks like paint.

I head back out. No Ulric yet. I can hear hundreds of kids laughing and chatting as they flow through the museum, enjoying all the things that I used to love. Ulrich would race towards the astronomy room. Me, I liked the one about warrior queens. I'd imagine their bracelets clinking and their shields clanging as they fought the enemies who'd invaded their lands. Mum reckons that most of the jewellery are replicas, made to look old. But Queen Nzinga's gold bangles are real. I used to imagine slipping them over my arm and racing into battle with a mighty scream.

I think about the gold smear in the sink. Those two women – that conversation was pretty sketchy. I feel nosy about it, but I can't leave here without Ulric.

'Have you set your time?' a woman asks. 'We need to be perfectly synchronised.'

I recognise that voice. It's one of those women from the toilet. I peer around the pillar. She's wearing a lanyard, like she's staff. I don't recognise her, but I suppose I haven't been here for a while. I can just see the other woman who's standing to her side.

'Thirty minutes and counting down,' that one says, tapping her tote bag.

'And the taxi's booked?' the first one asks.

'Of course.'

They split up and head off in different directions.

I really want to follow them! I know I haven't been here for so long, but I kinda feel protective towards this place. It's like some of my best memories are in those cabinets, alongside the bangles and pottery. And those women, I'm pretty sure they're not planning anything good.

But Ulric . . . How's he gonna find me? Ah! I have an idea. I take out my envelope of DBS stickers. I stare into DM – otherwise known as DreaM Boy's face – then peel him off the sheet. I stick him on the pillar so he's level with Ulric's eyes. Him and my little brother are going to be staring right at each other.

Which of these women am I going to follow? Well, I only saw which way one of them was going. She's the one that tried to fry my head. I don't know what she did, but I really don't want her to do it again, and I've got a feeling that's exactly what she's gonna do. I scribble on the sticker above DM's head with my new DBS pencil – *earworms.*

I glance at the toilet door again, but there's no Ulric.

OK, little brother, I hope you're ready because the next half hour's gonna be proper 'Explosive'.

ULRIC

There's a dad by the sinks who's brought his son and five friends to see the flute. They're washing their hands and, man, they're taking some time. They're turning their hands over and over beneath the tap, making sure every speck of soap is gone. I know that Evie's gonna be outside, checking the time and getting grumpy. But she's the one who taught me that you *always* wash your hands after you've been to the toilet. Your germs shouldn't go nowhere but down the plughole, so I'm waiting and waiting . . . And eventually, every boy has got every soap particle off his skin.

But before they finish, something weird happens. It feels like someone's screamed inside my head, like one of those high screams that only little kids can do. It doesn't last long, but it makes my eyes feel bulgy. One boy bursts into tears. Another stares at me impressed, as if I made that sound. I shrug and he kinda looks disappointed. The dad's really confused because it seems like he didn't hear nothing at all. He ushers them out and I wash my hands. I try and be quick – but the dryer's stopped working and I have to use toilet roll. Then I have to spend time peeling the wet, ripped paper from between my fingers.

When I get out, I can't see Evie. Maybe she's had to queue too. I wait. Then I wait some more. Then I ask a woman going into the toilets to see if my sister's there. The woman says it's empty. She looks worried and asks me if I'm lost but I'm not. I know where I am, I just don't know where Evie is. I force out a smile and say I'm OK.

I don't think the woman believes me. Man, Evie didn't want to come in the first place! Has she just gone and left me?

Then I spot DBS! Well, not all of them, and not in real life. It's one of them staring at me from the pillar. I know, because I've seen his face smiling from the billboard so many times. I go and have a closer look. There a couple of words in pencil above him – it's definitely Evie's writing.

Earworms.

Earworms? That's what Mum calls tunes that get stuck in your head and won't go away. Evie doesn't need to tell me that about 'Explosive'. It's gonna be stuck in my head until I'm eighty. Maybe she's gone to the museum cafe – it's called Grubs. A grub is kinda like a worm, but then why didn't she just say grubs? I don't understand!

Earworms, earworms, EARWORMS . . . My brain's being invaded by them and it still doesn't make sense.

Oh, maybe it does! Earworms! I think I get it!

I take my map out of my pocket and study it.

The room straight ahead is what Mum always calls the Pickle Room. It's full of shelves of animals and bits of animals in jars. Some of them are more than a hundred years old. I have to remind myself of that because I feel really sorry for a baby aardvark, all curled up behind the glass, its eyes closed like it's sleeping. I know what I need to find – it's a small jar with two thin worms curled up inside. Evie says they look like love hearts, I always thought they looked like ears.

Earworms!

I peel the DBS sticker off the pillar and dash to the pickle room. Is Evie here?

The Pickle Room's empty apart from me. There ain't nowhere Evie can hide to surprise me. A few people rush through, probably trying to get to the magic flute. Maybe I should do that – go straight there in case Evie's gone ahead to save me a place at the front, like a bribe so I don't change the Wi-Fi password again. But I'll just check on the earworms first.

I see it straight away, another DBS sticker on the edge of the glass cabinet next to the worms. There's tiny writing across it because she's making sure there's none on the singer's face. If it was me, I'd write it across the middle like a giant moustache.

U, follow that song!

U, follow that song? What does that mean? Maybe she's playing with my mind for making her bring me here. 'U' might mean me, Ulric. I don't suppose she's talking to anyone else and not many folks' names start with a U. But what song? I strain my ears, but can't hear no song to follow. What if Evie secretly believes the flute's magic and I should go to the music? That's what happened to the children in Hamelin – they followed the piper and disappeared. I know Evie wishes I'd disappear sometimes, but I'm pretty sure she doesn't think magic's real. So that's not it.

There *is* a song that's been following *me* though, on the billboards and on TV. It's the earworm that won't crawl out of my head.

That song is 'Explosive'. I sing the words to myself and look at my map.

My hea-ar-art is beating hard,
Shatters like a mighty shard.

I don't get it. There are three ways out of the Pickle Room. Which way am I supposed to take? I just came through one door, so I suppose I've got to choose between the door ahead of me and the one on the left. Why can't Evie just tell me where she's going? Or just wait for me?

Maybe it's a test. If I pass it, she'll be nicer to me. I'm gonna try and pass it then. I think hard. Does 'beating hard' mean drums? The music room's got djembes that they let us play, but it's way across the other side of the museum. What's 'mighty shard'? There's a model of the Shard building in the Map Room, but that's past the theatre. I don't think she means none of those – they're too far away.

I sing the song to myself again. *My hea-ar-art is beating hard.*

Is it 'heart'? Is that the clue? I still don't know if I'm supposed to go left or straight on. The left room's called

Eight Legs Good. It's full of spiders; there's some really old ones in jars and an animatronic tarantula that shows how their leg joints work. Melody won't go near that room.

The other room's Giant Friends. It's about big mammals like elephants and giraffes and whales. And . . . there's an elephant's heart in a jar! Bits of it are dyed different colours so you can see how it works. Mum says it weighs more than me – or it used to. I've grown recently. But it's so big that it must have beat really hard when the elephant was alive.

I race into the Giant Friends room and maybe because I'm looking for it, I see the sticker straight away on the panel below the elephant's heart. I peel it off. It just says *SONG*.

Evie? Man!

EVIE

No one wants their little brother trying to dance and sing like DBS, but Ulric, man, I hope you remember those lyrics. I'm gonna use code to help you follow me just in case the brain-frying woman's got sidekicks watching me. It's hard work trying to match up what I'm seeing with 'Explosive' while watching where the woman goes. Pickle Room, Giant Friends . . . Where next? She definitely works here because sometimes she sees other staff who say hello to her. Her name's Heather. Even though she tried to wash her hands, her fingertips are still stained with gold paint. I try and get close to her without looking suspicious. There's a bulgy, padded envelope in her bag. I reckon the brain fryer's in there.

OK, Heather's heading to Neolithic, the room full of old pots. The security guard chats to her and I stick my favourite DBS dancer, Rhythm, on the side of an explanation panel by the elephant heart before following her into the room. I just hope Ulric remembers *shards* not *Shard* – and the lyrics that come after, because I don't have time to scribble more than *SONG* above Rhythm's head.

Heather's on the move again. I got to be quick.

ULRIC

I check my map. There's two rooms leading out from here – Neolithic, full of boring old broken pots or Argent, where everything's made from silver. *SONG* must be 'Explosive'. It's the only song Evie's been singing to for months. The *shard* line follows the *heart* line, so I hope that's what she means. I still don't think it's the model Shard, as that is too far away.

I sing the line in my head again.

Shatters like a mighty shard.

Shatters means broken. None of the silver's broken, but most of them old pots are. I walk into Neolithic. The security guard smiles. I work my way along the cabinets. Every single pot is broken. I stop, not because I've seen a sticker, but because it's more interesting than I expected. There's some shards – *shards!* – found in east London that are more than 5,500 years old! Wow!

Next time I come back, I'm gonna spend more time looking, but now I've got to find if Evie's been this way. I see the sticker. This time it's half hanging off the panel as if she had to be super quick.

Oh my days! There's no writing on it at all! I thought I was working this stuff out, but now she's given me nothing. Does she just want me to know she was here?

'Excuse me?'

The security guard's talking to me, saying the words in a nice way. (Sometimes 'excuse me' means 'get out the way' or 'how dare you!'.)

'I just have to say,' he continues, 'that usually no one's interested in ancient pottery. But today must be potter day! First there's a young lady, and now you!'

Young lady? Was that Evie? There must be loads of girls who pass through here, but I may as well ask him.

'Have you seen . . . I'm looking for my sister. She's gone on ahead of me. I was wondering if the young lady could be her?'

I describe what Evie looks like, though I miss off her cross expression. The security guard screws up his eyes and stares at me.

'Yes,' he says. 'That could be her. She was with ...' He scratches his head. 'No, maybe not with, but close behind Heather.'

'Who's Heather?' I ask him.

'She's our guest curator. She's *the* expert on that flute.' He points to the room in front. 'They went that way.'

Is Evie following Heather, the flute expert? Why's she doing that?

I look at the sticker, but all it's showing me is that DBS have perfect teeth. I hope I find another clue in the next room. It's Evie's favourite.

EVIE

I've done as much as I can with the shard and the heart. It's time to move on to the verse.

Wake up! Get up out my bed,
Teacup, cornflakes, jam and toasted bread,
Suit donned, James Bond ...

Nah, I can't go no further than *bread*. Ulric doesn't know who James Bond is because Mum thinks the films are sexist.

I follow Heather into my favourite room, the one with

Queen Nzinga's bangles. When I was little, I wanted to be a warrior queen when I grew up. I glance at the bangles. They're under thick glass to protect them. This room's got a security guard too. There's two rooms leading out of here. I see where Heather's heading. The security guard's watching us, so I got to be careful. I turn my back on her and study a wall full of carved masks. I scribble two letters above Tee's face and peel off the sticker. I keep it with the sticky bit facing upwards on my palm, though with my fist slightly closed so the guard can't see it. I smile at the security guard and go back to the bangles. I push my palm underneath the table with the bangles. I just got to hope that Ulric looks there.

I walk casual and quick into the room called The Sky's The Limit. It's big and round. Heather and that other woman are talking quietly in the middle of the room next to the glass tube that holds the replica of Iron Man's first suit. They glance at me. I smile sweetly back and look around, trying to edge closer. Everything in here's about flying. A giant model of a bat hangs from the ceiling and there's a few more of those jars of dead animals – bird skeletons and a flying squirrel – and then a tank of real flying frogs.

Opposite the giant bat, they've hung a house being lifted into the sky by a bunch of balloons. It's pretty close to Heather and her friend. I move nearer, humming the sad music from *Up*. They both check their watches and nod at each other.

As Heather moves away, her friend says, 'You're sure I won't need earplugs?'

Heather pats the bulgy envelope in her bag and grins. 'I can guarantee that we're both immune.'

The women head in opposite directions, Heather towards the amphitheatre, the other one back towards the bangles room.

Right, so they're definitely planning to scramble our brains again. And by *our*, I mean all those excited kids in the amphitheatre. That's bad enough – but why? In the toilets, they'd said they needed 'a distraction not an ambulance'. So while the kids' brains are screaming and the families are freaking out, what's Heather doing?

I actually slap myself on the forehead. Heather will be standing on stage with the gold flute! The one that's so valuable it needs special guards! She can just grab it and run. I need to do something, but what? My brain's gonna be scrambled too – and so's Ulric's. My little brother can be a pain, but little brothers are supposed to be, aren't they? I'd never, ever tell him this, but he's like my extra heartbeat. I don't want nothing to hurt him.

There's a panel on the wall that explains why in real life balloons could never lift up a house. Long ago, me and Ulric decided that we were never gonna read it because we wanted to believe that the house can fly.

I peel off the last sticker. It's Lola's favourite singer, Honey. Just above Honey's face, I write one word. I stick it on the panel. Now I've got to run. I need to get to the amphitheatre.

ULRIC

Evie likes Marvel films. Her favourite character's Okoye from *Black Panther*. Once, Evie told Mum that when she was grown-up, she was gonna shave off all her hair and fight robots. She used to think that Queen Nzinga's bangles could give you superpowers. I'm sad Evie doesn't believe in magic any more.

I've checked my map and I already know that there's two rooms leading off here. I'm tempted to ask the security guard if she's seen Evie, but she's staring at her phone and smiling, tapping out a message, and I don't want to get her attention in case she asks why I'm by myself.

If Evie's left me a clue here, it's gonna be by the bangles. I pretend to be interested in the masks and headdresses, and shuffle towards the jewellery. The guard looks up then back at her phone. There's no sticker near the bangles – but why would Evie put it where the guard can see it? I run my hand beneath the table, hoping that no one's stuck their nasty chewing gum there. I feel wrinkled paper.

I find the edge and dig my nail underneath. The sticker comes away easy. I move to the other side of the table.

Wake!

I grin, because this one's easy! Evie's Marvel, but I like Pixar even more. When I was in year three, we used to watch the films together – me, Mum, Evie and Melody, all squeezed together on the sofa, with snacks. I go straight into The Sky's The Limit and stand beneath the flying house. Imagine ... imagine being able to soar away! I won't look at the explanation panel because it kills the fun.

Where do I go from here? I sing the 'Explosive' verse in my head. I don't know who James Bond is. Maybe's he's an inventor who knew about flying. I can't see nothing about breakfast in here, so the clue *must* be about him. I'm gonna have to look at every panel. I start with the one about the first hot-air balloons and I go around the room slowly reading everything, checking the glass cabinets for any stickers too.

Man, there's nothing. James Bond ain't in here. I look up at the house and balloons again.

Wake up! Get up ... Double *up.*

I turn around slowly and look at the panel behind me, the one me and Evie never read. The sticker was here all the time.

Chorus! Quick!

EVIE

I catch up with Heather in the amphitheatre. I feel like I've been locked in the Eight Legs Good room and every one of them spiders have come alive and crawled over me. My heart's beating so hard that I think every bone in my body's gonna shatter into shards.

I hope Ulric's found what I left for him. I hope he works out what to do, because right now, I'm not sure what *I* should do. The amphitheatre's filling up. There are so many kids here. There's loads of staff here too, with lanyards around their necks, chatting with the families and looking excited.

Maybe I should say something to them. But what?

Hey! I heard two women chatting when I was in the loo and I think they're up to no good!

Hey! I saw a smudge of gold in the sink!

Hey! A noise almost made my head turn inside out but adults didn't hear it!

If I say all that, they'll think I'm part of the entertainment.

Those Eight Legs Good spiders are doing choreo now, jumping and prancing across my skin. The countdown was thirty minutes. I check my phone. That was twenty minutes ago. In ten minutes time . . . I don't know everything that's gonna happen for sure, but I bet Heather's gonna blast out that noise again.

Why, though? And what can I do?

I wiggle my way through the crowds until I'm at the front. I squeeze on the edge of a bench next to a kid wearing a red-and-yellow checked hat and waving a plastic gold pipe. They're so excited they don't notice me. Heather moves closer to the mic. There's a blast of feedback and my heart almost stops. The kid next to me gasps and a baby cries behind me. Then the audio person apologises and moves a loudspeaker a bit further away.

'Welcome!' Heather grins. 'It's so wonderful to see so many of you here today. Are you ready for magic?'

'Yes!' The kid next to me cheers so loud I'm scared he's gonna swallow his pipe.

'Do you want to see if fairy tales really can come true?'

'YES!'

It's like Christmas time at the pantomime.

Heather waves at the side of the stage. Two guards walk on. They're so big, they look like they should be living at the top of a beanstalk. They're wearing dark uniforms with peaked caps and equipment belts. I don't know what half the stuff is, but I recognise handcuffs and a taser. They're carrying an old wooden box, and place it on the table. The kid next to me strains forward.

'Do you know what's in this box?' Heather asks.

'YES! The Child Whisperer!'

She asks if anyone knows the legend of the Pied Piper of Hamelin. Loads of hands shoot in the air and she points to kids to tell different parts of the story. As we reach the bit where the Piper realises that he's not gonna get paid, Heather turns the box around slowly. I can see the gold flute glistening behind the glass door. The mouthpiece is chipped. I check the flyer. Yes, they look the same.

Heather carries on telling the story – about how the Pied Piper magicked all the children away.

She says, 'Do you want to know if the flute really is a child whisperer?'

The kids shriek, 'Yes!' Some of the grown-ups look a bit nervous and then embarrassed by themselves.

'If you please, Mr Mayer.'

The guard rolls up his sleeve. There's a metal cuff around his arm. A long, thick chain's attached to it – and at the end of that, there's a key. He twists the key in the flute box's lock and gently opens the glass door.

Everybody in the amphitheatre leans forward at the same time. I'm surprised the whole place doesn't tip over.

'Well, of course, we're not allowed to use the real one.' She gives everyone a sad grin. 'We've examined the archive information about this flute and we think we've built a decent replica.'

The grown-ups go, 'Phew!' The kid next to me makes a disappointed sound.

Heather lays her bag on the table and opens the bulgy envelope. She pulls out a package wrapped in cloth. She's careful, like she's unswaddling a baby, until at last she holds up another golden flute.

She checks her watch and smiles. That reminds me. It must be nearly time! *Ulric! Where are you?*

Heather lifts the flute to her lips and leans closer to the mic. All the spiders stop partying because even they realise what's happening next. My hands hover near my ears, ready.

ULRIC

Chorus. That's easy. It's what I learned first, the words and the dance.

My hea-ar-art is beating hard,
Shattering like a mighty shard.
Burning through my body, lighting up the night,
Boom! Boom! It's gelignite.

I've found the *heart* bit and the *shard* bit already. *Burning through my body, lighting up the night* – that's easy. It's Our Universe – the astronomy room. There's a cabinet full of drawers with pictures of different space things on them – satellites, Jupiter, black holes and other stuff. She said *quick* so I run there and go straight to the drawer that says *Meteorite*. I've read the card a hundred times; it's about the Hoba meteorite that landed in Namibia. Even better, there's a chunk of meteorite that you can touch. It's on a chain in case anyone steals it.

I lift it up. Evie's left the folded sheet of stickers underneath it. As I lift them out, a sound blasts through me. It's so loud and high. It's like a screeching ghost. I don't know if it's inside or outside my head. I slap my hands over my ears, but I can still hear it like it's going straight through my bones. I'm kinda frozen, then I have one thing in my head: I need to find the noise and stop it. I glance back in the drawer and I see Evie's left something else – her DBS earbuds. Oh, Evie! How did you know this was gonna happen? I sweep the earbuds out of the drawer and shove them in my ears. The world turns silent and my body relaxes.

I race towards the amphitheatre.

EVIE

The kid next to me drops his pipe. His eyes are wide as plates. We all clap our hands over our ears at the same time. Some of the small kids are sobbing. The adults are confused, trying to comfort them. They obviously can't hear anything. There's only one thing in my mind: I have to stop that noise!

I try and stand up but it's like the screaming has muddled up my brain signals. My body won't work.

The mother of the dressed-up kid next to me yells at the stage.

'Help us, Mr Mayer! Please!'

The guard looks uncertain. But some of the adults have realised what's going on. The mother pushes past me and her dressed-up kid and runs onto the stage. She's not alone. Soon loads of adults are surging towards the stage like a DBS concert for real. I can't even see Heather no more.

My head feels – Explosive! There's the screeching inside it, and the adults yelling and children screaming outside it. I squeeze my eyes shut, but it doesn't help. When I open them, I see Heather's friend calmly walking off stage carrying a bag with a bulgy envelope.

ULRIC

The security guard from the warrior queens room almost knocks me down because she's running so fast. I sprint after her. The amphitheatre looks like market day when the cheap biscuit stall's there. The stage is jammed with shouting adults and the seats with screaming children, except it's all on mute for me.

I run down the aisle, looking around. *Where's my*

sister? Where's Evie? I spot her near the front, her fingers jammed in her ears and her face all creased up like she's got the worst ever toothache.

'Evie,' I yell, the sound even louder in my head because of the earbuds.

Evie spots me. 'Get her!' she mouths.

A woman's walking slowly out of the theatre. She's carrying a bag with a bulgy envelope in it.

'Flute!' Evie mouths.

All the grown-ups suddenly turn around. I don't know if Heather's turned the volume up because even though I can't hear nothing, I can tell the kids are shouting for the noise to stop! As the adults run back to them, I see Heather race off in the opposite direction, still playing the flute. The guards are left on stage staring at an empty box.

What am I supposed to do?

Evie tries to smile. 'Use your moves, little brother.'

I nod and run after the woman. She must have heard me, but she keeps walking without looking around as if she's totally innocent, weaving between all the staff running towards the theatre.

'Thief!' I yell. 'Give back the flute!'

The woman does stop. She turns around, looks at me and smiles. Her mouth moves, but of course I can't hear a thing. Then she turns back and carries on walking.

I've got to stop her.

Use your moves! I let them flow through my body like I'm DBS's guest member.

My hea-ar-art is beating hard . . . I wiggle my shoulders, then chest in and out like I'm breathing a hurricane.

Shattering like a mighty shard . . . Reach up – I'm a steeple, then another jump with my arms and legs straight out, trying to sit on air. It took me a while to learn this; I had to practise in the park so I didn't make no noise. The thief's getting away. I have to speed up.

Burning through my body, lighting up the night. Spin, spin, spin. Not all neat like DBS, but I get closer.

Boom! I look around.

Boom! I crouch.

It's gelignite. And I explode! I launch myself into the air, yelling as I fly forward. The thief spins around and we collide. Her mouth opens wide so I know she's screaming and she collapses. The bag drops from her shoulder on to the floor and my fists punches it away across the floor.

A hand grabs my shoulder. Fingers pull out the earbuds. I spin around. It's Evie.

'Sick moves,' she says, and hugs me.

EVIE

Thief-Woman sits up.

'Ouch!' She rubs her ankle and glares at Ulric. 'You made me pull a tendon!'

Now it's my turn to explode. 'My brother didn't hurt you! You were stealing the flute!'

A slow smile spreads across the woman's face.

'It's not just *"the flute"*,' she says. 'It's the Child Whisperer.'

I fold my arms. 'I don't believe in any of that!'

'Then bring it here,' she says. 'Let me show you.'

'No,' Ulric says. 'We won't.'

The woman keeps her eyes on me. 'If you don't believe it, there's no harm, is there? So why do you think it's guarded so closely? Imagine a secret weapon that you can whisper into and make every child in the vicinity do exactly what you want.' Her smile widens. 'Teachers would love it, of course. But remember the Pied Piper of Hamelin? If you have the Child Whisperer, you can threaten to steal a town's children if you don't get what you want! Oh, the power!'

I start to say No!' but the words are changing in my mouth.

'You are the best brother in the world!' my lips are saying. 'From now on, I will always do the washing-up for you!'

I look over at Ulric. His eyes are wide, staring at me as he holds the flute to his mouth, talking into it.

'I told you,' Thief-Woman says quietly. 'If you hand it over, I'll cut you into the deal!'

Suddenly, there's a small squeal and all the thoughts of washing-up disappear from my head. Mr Mayer, the guard, has swiped the flute from Ulric's hands.

'I'll take that,' he growls and marches off.

The other guard helps Thief-Woman to her feet and leads her away.

I glower at Ulric. He grins back.

'You can't blame me for trying,' he says.

Mum has to come to the museum and sit with us while we're asked loads of questions. Paramedics even examine us to make sure there's no permanent damage. When we're finally allowed to leave, Melody's outside waiting for us. She knows more about what happened than we do! Some of the adults in the theatre managed to get their phones out to film it all while Ulric was using his DBS moves to catch the villain. I'm a bit sad no one filmed that.

'They reckon the replica flute had a kind of dog whistle device in it,' Melody says as we head home. 'It used to be in shop doorways to stop kids hanging about. Adults can't hear it.'

'Rude!' I say.

'Agreed,' Melody says. 'The flute must have amplified it until it was really uncomfortable.'

'Yeah,' I say with feeling. 'Though I'd rather use the

word "torture". What happened to Heather?' She's the one I really want to see in prison after her brain-frying exploits.

'They caught her as she was jumping into a taxi,' Melody says. 'I wonder if it was worth it? No one knows if the Child Whisperer is real or not.'

Me and Ulric look at each other. He looks just a little bit embarrassed.

'Who knows?' I say. 'But Ulric did save the day!'

'He did indeed!' Mum says. 'How we can say "thank you"?'

Ulric sneaks me another look. I don't need a Child Whisperer to know what's in his head. I sigh.

'I'll do his share of the washing-up for the rest of the year,' I say, making the words 'rest of the year' a bit louder, so he doesn't try and push his luck.

'Thank you,' he mouths at me.

I give his hand a very quick squeeze.

'I don't need the Child Whisperer to think that you're the best brother in the world,' I say. 'Well, sometimes.'

SAY I
DUNNIT

TOP SECRET

SAY I DUNNIT

By Elle McNicoll

A wedding is a stressful affair at any time of year, but a wedding during a heatwave is enough to lead to murder.

Thirteen-year-old Briar entered the vast stately home her cousin had chosen to be married in and grimaced at the gaudiness of it all. Her basset hound Flute was by her side. They both stared up at the gauche chandelier in the reception room, while catering staff and helpers hurried all around them. Champagne flutes on silver trays flew over their heads and there were gargantuan bouquets of flowers arriving. The smell of the lilies, the pinch of the stuffy air and the sound of the fans set up in corners of the room, to try to create coolness through the incredibly soupy heat – it was all a little too much for Briar. She was overstimulated and wanted nothing more than to leave the grand house and jump into the lake outside, even if it was her only cousin's wedding.

But her additional sense was stinging. The same sense that had told her, last Christmas, about the poisoned ballerina. Something was afoot. Something in the swampy heat was waiting to happen.

'Briar!'

Her cousin appeared on the twisting staircase at the back of the entrance hall, her hair all in rollers, wearing a white satin robe.

Briar nodded once in greeting. 'Clover.'

'Where are your parents?'

'Parking the car.'

'And you brought Flute?'

'Of course.'

A bridesmaid appeared on Clover's left, eyeing Flute as if he were a bomb. 'She brought a dog.'

'Flute's special, Sofia, he keeps her calm,' Clover said wearily.

Amira, another bridesmaid, gave Briar a bright and sunny grin in greeting before making a face behind Sofia's back, earning a smile from Briar in return.

Briar's eyes usually narrowed at the use of the word 'special' but she said nothing. Her only job was to smile for photographs, and trust the innate gnawing in her gut that knew something was coming.

The hours leading up to the wedding were tremendously difficult. Clover, usually calm and collected, snapped at both of her bridesmaids and even threatened to kill one of them. The bridesmaid threw the threat right back at her and stormed out. The bridesmaid seemed to mean her promise of murder a little more than Clover had. Briar made a mental note.

There was a second rehearsal for the actual ceremony before most of the guests arrived. Briar found herself standing next to a young man she vaguely recognised.

'We've met before,' he told her, his friendly face becoming even more pleasant when he smiled in greeting. 'I'm an old friend of Clover's.'

Briar instantly remembered. 'Oh yes., reg. We met at Clover's university graduation. You pushed me on the swings.'

The two of them stood in silence and watched the rehearsal. The waiters were moving around them, on the outskirts of the large room, trying to get everything in place. Preparations had obviously taken longer than anticipated. A nervous wedding planner was hissing orders out of the corner of her mouth. She put two unity candles on the altar: one to use and one for backup. As she walked backwards, almost knocking over a bartender making his way to his station, she let out a little shriek.

'Oops,' Greg said to Briar, sympathetic to the bartender

who now had a trodden-on foot. 'No one ever pays attention to the help.'

Briar glanced at the red-faced wedding planner and said nothing.

Flute sat beneath Briar's chair as the ceremony began. A string quartet played and the groom, Jason, stood up at the front while the bridesmaids walked slowly down the aisle. They all carried white roses. The floral scents made Briar's nose, sting but she kept her eyes moving across the many guests. The wedding planner was at the back of the hall, looking purple with stress. Or perhaps it was the heat.

Briar looked up at the ceiling just before Clover made her entrance. There were lots of hanging lanterns up there. They dangled from thin ropes that had been painted gold. A large chandelier hovered above the spot where Jason was standing.

People stood as Clover entered on the arm of Briar's uncle Jack. There were coos and noises of approval, but Briar was still uneasy. Even Flute let out a small, unhappy woof under his breath.

As Clover reached the beaming groom, her veil got caught on someone's chair. Jason darted forward to untangle it. When Clover was free, they stepped back into their places.

Only, Briar noticed with a frown, they had *switched* places. She supposed it didn't matter, as long as they were facing each other. Jason had accidentally swapped their positions while straightening his soon-to-be wife's veil.

The ceremony continued with beautiful music and a receptive audience. Briar started to calm down a little, telling herself that her sense was wrong for once.

And that was when the large chandelier fell and knocked Clover out.

Everything happened quickly. Briar jumped to her feet and Flute let out a deep bark. Uncle Jack and Aunt Kemi rushed to Clover. Jason and the minister were both already checking on her. Briar could see her moving a little and being told to lie still. The photographer looked confused about whether or not to take a picture and the wedding planner had gone very pale. Greg was watching in horror, looking devastated for his old friend from uni. Briar's parents were calling for an ambulance.

However, one of the bridesmaids was looking down at Clover with a strange expression. An expression that made Briar uneasy.

'What a horrible accident,' an usher whispered to another guest.

Briar looked down at her basset hound, who was staring up at her in an almost knowing way.

Both of them knew it was not an accident.

Clover was awake and with the paramedics, which meant the wedding was on hiatus. Jason was with her, as were Uncle Jack, Aunt Kemi and Briar's parents. This gave Briar plenty of time and opportunity to inspect the scene of the possible crime.

Everyone had left the ceremony room and moved into the ballroom on the other side of the stately home. It was quiet and eerie as Briar made her way towards the large, shattered chandelier. She knelt down, inspecting the broken pieces. It had been suspended by a golden cord, just like the lanterns. However, *this* golden cord was fixed to the wall. When Briar looked closely, she noticed that it had been severed. It was blackened, a patch of ebony amid artificial gold.

Briar moved to the wall, while Flute sniffed the debris. The wall fitting, where the golden cord had been attached, sat above a sconce. And inside that sconce was Briar's smoking gun.

'Gotcha,' she whispered.

She showed the strategically placed unity candle to Flute. A candle that would have burned away the cord holding the chandelier aloft. It would have been easy to miss among the other tea lights all around the room, and the general smell of gentle fire. But there was no

mistaking its placement.

Briar snapped a quick picture on her smartphone. She stepped away from the wall and the broken fragments on the floor. The damaged pieces of a weapon.

'Attempted murder,' Briar told her dog as they made their way towards the rest of the wedding party. 'Not an accident at all.'

As they passed through the entrance foyer of the house, Briar spotted a bridesmaid consoling the wedding planner. The latter had her head in her hands as she perched on the stairs.

'Clover has worked you way too hard,' the bridesmaid, Sofia, said to the wedding planner in a consoling voice. 'She's been a nightmare for all of us.'

'And now she might be dead,' sobbed the wedding planner.

'She's not dead,' sighed Sofia.

Her tone made Briar frown. 'Try not to sound so disappointed,' she told the bridesmaid with a steely look. Flute let out a chuff of agreement.

Sofia stared at the young girl in horror. 'Briar! Of ... of course I'm upset about Clover. But she's going to be fine.'

'Is she?' Briar asked coolly, wondering if the memory of the fallen chandelier and the screams were as fresh in Sofia's head as they were in her own.

'Are you all right, Briar?'

The question had come from Greg, who still looked very disturbed by the whole thing. He gazed down at Briar and Flute with real concern in his voice.

'I'm fine because Clover will be fine,' Briar said, the words like a mantra. 'How about you?'

She knew how close Clover and Greg had been. It was clear from his reaction to Clover's screams, and his face as he stood before Briar now, that he was horrified about the whole thing.

'I've had better days,' he said shakily. 'I've checked in with your aunt and uncle, they say Clover will be fine. She's just in shock. It could have been so much worse.'

'It wasn't an accident.'

Briar told Greg this with great certainty. He looked appalled at the suggestion.

'Briar, lovely,' he said gently. 'The chandelier hitting your cousin most definitely was an accident. No one would want to hurt Clover.'

'I found the backup unity candle in the sconce under the rope holding up the chandelier,' Briar said firmly, refusing to be dissuaded from her findings. 'It was alight. Someone obviously placed it there, and lit the flame, to burn away the rope.'

'Attempted murder?' Greg asked, sounding strangled and unsure.

'Yes. Someone clearly meant Clover harm.'

'But . . . who? This is her *wedding* day. Everyone is here to support her.'

Briar's eyes flashed back towards Sofia, the sulking bridesmaid, who looked far more annoyed than worried about her friend. Then to the wedding planner who was crying a little too theatrically.

'Someone came to this wedding with a plan,' Briar said. 'I'm going to find out who. Will you help me?'

She looked up at Clover's old friend sternly and he swallowed. 'Yes. I'll help.'

Greg and Briar began their investigation by speaking to one of the venue staff members.

'Do you get a lot of weddings here?' Briar asked.

'Oh, yeah,' the young woman answered. 'There's one every weekend. And summer is our busiest time.'

'So, having seen a lot of weddings,' Greg asked, 'was there anything unusual about this one?'

The worker screwed her face up as she considered the question. 'Not really. It was a bit rushed and harried, but nothing out of the ordinary.'

'Did you have much interaction with my cousin?' pressed Briar. 'Was anyone behaving like they wished her harm?'

'I mean, nothing that was unusual,' the woman said.

'See, weddings are probably the most stressful events you can ever experience. There's just so much that goes into them, and so most of the people involved get irritable. And that can make other people irritable. You can occasionally witness the odd argument or snapped comment. But it's not a sign of there being something deeply wrong. People are just nervous and crabby.'

'No one had anything bad to say about Clover then?' Greg said. 'Checks out. She's the best.'

'Well, one of the bridesmaids was a bit shifty,' the employee said, frowning in memory.

Briar and Greg exchanged a look.

'Do you remember which one?' asked Briar.

'The unattractive one?'

Briar frowned but nodded. 'Sofia?'

'I think so,' the woman said. 'She demanded that the make-up artist do a different kind of eye look on her face, and when the bride reminded her that they were all wearing the same thing, she started mouthing off.'

'Mouthing off?' Greg's brow was furrowed as he repeated the phrase. He was proving to be a helpful assistant detective to Briar. 'How so?'

'Calling the bride selfish, saying she was a dictator and that she didn't look good in the agreed make-up look. Then the bride said she wouldn't look good in any look so it didn't matter.'

Briar shook her head. 'Clover's nice to almost everyone. It must be more than just wedding nerves if it made her say something like that.'

'Agreed,' Greg said. 'Clover is goodness personified. It would take quite a person to make her be mean.'

'Well, then, there you go,' the worker said with a shrug. 'That's the person who seemed to wish her harm.'

As Briar and Greg regrouped, Greg looked back towards the scene of the crime. 'It's quite a bit of effort. Causing a chandelier to fall. How do we know it wasn't an accident?'

'Nothing is an accident during a wedding,' a voice said.

Briar, Greg and Flute turned to see the wedding planner. Her tears were now dry and she looked exhausted.

'You think someone tried to hurt Clover on her wedding day?' asked the planner.

'The unity candle they were going to light after the vows?' Briar posed a question she knew the answer to. 'Where is it?'

'On the table by the altar,' the planner said without thought. 'Why?'

'Was there a backup?'

'Yes, of course.'

'Where?'

'On the table as well.'

'Can you point it out to me?'

The planner looked irritated but she stepped back into the ceremony room and pointed a finger towards the table at the back of the venue, by the altar. Her face froze as she noticed only one candle.

'But I set both there myself,' she breathed.

'Perhaps,' Briar acknowledged. 'But then someone moved it. They transferred it to the sconce directly beneath the chandelier suspension rope and they lit the flame.'

'Oh god,' sighed the planner. 'I . . . it could have been anyone, I set the candles ages ago and then checked them off my list. Anyone could have moved one.'

'A bridesmaid could have,' Greg reminded Briar. 'Or even the groom.'

'Jason would never,' the planner said, sniffing. 'He's obsessed with the girl.'

'Obsession can lead to danger,' Briar said, a ton of thoughts and possibilities entering her mind. 'I need to speak to Clover.'

'She's gone to the hospital,' the wedding planner said desperately. 'The groom has too.'

'Then I need to speak to everyone else.'

The wedding planner began to quietly invite everyone to congregate while Briar stood next to Greg.

'Are you all right?' she asked him. He looked torn up about the whole affair.

'I'm fine,' he said, somewhat restlessly. 'I just hate that someone did this.'

'You really care about Clover.'

It was a statement, not a question, but Greg nodded in answer. 'She's my best friend.'

'She's going to be all right,' Briar said firmly, for her own sake as well as his.

'I know,' he replied. 'But I hate that she was hurt.'

There was a pause before he spoke again. Briar had learned that keeping silent often invited people to share whatever it was they were feeling.

'In university, Clover and I used to break into the costume department of the opera school. We'd listen to the performances for free, hidden among all the clothes and props.'

Briar smiled. 'Did you have a favourite?'

'Mine was *Tosca*. She liked *La Bohème*.'

'That's really nice.'

'Yeah.'

Greg's face suddenly crumpled and tears spouted from his eyes. Briar was staggered and looked away quickly, uncomfortable at the sudden explosion of emotion.

'Sorry,' Greg said. 'I just can't stand thinking about someone trying to hurt her.'

'I know,' Briar said.

He looked at her with shining eyes. 'You have to find

who did this, Briar. Clover told me all about you and that ballerina. At Christmas? She says you solved the whole thing. I couldn't actually believe it. Now I hope more than anything it's true. And that you can find who did this.'

Briar gave him one last sad smile. 'I will.'

All of the wedding guests gathered in the drawing room of the stately home, without the bride and groom. The wedding planner looked awkward and unsure as she settled by the fireplace. Sofia had to be coaxed out of the bathroom. She looked up at Briar, very sullenly, from her chair by the window.

'What's going on, pet?' Briar's father asked. 'Why've you got us all gathered here?'

The large group of people all stared at Briar in perplexed expectation. Ties had been loosened, high heels had been removed, and there was a general feeling of nervousness among all of the guests.

'Clover was hit by that chandelier, but it was no accident.'

Briar's words echoed throughout the room they were all sitting in. They were met with confusion and even a little anger from the crowd.

'You're not serious,' Sofia said sharply.

'She is, actually,' Greg said. 'Briar alerted me to the fact that the chandelier fell because its rope was burned away.'

'Yes.' Briar stepped forward and Flute did the same. 'Someone, between the time of the rehearsal and the start of the ceremony, moved one of the unity candles to a hidden sconce beneath the chandelier rope and set it alight. It slowly burned away the rope, until the chandelier fell and landed on the bride. She could have been killed, which was no doubt the culprit's intention. Why else would you drop a large object on someone?'

'It was an accident, sweetheart,' Briar's father said as gently as was possible. There were murmurings of agreement from the other guests.

'No, it wasn't,' Briar said matter-of-factly. 'The chandelier was suspended safely. In a venue like this, it would be cleaned and checked regularly for any instability. However, the culprit managed to place the candle in the sconce between the rehearsal and the ceremony.'

'This kid is crazy,' sighed Sofia with a bored expression.

Briar was used to people talking about her in front of her. Sometimes they would do so over her head. She sat very comfortably in the lower end of people's expectations, and she enjoyed it, because it always allowed her to surprise people.

She loved proving people wrong. It was her absolute favourite hobby.

'Why would someone want to hurt Clover?' asked Amira, the other bridesmaid and one of Clover's good friends. 'She's perfect.'

'That's what Briar and I have been unable to ascertain,' Greg said with a look of regret. A few people in the crowd smiled sympathetically at him. 'Motive. We know someone tried to hurt Clover, but we don't know the why of it. We just know there were no accidents today.'

'Oh, there was one accident.'

When Briar said the words, the whole room stared at her. Greg looked as confused as anyone else. The wedding planner raised an eyebrow, Briar's parents looked concerned and ready to bundle her into the family car.

'There was one accident,' Briar repeated, moving into the middle of the room so that she became the nucleus, with everyone watching her as she surveyed their faces. 'But it wasn't the chandelier.'

'Briar?' Greg looked at her in nervous surprise, clearly wondering why his fellow detective was going off-script.

'There was an accident during the ceremony,' Briar continued as the room listened intently. 'Clover's veil snagged and Jason, the groom, leaped forward to help. In doing so, both became a tad disorientated, or flustered, and switched their positions at the altar.'

'That's true,' the minister said, speaking up from the back of the room. 'I didn't tell them to swap back because

I thought it would make more of a scene and upset things even further.'

'So they were NOT standing,' Briar said loudly, 'in the positions they had rehearsed. Earlier that morning, a quick rehearsal confirmed that they would stand in opposite positions.'

'This is crazy,' sighed Sofia. 'What's the point?'

'The point is, Jason was the intended target.'

Briar's words hit the room like a toxic gas. Some people reacted instantly, while others took a moment to understand what she was truly saying.

'Clover wasn't the intended victim?' the wedding planner asked, her voice sounding a little strangled.

'No,' Briar said softly. 'She wasn't.'

'She could have been,' Greg persisted. 'If the culprit was someone a little less obvious.'

'Who?' Briar's father asked.

'Jason, possibly.'

Greg's accusation caused a ripple of chaos.

'Not true!' bellowed the groom's father. 'Jason would never! What a thing to say!'

Pandemonium broke loose. It was not until Flute let out a sharp bark and Briar climbed onto a footstool that things settled once more.

'Jason was not the murderer. Or attempted murderer. He was the intended victim.'

Silence fell. Briar pushed ahead, her need to avenge Clover and her ruined wedding giving her courage.

'Jason was supposed to be beneath the chandelier. A moment of courtliness on his part saved him and he, unwittingly, put Clover in harm's way. The murderer could not alter their plans without everyone seeing. That rules out Sofia. She was a bridesmaid who could have easily blown out the unity candle and stopped the chandelier from falling.'

'So then who?'

Briar turned at Greg's question. She regarded her cousin's university friend, the man who had pushed her on the swings when she was younger. The one with the boyish smile and the gentle voice.

'You, Greg.'

There were horrified gasps. People were clearly shocked that Briar could say such a thing. Greg stared down at her in disbelief. 'Me? Briar, what are you –'

'It's like you said to me earlier today, Greg,' Briar said softly. 'No one ever pays attention to the help. And you've been very helpful to me today. I guess you thought that would stop me suspecting you.'

For the first time, something sinister entered Greg's face. Something unpleasant and unkind. Briar's father saw it too, and Briar watched from the corner of her eye as he slowly reached for the phone on the mantelpiece.

'I don't think you ever got over her, Greg,' Briar said. She was calm and composed as only a young detective could be. Flute chuffed from her feet, backing up her every move. 'You came up with a spontaneous plan to get rid of Jason. But it backfired.'

'You're a little liar,' Greg finally said, his voice sounding very different. 'You have no proof.'

'Actually, there is proof.'

The whole room turned to look at one of the bartenders. He stepped forward, his tie loosened and his eyes tired.

'I saw you move the candle and light it,' the bartender said flatly. 'I didn't have a clue why you were doing it. I assumed there was some secret wedding reason. Turns out you were trying to bring down the chandelier.'

'Very operatic,' said Briar. Her gaze shot back to Greg. 'Wow. You really don't pay attention to the help, do you, Greg?'

Greg looked like an animal in a trap for a brief second. His eyes were panicky, and it was clear to everyone in the room that he had been caught and was desperately working out how to get un-caught.

He lunged at Briar.

But before he was able to grab her, Flute launched himself into the air. His jaws clamped on to Greg's arm and he shook him like a doll. And while the basset hound was not large, like his owner he was strong.

'The police will be here soon,' Briar's father said. 'And, son, you've ruined one of the most expensive weddings this family has ever seen. Best get into the van before the father of the bride gets back from the hospital.'

Briar and Flute watched as Greg was handcuffed and walked to the police car. Amira and Sofia stood in the doorway of the venue, looking on as well.

'How did you work it out?' Greg asked her as he paused before the vehicle.

'*Tosca*,' Briar said with a shrug. 'It's an opera about a jealous lover. Baddies always tell on themselves.'

'What kind of twelve-year-old knows about opera?' whispered Sofia.

'Weird ones,' Amira replied, but she had a touch of admiration in her voice.

Greg gave Briar a small smile of acknowledgement. 'Love – it's the worst poison of all, kid. It's the only thing that kills you slowly and leaves no trace.'

The car drove away.

Briar's parents came out to tell her that Jason and Clover were both perfectly fine and coming back to the venue to have a smaller, quieter ceremony and that she and Flute had been promoted to the bridal party.

'Weddings, eh?' Briar's father said, squeezing her

shoulder and patting Flute on the nose. 'Never a dull moment.'

Briar watched the car disappear into the distance, with Greg watching her from the back window. She stared at his forlorn, desperate face and shook her head.

'I'm never falling in love, Dad. It looks awful.'

Her father watched Greg as well, and Flute let out a small bark.

Briar could code things together, and see things that other people thought they were good at hiding. However, the mechanisms of the heart were too unpredictable.

And they could easily lead to murder. So it would seem.

SUMMERTIME
AND THE
KILLING
IS *EASY*

E.L. NORRY

TOP SECRET

PROPERTY OF THE SUPER SUNNY MURDER CLUB

SUMMERTIME AND THE KILLING IS EASY

By E.L. Norry

I leaned out of the car window, wind whipping my hair, as Becky drove towards the seafront and the Superkids' Spectacular Summer Holiday Club where I'd be spending the week.

It was hard to believe I'd lived with Becky for almost a year without any trouble. Well, except for a teacher who got murdered on a school ski trip last October – but that wasn't my fault! And on that trip, I'd made friends with Ishan and Holly so, for me at least, it hadn't been *too* traumatic.

Becky was all right. She worked full-time and parented solo, so the only choice during school holidays was clubs or respite care. Respite is when someone else agrees to look after me if Becky needs a break. But this summer she'd found a multi-activity club held right on the beach, and had done the usual parenting speech: 'Luca, the fresh air will do you the world of good', etc, etc. I'd rather be gaming, sprawled on my beanbag, to be honest, but I loved the beach and sport, so maybe it wouldn't be *too* bad.

Becky slowed down and turned into the car park next to the seafront and my stomach suddenly twisted with nerves. I clutched the handles on my rucksack, wondering what the other kids would be like. She turned off the engine and a tall girl with a high blonde ponytail wearing a high-vis jacket jogged over to the car, holding a clipboard.

'Hiya!' She leaned through Becky's open window. 'Another one for the Superkids' Spectacular Summer Sports?'

Becky nodded her head at me.

'So who've we got here then?' the girl asked with a perky smile, her pen with a pink pom-pom poised over her clipboard.

'Luca Azoria,' Becky replied. 'He's with you all week.'

'Azoria?' She bounced the pom-pom against her lips. 'That name sounds familiar. Have you been with us before?' She cocked her head to one side, just as I shook mine.

'Nope. First time,' I replied.

'Hmm. I must be thinking of somebody else. Anyway, I'm Lisa.' Lisa passed Becky the clipboard. 'Just tick his name off, sign and then you can leave him in our capable hands! Any allergies or anything we should be aware of?'

'Nope, just your typical food-guzzling teenager!' Becky grinned, signing me in, and I climbed out of the car, slinging my rucksack over my shoulder.

'See you later,' I said.

'Enjoy!' Becky waved back as she sped up the hill and off to work.

'Follow me, Luca,' Lisa said. 'We've got loads of activities planned and the weather forecast is fantastic for the whole week.'

The way she was hardly pausing for breath, it was almost as if she was nervous about something. 'Sounds good.'

'Me and my boyfriend Marc have been running these clubs in the school holidays for three years; if there's one thing I *can* guarantee – it's total fun!'

As we walked towards the beach, I wondered if her idea of fun and mine were the same . . .

The morning was already warm, and the cloudless blue sky promised a scorcher. Even though I tanned easily, Becky said skin damage was still a concern and had made me slather myself in factor 30 before breakfast and insisted I bring a bottle of sun cream along too.

'What does the AI on your vest stand for?' I asked Lisa

as we walked along the promenade towards the beach. 'You some kind of robot?'

'AI?' Lisa glanced down at her high-vis vest and smiled. 'Oh, that stands for Arts Institute.'

'What's that?'

'It's the uni me and Marc go to. We're your group leaders, and we're training a new girl at the moment too.' As she said this, her voice dipped and the cheerful light in her eyes dimmed.

'What are you doing at uni?'

'Performing Arts. Acting is my life! Oh –' she stopped walking and stared at the ground, biting her lip. 'I shouldn't have mentioned that Marc's my boyfriend earlier. We're not supposed to . . .' Her voice trailed off, and she rubbed the back of her neck awkwardly. 'Just . . . forget I said anything. Please.'

'Don't worry,' I promised her. 'I can keep a secret.'

We passed a row of pastel-coloured beach huts nestled in front of the wall leading up to the cliffs and I counted nine other kids standing in a circle down on the sand. As we got closer, my heart sank; I was definitely the oldest here. *Oh no.* This week was going to suck. But then I spotted two people wearing backpacks running across the sand towards us; one of them running in a very familiar way. Those flailing arms were unmistakable.

'Ishan!' I yelled excitedly, jogging over to him. 'You

didn't tell me you were coming!' We fist-bumped. It was great to see him.

A small girl who looked exactly the same as Ishan, only with long, bushy hair, bounced out from behind him, jumping up and down. 'Hi! I'm Jiya!' she squealed.

Ishan stepped back frowning. 'Luca, this is my little sister.'

'I can see the family resemblance,' I said. Ishan's frown deepened. 'Hi, Jiya.'

'I like collecting things!' she said enthusiastically. 'What do you collect?'

'Oh, me? Nothing,' I said. 'I used to when I was your age, though. What do you like to collect?' I asked, trying to be friendly.

Jiya wrestled with the zip on her backpack. 'I like shiny things. And make-up. And pens. And shells!' She pulled out a handful of random items from the front pocket of her rucksack and thrust them at me. 'I'm six!'

'Seven, Jiya,' Ishan said with a sigh, pushing his glasses up his nose. 'You had your birthday party last weekend, remember?'

'Oh yeah!' She giggled. 'I got more lip balms as presents, to add to my collection. All different colours and flavours – I've got melon, and mango, and liquorice. Look!'

Ishan covered his face with his hands in embarrassment as Jiya unveiled her roll-out purse and proudly displayed her collection. 'These are my lip balms. I've got nearly thirty now, but some of them are doubles,' she announced happily.

'Wow, that is an impressive collection!' I said.

'Yay!' Jiya stuffed everything back in her bag and then spun round with her arms out, nearly knocking over two other kids who were setting up orange cones in the sand next to us.

I couldn't help but laugh. Jiya had more energy than those children's presenters you see on Saturday morning TV! And there was something very funny about how she annoyed Ishan, who usually was pretty unflappable.

'Be careful, Jiya!' Ishan rolled his eyes and muttered to me, 'This is going to be the longest week of my entire life.'

'Don't worry,' I reassured him. 'Hopefully, you won't be on babysitting duty the *whole* time. There's loads of younger ones here. She'll make friends soon and you'll be off the hook.'

All three group leaders stood in a huddle next to a tall red flag, chatting and pointing at their clipboards. Marc had a real surf dude vibe: shoulder-length bleached-blond hair, a wispy goatee, and tattoos running up and down his arms. The other girl looked very different to

Lisa, with short purple hair and a nose stud. She looked cheerful and relaxed. After a few moments, she nodded and turned to go, but Lisa stopped her and jogged off herself. She headed towards a VW van parked up at the promenade by the beach huts. When she came back, I saw she was carrying three small rucksacks.

Marc and the other girl were nudging each other and laughing together as Lisa returned. The laughter stopped suddenly when Lisa chucked a rucksack to each of them, a bit too hard. Marc dropped his bright yellow one and had to collect up a bunch of stuff that spilled out on to the sand.

'All right! Listen up, guys!' he shouted. 'My name's Marc, and I'm into surfing, paragliding and rock climbing. I don't know if any of you have noticed this yet.' He pointed to the long scar, which ran the length of his calf. 'But I got this by fighting off a shark with nothing more than a Swiss army knife near the coral reef in Sydney.' Then he brandished a big white curved pendant hanging from his neck. 'I wasn't the only one left with a scar that day!'

All the younger kids went, 'Oooh,' and gazed up at him with wide eyes. *Way to go, Marc.* They'd be eating out of the palm of his hand all week.

'Ever since then, they call me Marc the Shark!'

That was just too much. I struggled to hold in a laugh, and nudged Ishan. 'Is he for real?'

'Speaking of natural dangers, before we get started, we need to check that you've all brought your health and safety essentials,' Marc announced. 'Let's have a quick look through the inventory that we emailed to everyone. Sun cream. Water bottle. Hat.'

Everyone started checking their bags.

The girl with the purple hair chewed her lips. After a moment, I saw Lisa tap her on the shoulder and hand her a lip balm. The girl looked surprised, but then she smiled and took it. After covering her lips thoroughly, she went to hand it back, but Lisa shook her head and indicated she could keep it, so she nodded and tucked it into her shorts pocket.

'Right. Now that we've made sure we have everything we need, we're gonna find out a bit more about each other and then you should get ready to have the most fun you've ever had! All right!' Marc punched the air, grinning, as the younger kids shrieked, 'Yeah!' at the top of their lungs.

'OK. This is Lisa. We call her Mona Lisa, after the world's most famous painting.'

'That's because of my beautiful, mysterious smile, right?' Lisa said, raising one eyebrow, teeth gleaming.

'Nope – just the fact you moan a lot!' Marc cracked up and high-fived the other girl, while Lisa's smile changed to a grimace.

'Lisa and Marc are boyfriend and girlfriend,' I said, leaning into Ishan and whispering over the others' giggles. 'Though she's not supposed to tell anyone. They study acting together.'

'Strange choice, don't you think?' said Ishan. 'Learning how to be a professional pretender. Although she's obviously not that good at pretending to be happy.'

'Bet they do this routine all the time as part of their acting schtick.'

Ishan frowned, watching Lisa carefully. 'I don't think so,' he said. 'She seems really upset. I'd have guessed the one with the purple hair was his girlfriend. You can tell he's really into her! Just look at them.'

Ishan was right. Marc stood much closer to the purple-haired girl who kept fiddling with her hair, chewing her lip and looking up at Marc adoringly.

'What's *her* name?' Jiya piped up loudly, pointing at the other group leader. Ishan winced.

Marc smiled. 'This is Grace. I call her Amazing Grace – she really is amazing, very smart and athletic. And she can surf nearly as well as I can!'

Everyone grinned at this, including Grace; but I saw that Lisa's grin was fixed and her hand was clenched into a fist by her side.

'So,' Marc carried on. 'Our first game today is to come up with nicknames for each other. These will help us remember who you are and what you enjoy. But, remember, nothing mean, please.'

There were twelve of us altogether, so we were split into three groups of four. Me, Jiya, Ishan and a little boy with a ginger crew cut.

'I'm Ronan. I really like reading, especially poetry. I'll come up with some good rhymes,' he said enthusiastically.

Ishan pointed at me and then himself. 'He's Luca and I'm Ishan – good luck finding rhymes for us.'

'OK. Well, what are *your* favourite activities then?' he asked.

'I like swimming,' Ishan replied. 'I'm in the school team.'

'Swimming. Hmm . . .' Ronan said.

'Luca likes detective stories,' Ishan explained. 'Hercule Poirot is his favourite.'

A few minutes later, Marc and Lisa walked over to our group. He had tied his yellow jacket round his waist and his sunglasses were perched on top of his head. When he looked at me the smile dropped from his face. His eyes narrowed and he whispered something to Lisa who also glanced at me, a frown appearing on her face.

'How are you guys doing?' Marc turned to beam at Ronan.

'I've come up with a great nickname for Ishan!' Ronan exclaimed.

Marc raised his palm up in the air and shouted, 'High five!' Ronan jumped up to high five him. Yeah, this was definitely more for younger kids. 'So what is it? Remember – prizes for the winning team!'

Ronan pointed at Ishan. 'We can call him *Ish the Fish* because he's into swimming.'

Marc nodded and ruffled Ronan's hair. 'Nice work, sport,' he said. 'And you?' He pulled his shades down and turned his attention to me. But as he did so, his expression seemed to transform into something more serious. 'You're the Azoria kid, right?'

'Luca Azoria, yeah.'

'Let's hear what you've come up with then, Azoria.'

The way he kept staring at me and calling me by my surname made me uneasy. What was that about?

'This is *Ronan the Librarian*, 'cos he's into books,' I said.

'Mate.' Marc pulled a face. 'That doesn't rhyme, does it?' The way he said 'mate' made it sound more like 'idiot'.

'It's actually cleverer than a rhyme,' Ishan said, clearing his throat. 'Ronan the Librarian is a play on words – you've heard of *Conan the Barbarian*, right?'

'Mmm.' Marc's lip curled. 'What else?'

Ronan frowned. 'We couldn't think of anything to rhyme with Luca.'

'Luca.' Marc gazed at me, eyes narrowing. 'Luca, Luca, Luca.' Something about the way he kept saying my name gave me the creeps. 'What keeps you off the streets, hmm?'

I shrugged. 'I like reading detective stories.'

'So you like reading, eh, just like Ronan the Librarian here. Trying to steal his idea. That figures,' he sneered. I was so confused. Had I done something to upset him?

'I . . . I like gaming too,' I replied.

Marc laughed dismissively. 'Everyone likes gaming, mate! That's hardly unique, is it?'

This was getting really uncomfortable. I hated being put on the spot like this. Why didn't he just move on? 'I don't know. I like horror films, I suppose.'

'Oh! You like being scared, do you?' Marc's eyes glittered. 'I've got it!' He turned round on the sand and yelled over at the other two groups. 'Everyone! This is *Spooky Luke*!'

'That's not very good . . . it doesn't even rhyme,' said Ishan, shaking his head.

'It's not Luke, it's *Luca*,' I muttered under my breath, as Marc strode away across the sand with Lisa to see the other groups.

Jiya's lip wobbled. 'He didn't even ask me!' she wailed.

'Time for Capture the Flag!' Marc sorted out new teams and then stuck each team's flag at opposite ends of the beach. Grace made a pile of stones marking off where anyone who got tagged would have to stay until they'd got freed. She pointed to the stones. 'Try and stay away from prison!'

I always winced hearing that word – it made me feel strange because of my dad. He refused to let me visit him after he'd been put away for robbery, and I really missed him. Still, Grace didn't know that, and I preferred that no one knew.

After Marc explained the rules, we lined up in our teams, raring to get to where the other team's flag had been planted. He handed Grace a stopwatch, teasing her by pulling it away a few times and making her giggle before letting her take it.

Lisa's eyes narrowed, then she tossed her hair over her shoulder and headed down the beach towards the sea.

'OK, everyone! First competitive game of the day – so make it count!'

Marc blew the whistle and immediately I locked eyes with Ishan on the other team as he rushed towards me. I needed to tag him before he made a dash for our flag. I leaned over, ducking low and tagged him on the legs. Then I dodged the others and ran right for the flag, weaving in and out of the little kids easily.

'Yay! Luca wins again!' I yelled, doing a victory lap with my arms above my head.

Jiya laughed. 'You're good!'

Marc whispered into Grace's ear, and she came over and patted me on the shoulder. 'Could you give the younger ones a chance to capture the flag on the next round?'

Heat flooded my cheeks. 'Oh, yeah, of course – sorry.' It felt like I couldn't do anything right today!

After the last round of Capture the Flag, we all flopped on to the sand, guzzling from our water bottles. Ishan came over to me.

'What was that about with Marc earlier on?' he asked.

I shrugged. 'I don't think he likes me very much for some reason. I don't know why.'

'Yeah, he seems weird around you.'

'I'm SO hot!' Jiya whined, wiping her forehead.

Marc and Grace stood off to one side chatting and chuckling while Lisa walked around giving each of us either a number one or number two.

'Now it's time for a quieter activity in the shade where you can get your breath back and show your creative side. All the number ones pair up with the number twos and build the best sand sculpture you can!'

Jiya bounced over to me. 'I'm a number two and you're a number one so we can be a team!'

I didn't know what to say as she wriggled next to me. I glanced at Ishan who was carefully arranging a bit of driftwood to sit on, so he didn't have to sit on the sand. A very excitable Ronan handed him a spade.

Watching Jiya scoop up huge piles of sand and get stuck into making a mermaid, I decided to join in. 'I'll go and get some stones and shells to decorate her tail with,' I said, grabbing a bucket and heading towards the shoreline. After I'd collected enough, I turned back to look up at the beach and saw Marc and Grace standing very close together on the shaded side of the lifeguard huts. However, they quickly sprang apart when they saw Lisa heading in their direction. What was going on between those three? Something was up for sure. I'd ask Ishan what he thought . . .

When I got back with my bucketload, Jiya had already started to cover the mermaid in pebbles and shells.

'Where did you get those from?' I asked, impressed. She'd done most of the hard work.

She pointed to her pockets. 'Oh, I always have a few shells and pebbles; you never know when you might need them!'

'Lunchtime!' Lisa called out, waving at us all. 'Let's go and sit at the tables – no one likes sandy sarnies!' She pointed to the tables lined by benches on the promenade.

We grabbed our backpacks and Lisa and Grace headed up separate tables, helping the younger ones unwrap their sandwiches and open drinks without making a mess. Ishan and I decided to join Grace's table, with Jiya

skipping along behind us singing to herself. At the table, she squeezed herself right next to Grace.

'I love your hair!' Jiya exclaimed.

'Oh, thanks. I like yours too,' Grace replied kindly.

'It's exactly the same colour as my blackcurrant lip balm.' Jiya unrolled her collection again on the table and plucked out a small purple cylinder. 'See!'

It wasn't long before Grace and Jiya were exchanging lip balms and singing Taylor Swift at the top of their lungs. *Time to leave!*

'Ish, I'll be back in a sec, I want to speak to Marc.'

I wandered over to Marc, who was sitting by himself drinking from a paper cup. *Maybe I can figure out what I've done to upset him*, I thought to myself.

Pulling his shades down, he peered up at me. 'Everything all right, Spooky?' he said through a mouthful of thick green shake.

'Yeah. Can I sit here? The girls' table is too much.'

Marc glanced around and then shrugged. 'It's a free country, I suppose.'

I sat down, putting my backpack on the table. 'Why are you eating on your own?' I asked.

'Not that it's any of your business but I've got a severe nut allergy,' Marc grunted, pushing his fringe out of his eyes. He stared at me. His blue eyes were cold. 'You know what else I'm allergic to? Criminals.'

'What?'

'Don't play innocent. You and your family cost my dad his job, and his sanity too.'

'What are you talking about?' I asked indignantly. I'd never met Marc the Shark *or* his dad.

'You're Luca Azoria,' he hissed. 'Jacob Azoria's son. Your dad robbed the Tesco Metro on Percival Street last year.' He slammed his cup down and got up from the table, taking a step closer to me. 'It was all over the papers!'

A flush crept up my neck. He knew about my dad? Was that why he was being so weird with me?

Marc leaned in so close that I felt his hot breath on my cheek. 'My dad was the manager of that store. That day almost ruined his life and ours. Having that gun pointed at him. Even when he found out it was just a replica . . . he was never the same after that. Couldn't leave the house. Lost his job and started drinking; he was like some sort of zombie. He'd barely speak to us. In the end, he had to go into –' Marc broke off suddenly, struggling to continue.

A cold prickle rippled across my shoulders. He looked ready to burst and I felt really scared.

'Just stay out my way, all right?' he said, getting up and barging my shoulder as he went past me.

Oh man. This wasn't good. This wasn't good at all . . .

'Time for volleyball!' Marc and the other group leaders got busy moving everyone's bags and hoodies over to the lifeguard huts to clear a space for the court. We were still in the same groups from our Capture the Flag game.

Grace and Lisa opened a huge kitbag and unrolled the volleyball net. As they set it up on the beach, I heard their raised voices even over everyone else's excited conversation. *What are they arguing about?* I wondered.

'OK!' Marc shouted. 'Lisa, can you referee and keep score? I left my camera up in the van, and I wanna get some shots of the game for our new flyers.'

'Yeah, and I need to pop to the loo,' Grace chimed in. 'But I'll ref the next game when I come back.'

Lisa blew the whistle, and we were off, but I couldn't really relax or enjoy the game. I kept wondering if Marc was going to say anything else. I couldn't believe his dad had been so affected by what mine had done. I felt bad, but that was my dad's fault, not mine.

Suddenly, there was an almighty scream. Grace came dashing back down from the beach huts, almost falling over herself, eyes wide with panic.

'Help!'

Everyone stopped playing and turned to face Grace, who was sprinting across the sand.

She stopped in front of us, hands on knees, gasping. 'It's Marc. He's collapsed! He can't breathe!' Her chest heaved as she panted, out of breath.

The younger kids started to look around, worried. A few started crying. Ishan and I stared at each other, confused.

'It's all right,' Lisa said calmly. 'I'm a trained first-aider. Now go and sit on the beach in pairs, and I'll be back in a minute. I'm sure everything is fine.'

Ishan and I exchanged a look. 'What do you think has happened?' Ishan asked as we watched Grace and Lisa jog back up to the row of beach huts at the top of the beach, where the van was parked.

'Let's go and see,' I said.

'Jiya,' Ishan called, going up to her and getting out a packet of Fruit Pastilles from his pocket. 'Share these out.'

'And perhaps you can show them your amazing collection of treasures?' I added. 'Or you could organise a treasure hunt? Ronan will help.'

She grinned up at us. 'Course!' She skipped off.

Although we were following a little way behind Lisa and Grace, we heard everything as they disappeared behind the long row of beach huts.

'What were you both even doing back here?' Lisa hissed, annoyed. 'I thought you were going to the toilet?'

'Marc asked me to help with something,' Grace

stuttered, her cheeks flushing.

'I bet he did!' muttered Lisa.

When we reached the top of the beach, Ishan and I leaned forward to peer into the narrow space between the beach huts and the beach wall. Marc was lying on the floor clutching at his throat. His eyes were bulging, and his lips and tongue were horribly swollen and red.

Grace and Lisa leaned over him. 'Marc! Can you hear me?' Lisa knelt and shook him.

Marc's eyes were glassy, and his breathing sounded like a wheezing rasp. It was a terrifying sight!

'What's happening?' I blurted out.

Lisa and Grace spun round. 'He's having an allergic reaction,' Lisa said, her voice shaking. She glared at Grace. 'This is YOUR fault!' and she burst into loud, dramatic sobs.

Grace jolted backwards. 'What?! How is this *my* fault?'

Lisa wailed loudly, holding her hands either side of her head. 'He needs his EpiPen!'

'His what?' Grace asked, confused.

Lisa glared at her, and I noticed that despite the sobbing noises her eyes seemed strangely dry.

'EpiPen,' Ishan repeated. 'If someone has an allergic reaction, they can give themselves a dose of adrenaline which is inside the EpiPen. It can literally be life-saving.'

Life-saving – the word reverberated in my head.

'Marc needs a shot of adrenaline right now,' Lisa said coldly. 'You two have been all over each other today. You must have known about his allergy?'

'We haven't got time for this,' I shouted. 'We need to do something!'

'Lisa, where does Marc keep his EpiPen?' Ishan roared.

'In his rucksack – the bright yellow one. Be quick!'

Ishan and I sprinted down the beach towards the pile of coats and jumpers by the lifeguard huts. I dug around under the clothes, pulled Marc's bright yellow rucksack out of the pile and ran back with it as fast as I could.

Lisa snatched it out of my hands and unzipped one of the side pockets. Her face fell. 'It's not here,' her voice cracked. 'His pen is *always* here!' Now the tears flowed down her cheeks. This time, her distress seemed much more convincing.

'Maybe it's in one of the other compartments,' Ishan said, grabbing the rucksack from her and searching through each pocket. Eventually he admitted defeat.

Lisa's face drained of colour and her eyes looked wild as she pointed at me. 'It was here earlier . . . but I reckon *you* know that already, don't you? Marc told me who you are, after you went bothering him at lunchtime. You've got it in for Marc and his family. You better tell me what you've done with his EpiPen!'

'Me?' *What was she on about?* 'I haven't done anything!'

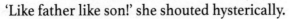

'Like father like son!' she shouted hysterically.

'But I haven't been anywhere near his rucksack. The other kids in my group can tell you – ask them!'

'Look, if there's no pen then we need to call an ambulance now!' Ishan interrupted.

Lisa pulled her mobile out of her pocket, but her hands were shaking so much that she couldn't dial properly. Ishan snatched the phone out of Lisa's hand and called 999.

'Maybe the pen fell out of his rucksack when all the bags were moved out of the way for volleyball,' I suggested to Lisa. She stared at me for a moment, then hurried down the beach towards the big pile of belongings.

'I don't understand . . . what's happening?' Grace said, weeping and wiping at her nose. 'Is he going to die?'

'He told me he has a nut allergy,' I said. 'That was why he sat away from everyone at lunch. Maybe he's eaten or drunk something by mistake?'

'I guess that explains why Mona Lisa's pointing the finger at you,' Ishan said. 'You knew about his allergy, and you were the only person to spend any time alone with him.'

I tried to stop the panic threatening to flood me. 'We know it wasn't me.' I paused, thinking. 'But what if it wasn't an accident?'

Ishan raised his eyebrows and stared right at me; I could almost see the cogs whirring in his brain.

Grace held Marc's hand. He was breathing shallowly and looked very pale. 'I'll stay with him,' she said, trying to pull herself together.

Ishan and I jogged down the beach to catch up with Lisa. The children flocked around Jiya and Ronan like bees around an open jam jar, collecting their sweets.

We'd already searched twice through the pile of belongings by the time the ambulance pulled up by the beach huts. Two paramedics jumped out, opened the back doors, and pulled out a stretcher and a large orange bag. We watched as Grace beckoned them frantically, and they disappeared behind the hut. Moments later they returned, scuttling along rapidly with Marc lying on the stretcher between them, a transparent plastic mask over his nose and mouth. His face seemed to be returning to its normal colour.

Grace stood like a statue, watching as the ambulance sped away up the promenade. Ishan and I turned to a horrified Lisa who was also watching the ambulance drive off, hand clapped over her mouth.

'We'll see how Grace is,' I said, and Ishan and I abandoned the now pointless search for the missing EpiPen.

'I should stay here and keep an eye on the little ones,' Lisa said, despondent.

'What did the paramedics say?' I asked Grace.

'Huh?' Slowly, Grace emerged from her trance. 'They got to him just in time, they said. Another few minutes and he would have been . . .' She broke off and started sobbing.

'It's OK. He'll be fine,' Ishan tried to reassure her.

Something was still playing on my mind about this so-called accident. Marc had been so careful. And there'd obviously been tension between Lisa, Marc and Grace. But what could have caused his allergic reaction? The questions wouldn't stop bubbling up in my brain.

'I can understand why you're so upset, Grace,' I said sympathetically. 'You and Marc are obviously good friends.'

She gave a guilty look towards where Lisa was. 'Er, yeah,' Grace replied hesitantly. 'He's a cool guy.'

Ishan grinned and nudged me. 'Here we go . . . Hercule's up to his old tricks again,' he said under his breath.

'Lucky you were with him back there to raise the alarm, though,' I observed. 'Otherwise he definitely would have been a goner. Why were you with him again?'

'I . . . he . . .' Grace searched for an explanation. Finally, her shoulders slumped and she sighed. 'OK, look, we just . . . had a little kiss. We've been getting so close! Marc said he'd been planning to split from Lisa but wanted to wait till after the summer clubs, so it wasn't awkward for them working together. Please don't tell her!'

'But he was fine up until then?' I asked.

'Yes. I didn't do anything to him, honestly! I don't know what happened.'

Suddenly, I felt the jigsaw pieces slot into place.

'Don't worry, Grace. I think maybe I have an idea of what happened. Let's get everyone together.'

I turned to Ishan with a quick smile and a wink.

When we got back down to the beach, the younger kids were gathering around Jiya and Ronan, showing off the 'treasures' they'd discovered. Ishan and I went over to see how they were doing.

'How did your minions do, Jiya? Did they manage to find your treasures?' Ishan asked.

'Yep, and a few extra ones too,' she explained. 'Look!'

But before any of us could look at Jiya's new discovery, an urgent voice was screaming from the promenade.

'Hey! Lisa!' A woman around Becky's age, wearing a long white dress and a worried expression, came marching towards us.

'*Molly?*' said Lisa. 'What are you doing here?' She sounded surprised, but there was also a note of panic in her voice.

'Someone called on your mobile and told me about Marc's attack!'

Ishan piped up. 'I saw *Marc Home* on your contacts,

Lisa, and thought I'd better let her know.'

'Where's my son? Is he OK?' Molly asked frantically.

'He's on his way to the hospital. The paramedics said he's going to be OK. No thanks to that one,' Lisa sneered, pointing straight at me. 'That's Luca Azoria – *Jacob* Azoria's son. I'm sure he had something to do with this.'

'Azoria?' Marc's mum repeated my surname quietly, and her face paled. Something about the expression on Lisa's face made me feel really weird.

'Marc figured out who he was. Of course, Luca wouldn't want anyone else knowing about his corrupt family. He was the only one who knew about Marc's allergy, and the only one who spent any time alone with him today.'

They both stared intently at me. I took a deep breath.

'Lisa's right,' I announced. Molly gasped.

'Eh?' Ishan blurted, his brow knotted in confusion.

'She's right about Marc's allergic reaction. It wasn't an accident,' I continued. 'He's a careful guy. He was all over the health and safety stuff, first thing, making sure everyone had their sun protection. He sat away from everyone else at lunch, avoiding any contamination risks. And he was watching me like a hawk; he wasn't taking any chances with me, that's for sure.'

'So, if you weren't responsible, how did it happen?' Molly demanded.

'A little kiss,' I replied.

Grace gasped, eyes widening in horror. Lisa stared at her with a look of pure anger, but not a hint of surprise. 'Luca, stop!' Grace implored.

'Grace, I hate to say it but I'm pretty sure Lisa already knows.'

'What the hell are you talking about!' cried Lisa.

'As soon as Grace confessed to Ishan and me about her little secret, I pieced together what had happened. When we were all first together, Lisa gave Grace a lip balm.'

Lisa frowned. 'Yeah, she had sore lips so I did her a favour. So what?' She crossed her arms, defensively.

'I also remembered that you volunteered to collect the rucksacks from the van before we got started, even though this allowed Grace to carry on chatting and laughing with your boyfriend. I wondered why you'd do something like that, considering how jealous you seemed to be about how well they were getting along.'

'Jealous?!' she protested.

'Well, you threw those rucksacks at them pretty hard when you saw them having fun together. In fact a bunch of stuff fell out of Marc's bag . . .'

'Look what I found!' Jiya thrust her way in front of me, holding up a fluorescent green pen. 'Isn't it cool? Definitely going into my collection!'

'Windy Cindy found it down by the red flag, the meeting point from this morning,' Ronan explained.

'Jiya – mind if I take a look at that?' When she handed it over, I held it up. 'This is the missing EpiPen!'

Ishan and I looked at each other. 'I think you're off the hook,' he smiled.

Grace, Lisa and Molly stared at the pen, wide-eyed, and I felt the dark cloud that had been hanging above my head disintegrate.

Molly said, 'I'm heading to the hospital. I'll call you as soon as I know anything more.' She rushed off back towards the car park. Once she was out of earshot, I turned to Lisa.

'Also, you really need to take more acting lessons, Lisa. You're not very good at *distressed*,' I commented. 'Ishan noticed that you only seemed to cry real tears after the pen couldn't be found, but not when you saw Marc gasping for air. It was almost as if you were . . . *expecting* to see him in that condition.'

'What? That's rubbish!' Lisa shouted. 'I was terrified. I love Marc.'

'Maybe too much,' Ishan said. 'Jiya, come here a minute. I think you've got something really interesting in your collection to show us.'

Jiya gave a big smile, happy to be the centre of attention once more, and hurried over. 'What would you like to see?'

'Where's that lip balm that Grace traded you at

lunchtime?' I asked. 'The one Lisa gave her this morning.'

Jiya shuffled around in her bag and pulled out the long purse. 'Ah, here we go!'

'What flavour is it?'

Jiya inspected the label on the lip balm closely. 'Peanut butter.'

A look of realisation crept across Grace's face. Lisa started biting her nails.

I had her now!

'This secret poison was all over Grace's lips during that little kiss. But neither of them knew. You wanted to use the lip balm to prove that there was something going on with Marc and Grace, and I think to punish him. But you ALSO wanted to come to Marc's rescue and make him love you again by being the hero and saving his life. *That's* why you only got genuinely upset when you couldn't find the EpiPen.'

Lisa was looking at the ground now, with real tears dripping from the end of her nose. 'I didn't mean to hurt him. I love him. I've always loved Marc, ever since we were doing A levels together! I just wanted him to stay with me.'

Grace's head was hanging now as well, as she chewed one of her thumbnails.

Suddenly, my feelings of victory and self-congratulation at having solved the mystery melted away, and I felt really sorry for Lisa too. It was hard when someone wasn't really who you thought they were.

As we all waited up at the car park for our parents to come and collect us, Ishan continued to marvel at my powers of deduction. 'That was some top-level detective work there, Luca.'

At that moment, Jiya came hurtling between the two of us, brandishing something which caught the sun and sparkled.

'Look what I found, Ishan!' she screamed happily. 'An old coin for your collection!'

I turned to him and raised an eyebrow. '*You* collect stuff too?' I said. 'You kept that quiet.'

Ishan rubbed the back of his neck and stared at the sand. 'Well, yeah. Collecting sort of runs in our family.'

He took the coin from Jiya, unable to hide his excited grin as he turned it over and read the date. 'Don't mention it at school though, will you?'

I grinned at him. 'Course not – my lips are sealed!'

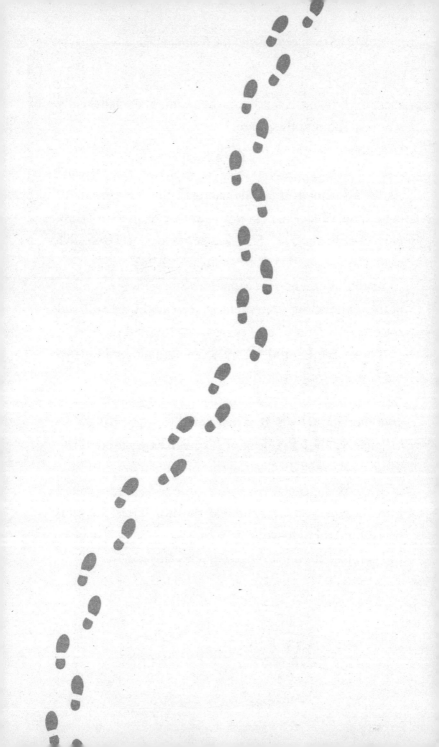

DEADLY DEPARTURE

PROPERTY OF THE SUPER SUNNY MURDER CLUB

DEADLY
DEPARTURE

By Serena Patel

Ela knew the holiday was going to be a disaster. Something *always* went wrong whenever they went anywhere as a family. But of all the things that she thought might go wrong, she definitely was not expecting there to be a murder. And especially not before they had even boarded the plane.

That morning had already been stressful. Mum had been panicking, waving a list of things they needed and should have already packed, shouting instructions and weighing the suitcases on their old scales about a hundred times. At the airport, she huffed as she heaved the suitcases out of the boot of the taxi onto the pavement. 'Ela, you take your backpack and the small case. Joshie, you carry your stuff too, please. It's busy, stay together.'

Josh jumped up and down. 'This is SO cool! We're actually going on a plane!'

Ela winced as a noisy plane flew overhead, and pulled

a face at the hundreds of people bustling in and out of the airport. She put her headphones on over her ears and pulled up her hood as they followed Mum into the crowd.

This was their first holiday in three years, so it was a big deal. But Ela was not looking forward to it at all. Holidays made her anxious. New places in general were difficult to deal with. But the travelling, lots of people she didn't know, the noise of the airport . . . it was ALL a lot.

Ela had been diagnosed with ADHD last year. The doctor had been really nice and explained everything, and all the things she'd felt made her different to her friends had suddenly made much more sense. But it didn't mean they got any easier. Mum had bought Ela the noise-cancelling headphones, which helped a bit, but she still hated travelling.

Ela knew how much Mum had been looking forward to getting away though. She worked really hard as a nurse at the local hospital and it was rare for her to have a whole week off. Ela also knew that her mum badly wanted them all to *enjoy* the holiday, so Ela had to at least try.

Her brother Josh, on the other hand, was buzzing with excitement. He loved exploring new places. The travel didn't bother him at all. Ela sometimes wondered how they could be so different.

The only thing they *did* have in common was a love of mystery stories. The ones where there was a puzzle, something to figure out. Murders, thefts, conspiracies, they loved them all! Their favourite book was called *The Mystery of the Missing Moon Gem*. Mum had bought them a copy each so they could read it at the same time. Ela was pretty sure she had figured out who did it after the third chapter, but Josh said he knew after the first chapter.

Ela rolled her eyes at the memory. She could have done with a mystery book now to distract her. The airport was every bit as big, noisy and chaotic as she had feared.

As they looked up at the large screen which listed all the flights, a man in a red turban and smart business suit rushed past them, pulling along a huge black suitcase which knocked into Ela's foot.

'Ow! He didn't even turn back to say sorry!' Ela shouted, wiggling her sore foot and hoping the man would hear her. But he carried on racing through the crowd towards the long line of check-in desks. '*Muuum*, can we find somewhere to sit down?' she pleaded.

'I need the toilet!' Josh complained.

'You always need the toilet!' Ela commented.

'Stop, you two! We only left the house an hour ago and we've got a whole week together yet!' Mum looked up again at the big screen, fumbling at the same time to get her backpack on. 'We need desk twenty-four, come on. We can sit once we've checked our bags in. And I'm sure the toilets are that way too.'

Ela noticed straight away that the man who had almost run over her foot was a few people in front of them at desk twenty-four.

'Typical, he's going to the same place as we are,' she muttered. 'I hope he's not staying at our hotel.'

'It's unlikely. There are lots of hotels in the part of Egypt we're going to,' Mum reassured her.

There was a sudden kerfuffle behind them. Ela looked around to see a woman in a pink sari and sunglasses, carrying a large tote bag that had the initials R.T.J. monogrammed on the side. She seemed to be arguing with another woman in a business suit, who was tightly clutching a briefcase.

The woman in the suit was gesturing a lot and pointing at the front of the line. 'Reena, as your friend, I'm asking you, please just let it go. What are you actually going to achieve by getting on that plane?' she shouted.

'This is important, I have to go. I won't let him go through with it. You can help by looking after business here,' the woman with the monogrammed tote bag replied.

'You're just going to make a fool of yourself. Don't say I didn't warn you!' the other woman retorted and stormed away.

'What do you think that's all about?' Ela asked Josh.

'They seemed pretty angry,' Josh replied, shifting awkwardly from one foot to the other. 'Maybe the woman in the suit really needed the toilet and didn't want to wait in this flipping queue.'

Ela huffed. 'It wasn't that and you know it.'

'It's not my fault all I can think about is needing the toilet right now!' said Josh. 'I wish this line would hurry up!'

'We'll be through soon,' said Mum. 'Anyway, look around you. Airports are so interesting! There are so many people, so much to see!'

'SO many people,' Ela muttered, pulling her case closer. The queue for desk twenty four seemed to squeeze even more tightly around her. She wondered, not for the first time, why some people didn't understand personal space.

The rude man in the red turban now looked like he was having a debate with the lady behind the desk. Ela took one side of her headphones off to listen properly.

'I'm sorry, Mr Singh, the bag is over the weight limit. You'll have to pay.'

Mr Singh sighed loudly. 'How much?'

'It'll be an extra one hundred pounds,' the woman behind the desk replied. 'Or you could try opening it up and taking out anything you don't need?'

She reached for the case, which was sitting on the conveyor belt beside her. Ela noticed it had a heavy padlock on it.

Mr Singh pulled it back. 'No, no, that's fine. I'll pay,' he said quickly.

'Wowsers,' Ela whispered. 'A hundred pounds extra? What does he have in that case?'

'A body!' Josh joked.

'You never know!' Ela murmured, her brain tingling like it always did when something suspicious was happening.

The departure gate was basically a big area with lots of seats and glass windows looking out on to the runway. Ela groaned inwardly. Of course, Mr Singh was sitting there, legs stretched out and scrolling on his phone. He'd got there quickly, considering he was behind them through security. Ela had spotted him getting frustrated with a young woman who had dropped all the bottles out of her toiletries bag and slowed the security queue down. Ela had felt the woman's pain as she'd put the toiletries back in her bag, which jingled with collectable key rings. And then Mr Singh had shoved past an older man with a little dog in a bag, and made the dog yelp. Her first thoughts about Mr Singh had most definitely been right!

A few seats to the left of Mr Singh was the woman in the pink sari. Across from them was a young man reading a book. There was also a family with two young children, and the older man with the dog, who glared at Mr Singh as he stroked his dog's ears. At least it was going to be a quiet flight. Ela was relieved to see that. A packed plane would *not* help her anxiety.

'Don't eat everything already. It's a five-hour journey, remember!' Mum warned as Josh got his snacks out. 'And I'm not buying food on the plane, it's always so expensive!'

An announcement burbled over the speakers. 'Passengers for flight number GB405, please be advised that this flight has been delayed. Update to follow.'

'What? Oh no!' Mum sighed. 'How long will it be?' she asked a woman in airline uniform standing by the gate.

'Not too long, I hope,' came the answer. 'But if we can ask you to stay in the lounge for now.'

'Great,' Josh moaned. 'That means I can't even get more snacks.'

Mr Singh was speaking loudly into his phone. 'It's been delayed,' Ela heard him say. 'No, I don't know how long. I know I said today but I can't help it if the plane is late, can I? Yes, yes, you'll get it. OK, I'll be there.' He caught sight of the man with the dog, who was still glaring at him as he finished the call. 'Want me to pull your mutt's tail again?' he jeered. 'See if it yelps a bit louder?'

Mr Singh rubbed his hand, which looked quite red and sore. He was sweating too, even though it wasn't that hot. He went to stand up but swayed and almost lost his balance so he sat back down again. Maybe he'd had a head rush. That happened to Ela sometimes.

He glanced up, catching Ela gawping at him. She looked away quickly. Something about the dead stare he gave her made her shiver.

The lounge settled down. Mum was reading her book. Josh was spotting planes on the runway, his face pressed to the glass. Mr Singh seemed to have dozed off. The family with children was playing a card game. The woman in the pink sari was clearly agitated and got up to complain to the boarding-gate staff. She came back to her seat after a few seconds, red-faced.

'What's the point of staff if they don't have a clue what's going on?' she muttered to herself. She flashed Mum a perfect smile. 'Hi, I'm Reena Taylor-Jones, lawyer – mainly high-profile divorces, celebrity murders, that kind of thing. Here's my card.'

Mum blushed. 'We're just going on holiday, I'm not sure we need . . .'

But Reena Taylor-Jones insisted and pushed her card into Mum's hand. It was black and embossed, very fancy.

The young woman who had dropped all her stuff in the security area hurried into the lounge and sat down opposite Ela and Josh. She seemed anxious.

Ela leaned forward, taking one earphone off her ear. 'Don't worry, the flight's delayed anyway,' she said. 'We're just waiting.'

The young woman smiled tightly but said nothing, picking at her nails nervously. She seemed to be shaking – or at least, the key rings on her bag were tinkling. Ela felt a rush of sympathy. Maybe she didn't like flying either.

'This is boring now,' grumbled Josh, sitting down again. 'I've spotted at least ten planes taking off. How come ours is still sitting there?'

'How am I supposed to know?' Ela snapped. She instantly felt bad as Josh flinched. 'Sorry, I didn't mean to snap. You know how I get when we have to wait for anything.'

Josh grinned. 'It's all right. Waiting is the worst! Here, use my fidget, I know they help sometimes.'

Ela took it gratefully and ran her fingers over the bumps and ridges.

'Passengers for flight GB405, please get ready to board the plane,' crackled the speakers. 'We apologise for the delay.'

'Finally!' Josh shouted. 'Let's go!'

Everyone started to gather their things together and stood up, ready to queue for the plane. Apart from Mr Singh, who stayed slumped in his chair.

Ela nudged her mum. 'I think that man's fallen asleep. We should wake him, or he'll miss the plane.'

'I thought you didn't like him?' Josh said. 'He ran over your foot!'

'Yeah, but still,' Ela replied.

'You're too nice to people sometimes, Ela,' Josh told her.

Mum went over to wake the man gently. As she touched his shoulder he fell forward in his seat. Mum gasped.

'What is it, Mum?' Ela asked.

'Er . . . nothing. Stay there,' Mum said, covering her mouth and putting her other hand up to keep them away.

An airline attendant noticed and walked across the lounge towards Mum and Mr Singh. Instantly she screamed. Everyone in the lounge stopped what they were doing.

The airline attendant shouted, 'He's dead. He . . . he's dead!'

Everyone stood in stunned silence. This must be some sort of joke. The passenger couldn't be dead. Could he? Ela strained to see – but Mr Singh was now surrounded by Mum, the airline staff and two security guards who had come running when they heard the scream.

Most of the other passengers looked horrified. Some looked curious. One little girl was crying and being comforted by her grown-up. The nervous young woman who had been sitting opposite looked pale and scared. Reena Taylor-Jones was marching around, shouting, 'This had better not delay our flight. I need to get to Egypt today! There's a very important matter I need to attend!'

'Please, madam, everyone, if you could just sit back down and allow us to sort this out in a calm and proper way,' the airline attendant gulped. 'We're just trying to find another lounge we can move you all to. This is a crime scene now.' She looked like she was going to throw up.

Josh nudged Ela. 'What do you think happened? Heart attack?'

Ela frowned. 'He seemed fine in the line for check-in. Just twenty minutes ago, he was chatting on his phone. Something feels off.'

Josh nodded. 'Like, murder vibes.'

'We don't know that,' Ela said but her head was tingling with the idea that they might just have been witnesses to a crime. And not just any crime. *A murder.*

The crowd parted. Ela saw Mum still looking at the man, slumped in his seat. She checked his hands and then pointed something out to the security guard. They were whispering, Ela couldn't hear exactly what. But she could tell from the look on her mum's face that it wasn't good.

Things happened quickly then. More security staff arrived, and two police officers. Someone brought a sheet to cover the body. A few moments later a white tent was placed over the space, as if they could forget what was in there, and safety barriers were erected to stop anyone coming too near. Ela heard someone say an ambulance was on its way. She shivered, but couldn't stop her brain from trying to figure out what could have happened.

Mum sat down with a massive sigh. Josh was on her immediately.

'What happened, Mum? Who do you think did it? What did he look like?'

'Joshie, please. It's an awful thing that's happened. That poor man.' Mum rubbed her temples. 'It's in the hands of the police now.'

'So it *was* foul play!' Ela breathed.

Josh snorted. 'Who calls it "foul play"?'

Ela puffed out her chest. 'The person who solved *The Mystery of the Missing Moon Gem* way before you did!'

'You so did not!' Josh exclaimed, a little too loudly.

Reena Taylor-Jones came to sit next to Mum.

'Terrible business this, very inconvenient. I need to be in Egypt urgently, and this is just holding everything up!'

She looked curiously at Mum. 'You seemed to notice something about the body. Do you think there has been foul play?'

Ela smirked at Josh, who stuck his tongue out at her.

Mum shook her head. 'I don't know if I should say,' she said. 'And I'm not an expert, but he had a fresh puncture wound on his hand.'

'Like a bullet?' Reena Taylor-Jones gasped.

'No, small, like something sharp – a needle, or a dart – had broken the skin. I'm wondering if he was poisoned,' Mum whispered. 'I shouldn't have said anything, don't tell the other passengers, please. I could be wrong.'

'Of course, of course, I won't tell a soul!' Reena Taylor-Jones smiled conspiratorially. She glanced then at Ela and Josh. 'Are these your children? Aren't they just the cutest!'

Ela winced. She hated when people called her cute. Josh on the other hand smiled sweetly. He was good at playing up to grown-ups. Ela just couldn't be fake, or pretend to like someone.

Reena reached over and touched Ela's hand. Ela fought the urge to snatch it away.

'Those headphones look just the bee's knees on you! I love the colour! So retro!' Reena enthused.

'I don't wear them for fashion,' Ela replied pointedly. 'They're noise-cancelling, to help me when I get overstimulated.'

Reena looked confused. 'Overstimulated?'

'I have ADHD,' Ela said, and then pulled her headphones up.

Reena's face went a little red. 'I didn't mean ... I didn't know ... She doesn't look ...'

'It's OK,' Mum said wearily, as she always did.

'I, um, I just remembered I need to make a call,' Reena mumbled, getting up to return to her seat.

Ela didn't care that she'd made the woman feel awkward. She had spent her whole nine years feeling awkward in most situations. Now she just felt proud to be herself.

Ela thought a bit more about Reena Taylor-Jones. Before all the bumbling, she'd seemed very eager to leave for Egypt, and didn't seem horrified or shocked by the idea that the man might have been poisoned. What about the argument she'd been having earlier in the queue? What had the other woman said? *Just let it go. What are you actually going to achieve by getting on that plane?* What did that mean?

Ela's mind raced, more than usual. Did Reena Taylor-Jones know Mr Singh? Did she have a reason to kill him? Could she be in a rush to board the plane because she had just committed the ultimate crime? She'd said she was a lawyer for celebrity murders, she'd probably know the best way to kill someone! And now she knew that Mum knew it was poison . . . oh no!

Ela grabbed Josh, who was scribbling something on his notepad.

'Josh, we have to do something!' she whispered. 'That man was definitely murdered and Mum could be next!'

'WHAT!' Josh yelled.

Everyone turned to stare at them. Ela dragged him over to a quiet corner and repeated what she'd just heard.

Josh looked unconvinced. 'So you think the woman in the pink sari murdered that man and now she's gonna come after our mum? There are police everywhere, for one. I doubt she's that silly.'

'I guess,' said Ela after a moment. 'But we need to be on the lookout, OK? If she did kill him, then she'll have slipped up somewhere. Murderers always do. Like in *The Mystery of the Missing Moon Gem*, when the thief left a footprint in the mud outside the broken window.'

'Um, I hate to break it to you, but there's no window that opens in this departure lounge, and *def* no muddy footprint, sis,' Josh pointed out.

'So we look for other clues,' Ela insisted, pulling her brother's sleeve. 'Come on, we don't have much time. They'll have to move the body soon. We need to try and get into that tent!'

Josh screwed up his nose. 'Are you sure? I mean, you get squeamish if you even get a nosebleed. This is a dead body!'

'That happened once and I'm a whole fourteen months older now,' Ela hissed. 'This is important, come on!'

Josh groaned. Once Ela got something into her head, there was no disagreeing with her. It was better to go along with it. Besides, who knew how long they were going to be stuck here now? Might as well do something with their time.

As they walked round the edge of the room, trying not to draw any attention to themselves, Ela overheard Reena Taylor-Jones talking to one of the other passengers. A very tired-looking man who seemed to be barely listening to her.

'My business partner and friend said I shouldn't, she said I should let it go. But how can I?' Reena was saying fretfully. 'My foolish father is about to marry a gold-digging monster! I can't allow it. I have to stop the wedding!'

So *that's* why Reena Taylor-Jones was going to Egypt. Ela sighed. Perhaps she wasn't the murderer after all. She had to get into that tent and look for clues.

Mum was busy on the phone talking to Grandma in a hushed tone, probably about what had happened. All the other grown-ups seemed occupied with each other, with the police or with their phones. Literally no one was paying any attention to Josh or Ela.

'OK, let's go,' Josh said, getting up from his seat. 'I'll walk round this side like I'm looking out of the window at the planes. You go that way and look for any clues on the floor or the seats.'

'Don't be obvious, though,' Ela warned. 'The grown-ups won't want us involved. And we have to hurry because they'll be moving us soon. Let's get as close as we can to the body. Then you distract the police officers and I'll go under the barrier and try to get into the tent and look at the puncture wound Mum mentioned. There might be another clue she didn't notice.'

'Mum says I'm good at being a distraction so I've got this.' Josh grinned. 'This is just like in *The Mystery of the Missing Moon Gem* when they're investigating at the ball!'

'Except wearing ball gowns and knowing how to waltz is probably not going to help us here!' Ela muttered to herself as they parted ways.

She walked round the seated area and past the entrance to the lounge, which now also sported a safety barrier to keep people out. OR keep a killer IN.

Ela looked around the room. One of these people was a murderer. A shiver ran up her spine. They probably thought they were going to get away with it too. No one LOOKED like a killer. What did a killer even look like anyway? And why had they murdered this Mr Singh guy?

She walked casually towards the tent. Josh was hanging around on the other side, beside the two police officers guarding it.

'Officers!' Josh beamed and launched into a stream of questions about being in the police.

Ela took her opportunity and dived under the barrier and into the white tent.

It was weird being in there. Eerie. Like the hustle and bustle of the airport didn't exist. She pulled down her headphones and took a deep breath. Mr Singh was laid flat across three seats with a sheet covering his whole body. Ela was kind of glad. She didn't want to see the face of a dead man. There were enough things in the world to be scared of already.

She could hear Josh waffling on to the police officers outside the tent about some documentary he'd watched about crime scenes. Mum was right. He *was* good at being a distraction.

Ela crouched down to look underneath the chairs. Maybe there was a clue that no one else had seen? As she ducked her head, she accidentally knocked the sheet that was covering Mr Singh . . . and his hand dropped down!

Ela covered her mouth to stop herself from shouting out. She made herself look closer, trying not to touch the hand because that was just too gross to even think about. Mum had been right, there was a puncture mark. But it wasn't round, like a needle prick. It was triangular. What on earth would leave a mark like that?

Outside the tent, she could hear the police officer telling Josh to run along because another more important officer had arrived, wanting to see the body. She had to get out of there! Ela scrambled on her hands and knees out of the tent as quickly as she could.

Josh was lurking by some chairs, waiting for her. 'What did you find?' he asked eagerly.

'Keep your voice down,' Ela hissed. 'I didn't find any evidence, but I did see something weird. The puncture mark on his hand was triangle-shaped!'

'That *is* weird,' Josh agreed. 'So what's your theory then?'

'Well,' said Ela. 'If he was poisoned, it must have been while he was at the airport. We saw him when he arrived . . .'

'When he ran over your foot,' said Josh.

Ela didn't need reminding. 'Then we saw him in the queue for check-in, again in the security area - and finally, here at the departure gate.'

'So?'

'So the poisoning must have happened in one of those places,' said Ela, thinking. 'I'm sure I read that most deadly poisons work quickly. He didn't speak to anyone except the woman at the check-in desk. Then the security area was busy and chaotic, you don't really speak to anyone there, you just keep moving forward with your stuff. When we got here, he was on a phone call, but I didn't see him speak to anyone in person.'

'OK,' said Josh. 'So what does all that mean?'

'I don't really know,' Ela admitted. 'They'll move us out of here soon, so we have to act fast. Let's split the people here between us and try to talk to everyone. See if you find out if they knew Mr Singh, or if they saw anything suspicious.'

'OK. Be careful, though. You don't want to make the killer angry!' Josh said.

'Agreed. Let's do this!' Ela said, fist-bumping her brother.

Ela looked around. Mum was talking to one of the police officers. There were about fifteen people there in total. Talking to them all was going to be tough. She needed to get tactical.

In *The Mystery of the Missing Moon Gem*, detective Lia only questioned people she knew had been in contact with the gem. Who had been next to Mr Singh in the queue for the check-in desk? Ela couldn't recall. She moved on to who had been near him in the security area. Then she remembered the nervous young woman who had dropped her things!

The woman was sitting alone, in the corner by the window, looking out at the planes. Ela walked over and sat next to her.

'Hi, I'm Ela,' she said.

The young woman almost jumped out of her skin at Ela's voice. 'Oh! Er, hi,' she said.

'This is a nightmare, right?' said Ela. 'Can't believe what's happened. What's your name?'

'Afsa,' the girl replied.

'Are you travelling alone?'

'Yeah, I . . . um . . . Well, it was a last-minute thing.'

'Cool!' Ela looked around the room. 'So who do you think did it?'

Afsa stared at Ela. 'Did what, the murder? I don't know. Why would *I* know? You'll have to excuse me, I need to go.'

'Go where?' asked Ela. 'We have to stay here!'

Afsa picked up her stuff. She almost clunked Ela in the head with all the key rings attached to her backpack.

'Watch out, you almost took me out then!' Ela said with a grin.

Afsa didn't smile back. She just seemed to be frozen.

Ela focused more closely on the key rings, now dangling by her nose. There was a teddy bear one, a Paris one and one in the shape of a bottle with a pointy end. Wait – the end wasn't pointy. It was *triangle-shaped*. And the bottle looked half full of some kind of liquid.

'It was you!' Ela gasped quietly.

Afsa flinched. 'Me? Don't be silly. I didn't even know him!' Her cheeks flushed red and her eyes darted from side to side, looking for a way out of this conversation.

Ela knew she was right. 'Mr Singh was poisoned,' she said carefully. 'He has a triangle-shaped puncture wound on his hand, which is most likely where the poison went in. And here you are with what looks like a vial of liquid with a pointy triangle thing on the end!'

Afsa's face dropped. She sat back down, defeated. 'I . . . I guess you've got it all figured out.'

'Not really,' said Ela. 'I don't know *why* you did it.'

Afsa gave Ela a cold, hard stare. 'He was a bad man.'

'What did he do to you?' Ela asked.

'He took everything from me and my family,' Afsa replied, clenching her fists and making her knuckles turn white.

Afsa didn't need to reveal anything more. It already made sense. Ela had got the feeling Mr Singh was up to no good when she overheard his phone call.

'He was telling someone on the phone that he'd be there soon and he'd give them something,' she murmured.

'Money,' Afsa said simply.

'There was *money* in the suitcase!' Ela accidentally shouted out too loud. She lowered her voice when a few heads turned to look at her. 'He had money in the suitcase, that's why it was so heavy and why he had a padlock on it!'

'Dirty money, stolen money,' Afsa muttered.

'He stole from your family?' Ela asked.

Afsa nodded. 'He was a con artist. He befriended my parents, made them think they could make a load of money on this investment thing. And they believed him. "Nice Mr Singh, isn't he helpful," they used to say. Until he ran off with their life savings in cash!'

'But you could have reported him to the police!' Ela

argued. 'They would have arrested him. You didn't need to murder him.'

Afsa laughed bitterly. 'We tried. The police wouldn't listen. We had no proof. My parents kept their money in a cupboard under the stairs and handed it over to him willingly. There was no record of a transaction.'

Ela shook her head. 'So you decided to take things into your own hands?'

'I heard he was flying out to Egypt. I knew this was the only chance to stop him.' Afsa looked frightened. 'I just meant for him to get ill so he wouldn't get on the plane. I didn't think he'd die! But I was so nervous, and when I knocked into him in the security line, I accidentally pushed most of the liquid into him.' She looked like she was about to cry. 'And now I don't know what to do. My job is the only thing supporting my mum and dad right now. They'll lose the house if I go to prison! I hoped by coming here, I'd get the money back from Mr Singh, somehow. But I've just made everything a million times worse!'

'We need to tell someone that can help,' Ela said as Afsa burst into tears. 'Come on, I think I know who.'

Afsa sniffed but followed Ela over to where Mum and Reena Taylor-Jones were talking.

'Mum? Ms Taylor-Jones? We need your help,' Ela said.

Ela and Afsa explained what had happened. Reena Taylor-Jones turned out to be really nice about it all. She said she would talk to the police with Afsa and represent her while they sorted things out. If they could prove Afsa hadn't intended to murder Mr Singh then they might get a manslaughter charge rather than a murder one. She didn't know what punishment Afsa would receive, but she promised to do her very best for Afsa and her family.

As Ela watched Afsa and Reena Taylor-Jones explain everything to one of the police officers, Josh came running over.

'I know who did it!' he squealed.

'So do I,' Ela said.

'Me first, me first!' Josh said, jumping up and down. 'See that man over there?'

'The one with the little dog in a bag?' Ela asked.

'Yeah, him! It's definitely him!' Josh said proudly.

Ela pulled a face. 'Sorry, bro, but I already solved the murder and got a confession. The *actual* killer is over there right now with Reena Taylor-Jones, telling everything to the police.'

Josh slumped. 'Oh man!'

'Told you I'm the better detective,' Ela said.

'You just got lucky.'

Ela folded her arms. 'Next time we let Mum decide who's the better detective.'

FLIGHT	NO	STATUS
GDAŃSK	FD372	GATE CLOSED
CAIRO	GB405	READY TO BOARD
GLASGOW	GB135	DELAYED
ATHENS	GR2271	DELAYED
STAVANGER	NR7694	WAITING FOR GATE NO
NEW JERSEY	AM923	— —
VALLETTA	MT9031	— —

'Next time? What do you mean NEXT TIME?' Josh complained.

Ela pulled her headphones back up, watching the hustle and bustle of the airport around them.

Maybe a week's holiday in Egypt would be nice after all! It would be quiet there, wouldn't it?

ANNABELLE SAMI

A
BERRY
JUICY
MURDER

TOP SECRET

PROPERTY OF THE SUPER SUNNY MURDER CLUB

A BERRY JUICY
MURDER

By Annabelle Sami

E veryone seemed to think summer was about
frolicking on the beach and eating chocolate
ice cream.

But not Inaya.

She wasn't convinced of the summer-fun thing.
Sure, she used to go to the park and run carefree with
her friends. But since turning twelve in July, she'd had
a hard time enjoying anything. It was largely to do with
a girl at school starting a rumour that Inaya had 'creepy
vibes' whatever *that* means. Since then, the other kids
had taken to calling her Wednesday Addams. It came
out of nowhere (she didn't even own black clothes, for
goodness' sake) but it stuck. All summer, Inaya had just
laid in bed, curtains drawn, watching endless YouTube
compilation videos of dogs. Not exactly the most exciting
summer holidays.

It was a particularly hot August morning and Inaya was halfway through a bowl of cereal and the latest *Dug the Skateboarding Pug* video when her mum Bryony burst through the kitchen door in a floral dress.

'You need some sunshine, Inaya!' Bryony said, hands on hips. 'So I've decided you're going out today.'

'What?' Inaya protested. 'Where?'

'The pick-your-own farm,' Bryony chirped. 'I can drop you there on my way to Grandma's house and Dad will pick you up later. Text Joss and see if she'd like to go with you.'

Inaya sighed. Still, she trusted her mum, even if she could be a little demanding.

> Inaya:
>
> *Hey Joss, Mum's making me go to the pick-your-own today. Want to come with me? Collect you in half an hour? X*

> Joss:
>
> *Uhhh, YES. I've been trying to get you outside all summer. I'm there. See you soon.*

A little after midday, Inaya and her mother were blasting the air conditioning at full throttle and speeding down narrow country roads lined with thorny bracken that threatened to scratch the car with every turn.

They turned onto a residential road and screeched to a halt outside Joss's house. Joss appeared at the doorway and ran over, holding on to her floppy hat to stop it falling off.

'Hi, Inaya! Hi, Bryony!' she said brightly, sliding into the car in a white summer dress.

'Hiya, Joss, had a good summer?' Bryony replied, already pulling away from the house at breakneck speed.

'Yeah, we went on holiday *and* I finished all five seasons of that new true crime show *Never Seen Again*. It's so creepy!'

Inaya flinched at that word but Joss didn't notice. She went on to fill Inaya in on the most terrifying episodes of the show and her theories about what happened. Joss loved that kind of stuff – though she'd never managed to get Inaya to watch an episode with her. It was a wonder that *she* didn't get branded the 'creepy' one.

The roads became twistier and turnier as they neared the farm. Bryony suddenly hit the brakes when a small rickety sign came into view.

McCRAG'S PICK-YOUR-OWN

'They should really get a clearer sign. How's anyone supposed to find this place?' Bryony tutted as she turned onto the dirt-track road.

McCrag's was a ramshackle operation three fields wide that had seen better days. The field furthest to the right was where the farmer kept his small herd of cattle – visitors weren't allowed there. The middle field was a bright screaming yellow – a maize maze about as tall as a fully grown man. The field where the entrance was located was the largest, and sectioned off into the pick-your-own patches. This is where the farm shop was, and the farmhouse – though that building was tucked away in a shady forgotten corner, far from the farm shop and small cafe.

Inaya was surprised by how quiet it was. She could only see a few visitors out in the pick-your-own field and a handful of people eating at the cafe.

'OK, girls, I'll give you ten pounds for three large punnets,' Bryony said, fishing the money out of her purse. 'Have fun and –' she turned around in her seat to look at the girls – 'stay away from Farmer McCrag.'

Joss gently squeezed Inaya's hand in the way they did when something funny happened, but Inaya was locked in on her mum's expression.

Bryony shuddered. 'That man gives me the creeps. But this place is the best pick-your-own in the area and he's not usually around, so you should be fine. Just be careful.'

'OK,' said Inaya. 'See you later, Mum. Thank you.'

She took the money and hopped out of the car into the heat. Then she and Joss headed over to the farm shop to get their empty punnets.

The radio was playing quietly as they entered the shop, and a rusty fan blew hot air around. A teenage girl with jet-black hair was behind the counter speaking into her phone. She appeared to be leaving someone a voice note.

'Just give him some time to cool off,' she was saying in an urgent whisper. 'Then we can all chat –'

She looked up.

'Oh . . . ' She quickly cancelled the message and looked at the girls. 'Hi. How can I help?'

'Three punnets, please,' Joss said brightly, nudging Inaya to hand over the money.

As the girl handed them three large plastic containers, Inaya looked closer at her name tag. It said 'India'.

'The greenhouse, cattle field and farmhouse are off limits,' India began.

Joss laughed. 'Is that where the scary farmer lives?'

India's face changed and her cheeks went red. 'The pick-your-own sections are marked with signs,' she said abruptly. 'Bye.'

Inaya wondered why India had been so awkward about Joss's joke. Then again, Farmer McCrag was technically her boss. She couldn't be seen making fun of him.

As Inaya and Joss left the shop, they passed the small

cafe. A man in a smart suit sat at the table closest to the exit, a half-drunk cup of black coffee in front of him as he tapped the table with a silver pen.

'He's a bit overdressed for a farm, isn't he?' Joss whispered as they passed by.

'And he must be boiling in that suit,' Inaya whispered back.

They left the cafe area and walked back out into the clearing where the pick-your-own patches began.

'Let's start with raspberries, they're my favourite,' said Joss. 'Race you!'

She sprinted towards the rows of bushes, which had a little wooden sign painted with a raspberry. Inaya thundered after her, a big grin on her face, nasty school rumours forgotten. At least for the time being.

'I definitely won,' Joss panted as Inaya caught up. They were now standing between two rows of raspberry canes, tied up to wooden trellises, that ran like corridors all the way to the edge of the field.

'Well, you got a head start!' Inaya panted back, handing Joss one of the punnets.

The girls bent down and immediately started picking. Inaya popped one berry in her mouth for every berry in the punnet. After ten minutes, her fingers were stained red and sticky.

'Look, the *bloooood of the raspberriiiees,*' Joss said,

wiggling her own red fingers in Inaya's face.

'It's a berry massacre,' Inaya said, holding her hand to her forehead and pretending to faint.

They both giggled as they walked to the end of the trellis.

They had turned onto the next row and begun working their way towards the centre of the field when a sudden piercing sound ripped through the air.

A scream that could only be described as *blood-curdling*.

On instinct, Joss and Inaya grabbed on to one another. A young woman with a sharp-cut bob had run screaming out of the strawberry patch directly opposite the row they were in.

'Help! Help!'

The young woman desperately looked around, but they were far from the cafe and shop where most of the visitors were. Inaya and Joss rushed over to her.

'I saw a h-hand,' the woman sobbed.

'Where?' Inaya and Joss said in unison.

The young woman pointed at the patch of strawberries she had just left. Her hand shook wildly. 'I-in the ground, sticking up out of the mud ... and it was covered in –' the young woman took a few gasps of air – '*b-blood*.'

Suddenly, Inaya was aware of people surrounding them. India from the shop, the businessman with the silver pen, and a couple of older women Inaya thought she'd seen eating in the cafe.

'It's all going to be OK,' the businessman said in a soothing voice, one hand on the screaming woman's shoulder. 'Let's get you back to the cafe to sit down.' Inaya wondered if he was her husband.

'We should go look at the hand,' Joss said subtly to Inaya. But one of the older ladies overheard.

'No, you should come back to the cafe with us,' she said firmly. 'That's not for a child to see.'

Then she put her arm out and ushered Inaya and Joss along with her, to stop them from checking out the crime scene.

Back at the cafe, the screaming woman, whose name was Francesca, told everyone what she'd seen. The older ladies turned out to be her mum and aunt.

'A bloody hand, sticking up out of the earth where the strawberries were,' Francesca gasped. 'It was horrible.'

An unfamiliar voice suddenly chimed in. 'And you saw only one hand?'

Everyone whirled around to see a tall lady with voluminous hair, smartly dressed in a blue linen suit.

'Yes, just one,' Francesca's mum replied on her trembling daughter's behalf. 'Sorry – who are you?'

'I'm Amy,' said the tall lady after a pause. 'I was just picking up some blueberries from the shop a minute ago, and overheard you.'

Inaya frowned at the woman's odd response. Firstly, where were the blueberries she'd supposedly just bought? Secondly, she wasn't even carrying a purse. She only had a phone in her pocket – Inaya could see the screen glowing through the thin material of the lady's blue linen trousers. And, wait – was the voice recorder app open? Was this Amy lady recording the conversation?!

'Has anyone called the police?' Francesca whimpered.

'I was too busy comforting you, darling,' her mum said.

'I can't get any signal,' her auntie replied, looking at her phone.

'Neither can I,' said the businessman.

Inaya and Joss checked their phones. No signal either.

'Do you have any reception here?' Francesca's mum shot at India, who was standing behind the cafe counter.

India shook her head. 'No. But there's a landline over in the farmhouse –'

'Well, go and call the police!' Francesca's mum yelled.

Inaya remembered seeing India on the phone when they arrived. The teenager had enough reception then to send a voice note. Weird.

As soon as India had gone, the businessman clapped his hands, startling Inaya.

'Right, I'm going to spread the word to the other visitors,' he said briskly. 'You know, warn them to not go over there. And you two –' he pointed at Inaya and Joss –

'you're young. You should post about it on social media.'

Inaya raised an eyebrow. 'Why?'

'So people don't come here and get scarred for life!' said the businessman. 'This place is a death trap!'

That was a bit dramatic, Inaya thought as the businessman stalked out of the cafe.

Joss immediately pulled Inaya behind a large shelf. Her eyes were wide and practically sparkling. 'Inaya,' she said. 'There's something strange going on here.'

The hairs on Inaya's arms were standing on end. She felt it too.

'Definitely,' she answered in a hushed voice. She grimaced. 'Do you think the hand is attached to . . . well, you know. A body?'

'Maybe . . .' said Joss. 'This is just like an episode of *Never Seen Again*! They find the body at the beginning and then they piece together the rest of the case. We could do that, Inaya. We could be the ones to put the whole story together!'

Inaya's heart beat a little faster. Was she actually feeling *excited* about this? She bit her lip. 'I don't want to do anything that might be dangerous, and I'm worried that if people at school find out I was involved, it will make the rumour worse –'

'Oh, stuff them!' Joss said, her eyes blazing, 'Once the summer's over, everyone will have forgotten about that stupid nickname, I promise. And we'll be safe – we'll stay on the farm. Whatever happens, your dad is coming to get us at four o'clock, right? That's in three hours.' She tapped her phone. 'It's not like we can call him to come get us early anyway. No signal, remember?'

Inaya felt an energy building in her body, filling her with adrenaline. She hadn't felt like this all summer. Perhaps Joss was right . . . if she could move on from the rumour, then maybe everyone else would too.

'OK,' she blurted out, before remembering to keep her voice down. 'We're here already, so we might as well investigate.'

'Yay!' Joss squeezed Inaya in a big hug, jumping up and down.

'First, we should question the witness,' Inaya said, leaping into detective mode. It came surprisingly naturally. 'Then we'll move on to the suspects, who at the moment are –'

'That Amy lady and the businessman?'

Inaya nodded. 'There'll probably be more, but we have to move fast. India, the girl who works in the shop, might already have called the police and they definitely won't want us snooping around.'

Joss stood back with her arms folded, smiling at Inaya. 'What?' Inaya said, blushing.

Joss beamed. 'Look at you being a detective. I love this!' Inaya rolled her eyes, but couldn't deny that something had been unlocked in her following the grisly discovery. Now it was time for some hearty interrogation.

At one of the wobbly tables in the cafe, Inaya and Joss sat down with Francesca (who had ceased crying but was still red in the face), her mother and auntie.

'That must have been so scary,' Inaya began. 'At least your mum and auntie and husband are here.'

'Husband?' Francesca sniffed. 'I'm not married.'

'Then who was that man in the suit that was comforting you?' asked Joss.

Francesca shrugged. 'I don't know. He said his name was Mark, I assumed he was here with someone else. He kept telling me I should sue the farm. Maybe he's a lawyer or something.'

Inaya took notes in her mind. They would need to interrogate this Mark person too.

'Sorry to ask but . . .' Inaya searched for the right words. 'What did the hand look like?'

'Big.' Francesca shuddered. 'Like a man's hand. It was sticking up from the ground like this.'

She formed her hand into a claw shape and then thrust it into the air, before breaking down into tears again.

'So it was a right hand?' Inaya asked.

Francesca nodded as her auntie and mother consoled her.

'She needs some space,' the auntie said sternly. 'Why

don't you go wait for your parents in the shop?'

Inaya looked awkwardly at Joss. They'd pushed their first witness to floods of tears … They might need to work on their technique.

'We should interrogate this Mark guy next,' Inaya said, scanning the field as they left the cafe and walked over to the shop.

There was no sign of the man in the suit. What Inaya did see, however, was India, skulking around by the large rectangular greenhouse located to the far left of the farm shop.

'Or we could start over there with India?' suggested Joss, who had seen her too.

As they got closer, Inaya realised India was on the phone and trying to lock the door to the greenhouse with a long brass key.

'Argh … pick up …' she was muttering as she struggled with the lock. 'Stupid thing, can't believe I left it unlocked … Harry, where are you? I'm freaking out. Call me back.'

India had said there was no reception here. And yet here she was again, talking to someone. At the very least, she must have internet connection. Inaya frowned.

Turning to see Joss and Inaya standing behind her, India shrieked.

'What are you doing?' she said, clutching her chest.

Joss jumped in. 'We just wanted to check if you're OK.'

India scowled. 'I'm fine. You shouldn't be by the greenhouse. It's for employees only.'

Inaya looked around. 'What employees? You seem to be the only one.'

India snorted. 'Yeah, people don't last long around here . . . I mean, Farmer McCrag isn't an easy boss. Our last farmhand left because they had a huge argument.'

'Has anyone . . . heard from him since?' Joss asked quietly.

India's face drained of all its colour.

'Excuse me,' she said and ran off, back in the direction of the farm shop.

'Well, India is definitely hiding something,' said Inaya. 'Why did she say there was no reception when there clearly is?'

'And who was that "Harry" she was leaving a voicemail for?' Joss wondered.

India had run off but the greenhouse door was still ajar. Inaya reached forward to push it and the lock fell off entirely!

'Someone's damaged it,' Joss gasped. 'They forced their way in. Who would do that? And why?'

'There's only one way to find out,' Inaya answered.

They crept inside, Inaya leading the way. There were hundreds of plants and workbenches covered in tools and pots. A water sprinkler system kept up a fine mist that made the inside feel like a rainforest.

A large storage bench caught Inaya's eye. It was partially closed, but there was a strong whiff of strawberries and the handle of what looked like a garden shovel was wedged under the lid, as if it had been thrown in there in a hurry.

Inaya pointed. 'Look, Joss, over there.'

She moved quickly to the bench, not wanting someone to come in and find them where they shouldn't be. They'd already come so far.

She reached out and gently lifted the lid of the storage container to reveal –

'A bloody shovel!' Joss gasped.

The shovel gleamed at them, red and sticky. Inaya dropped the lid instinctively and turned to Joss, whose eyes were gleaming.

'This is *better* than any episode of *Never Seen Again*,' Joss breathed.

'I don't know whether to be impressed or scared of you,' said Inaya. 'Let's take a picture of it for evidence and then get out of here.'

Inaya and Joss regrouped back by the cafe.

'The only people who have a key to the greenhouse are employees – so just India right now. But it did seem like the lock had been broken,' Joss said, munching on a doughnut she'd bought.

'India's not the only person,' Inaya said gravely, turning to look at the old farmhouse. 'I think Farmer McCrag just became our number one suspect.' She pushed the image of her mum's serious expression when warning them about the farmer to the back of her mind.

'So we interview him next?' Joss mumbled, her mouth full.

'I really wish you hadn't chosen the jam doughnut, Joss. Doesn't that gross you out after what we just saw?' Inaya said, half laughing.

'Oh. I hadn't thought of that,' said Joss, licking her fingers.

On the table a few metres away from them, Amy was sitting on her laptop tapping away in a frenzy. Her coiffed hair bounced as she hit the keys.

'As if she was just "picking up some blueberries",' Inaya said, rolling her eyes. 'We need to see what she's writing, it seems important.'

The girls tiptoed over to the shelves near where Amy was sitting. As they got closer, Inaya could just make out the subject of the email Amy was writing: *This is going to be huge.*

Inaya was standing only a metre or so behind Amy now. Her hair had fallen forward over her shoulders and Inaya could see a lanyard around her neck, tucked under her shirt. She could just make out the initials JHTV. What did that stand for?

But before Inaya could read the rest of the email, Joss sneezed and their position was compromised.

Amy snapped her laptop shut before turning to the girls. 'Can I help you?'

'Oh . . . we were wondering if you know when the police will arrive?' Inaya asked, thinking on the spot.

Amy sighed, standing up from the table. 'I've no idea. The farm shop girl rang, not me.'

'It's a long time to wait around,' Joss said quickly. 'You've been here for a while, haven't you?'

Amy's eyes narrowed and she crossed her arms. 'Not really.' Inaya decided to test the woman. 'But you were here when Francesca found the left foot, weren't you?'

'You mean the right hand?' Amy scoffed. 'Yes, I was here buying some blueberries. But I'd only *just* arrived.'

'How do you know it was the *right* hand?' Inaya pressed, alert. Only she and Joss had heard that conversation with Francesca. 'Did you go see the crime scene?'

Amy's cheeks went bright red. 'Well, no, of course not. I just . . . uh – it was a lucky guess. Now I really have to go.'

She gathered up her smart brown leather handbag and strode off.

'She's shady,' Joss said, shaking her head.

Inaya sighed. 'Yeah, she is. Why would you bring your

laptop to buy blueberries? I do want to know how long the police will be, though. Once they get here, we can't exactly keep investigating.'

'Then we'd better hurry up!' Joss said, turning to Inaya. 'Where to next, detective?'

Inaya felt her heart beating faster. She thought of her mum's warning once again. 'I can't believe I'm saying this,' she said. 'But . . . we need to find Farmer McCrag.'

The farmhouse loomed in its own corner of the field: a single-storey stone building with a dark slate roof and tiny windows. It was impossible to look inside, but the front door was, alarmingly, slightly open.

The hairs on the back of Inaya's neck stood up as her mother's words rang through her mind. *Stay away from Farmer McCrag.* Her mother had just thought the farmer was weird. But now he was potentially a murderer! Was Inaya really going to go inside the old farmhouse?

A breeze blew the door fully open, as if answering her inner question.

'We'll just take a peep and then come straight out,' Inaya said, her voice slightly shaking.

'If you're going, I'm going,' said Joss, firmly taking Inaya's hand.

They tiptoed into the farmhouse.

The room they entered was a living room, with a stone floor and sparse furnishings. Hanging on the wall over the sofa was a framed photograph of a man, woman and young girl, which looked like it had been taken on an old film camera. There was clutter on every surface in a surprisingly normal, homely way. The inside of the house really didn't match its scary exterior.

Joss pointed to the far side of the room. 'Who has a fire burning in the middle of summer?' she asked.

The fireplace was indeed lit and beside it was a small pile of paper.

'Someone who is trying to get rid of something,' Inaya answered.

They picked their way over to the fireplace and squatted down next to the pile of paper. The pieces were torn up, but Inaya managed to pick out a few larger ones that still had writing clear enough to read.

*£500,000 . . . 3rd August. Lawyers for Mr . . .*Inaya read the words aloud but there were too many missing pieces to understand what it was saying. One thing was clear, though. This was a letter.

Suddenly, a clanging sound came from somewhere at the back of the house. Inaya collected up as many pieces of the torn-up letter as she could and stuffed them in her bag, before they both scampered out of the house as quickly as possible.

'Who's there?!' a gravelly voice boomed from behind them in the house.

The girls froze.

Turning slowly, Inaya and Joss were confronted with the silhouette of a huge man in the farmhouse door. He had a smattering of white hair under a tattered flat cap, and gnarled features with sunburnt cheeks. He was tall and wide but hunched at the shoulders, a pair of dirty faded overalls hanging off his frame.

'What are you doin' over 'ere?' Farmer McCrag snarled. 'No customers allowed!'

'Sorry, sir, we just, er . . .' Inaya racked her brain. 'We wondered if the police were on their way?'

'Now listen 'ere,' Farmer McCrag growled, walking closer. 'We don't need no police snoopin' around, and no little girls either! I told Indy to make sure you lot stay away from my house! Not like anyone *wants* to come here usually.'

Even though her legs were shaking, Inaya felt strangely sorry for the farmer. His voice was angry, but his eyes looked sad.

'Yes, sir,' said Joss, pulling Inaya back by the arm.

The farmer grunted and disappeared into his house, slamming the door behind him.

The girls ran all the way back to the farm shop, then stood panting while they collected their thoughts.

'OK,' Joss said finally. 'He is weird and *terrifying*. He did it. Case closed.'

Inaya shook her head. 'He seems kind of sad to me. Just because you spend all your time in a dark house alone, doesn't mean you're a murderer.'

Inaya thought of how she'd spent her summer. Sitting alone in her pyjamas, not wanting to do anything but sleep and watch YouTube videos. If the people at school knew, they'd call her weird too.

She decided to pursue another train of thought.

'Did you notice the old family photograph in the farmhouse?' she said. 'What if Farmer McCrag doesn't live here alone? What if the only member of staff he's managed to keep *has* to work here? He called India "Indy". Farmer McCrag doesn't seem the type to give nicknames to his employees. Unless, of course, that employee is . . .'

Joss gasped. 'His daughter! India is his daughter!'

Something caught Inaya's eye in the distance. A figure running towards the middle field, followed by another figure with jet-black hair.

'A daughter currently running into the maize maze,' she said. 'Come on, let's go!'

The towering stalks of corn felt even larger when you were standing inside the maze. The green leaves unfurled and stretched outwards like creeping fingers.

Inaya looked down at the dirt pathway and noticed that some of the stalks on the right-hand side had been trampled underfoot. *Aha!*

'These look like someone has accidentally crushed them while in a hurry,' she said, pointing out the debris to Joss. 'If we follow the path of destruction, we'll find India, and whoever she was chasing.'

They set off again, running down the twisting and turning pathways and keeping an eye on the trampled corn. The path grew wider – until they found themselves in the centre of the maze.

The sound of two voices, one India's and one deeper, floated through the walls of corn. Was India in danger? Inaya and Joss looked at each other.

There was only one thing to do.

They stormed their way into the clearing, ready to face the battle, only to find India and the potential murderer . . .

Hugging?

'Thank goodness,' India was saying, teary-eyed, to a young man with tanned skin, wearing denim overalls and welly boots. 'I thought it was you!'

'Um, who are they?' the young man said, pointing straight at Inaya and Joss.

India whirled around.

'*We*,' Joss announced, 'are investigating the case. Who are *you*?'

'I'm Harry. I used to work here,' the young man said, scratching his head.

Inaya's eyes widened. *The missing farmhand!* And he still had both his hands!

'I thought maybe the hand really was his after he'd had the argument with my –' India stopped short.

'With your dad,' Inaya said, finishing her sentence. 'We know Farmer McCrag is your dad. What were they even arguing about?'

'McCrag thinks I've been spreading rumours about the farm online,' Harry said, shaking his head. 'Stuff about the food being poisonous, rat infestations, calling the place "a death trap".'

A death trap . . . Where had Inaya heard that phrase recently?

'I mean, why would I do that?' Harry protested. 'I liked working here. But the rumours affected business and McCrag got so angry that he started blaming me. We had a pretty bad fight so I quit. India's been trying to help me clear my name.'

Inaya's mind suddenly flashed back to the voice note India had been sending when they first arrived. She was telling Harry to wait until Farmer McCrag had cooled off. Their story checked out.

'If it wasn't you buried under the mud, I did wonder if somehow this hand thing might be you trying to get revenge,' India said, her cheeks a little red. 'I'm sorry, Harry!'

Harry shrugged. 'I only came today, after I got your message, to check you were OK.'

Inaya tried to put all this new information into place in her mind.

'India, how much longer do we have until the police arrive?' she asked.

'I haven't rung them yet,' India admitted. 'I wanted to make sure Harry wasn't involved first.'

'So *that's* why you said there was no reception!' Inaya exclaimed.

India looked embarrassed. 'Yeah. I have signal on my phone. I'll ring them now.'

'If the farmhand isn't dead, then who is the body?' Inaya wondered as India and Harry moved away to phone the police.

Joss sighed. 'No idea. Looks like we're back to square one!'

'Not necessarily,' said Inaya. She patted the bag, which hadn't left her side the whole day. 'Let's put this letter back together.'

Exactly fifteen pieces of crumpled paper were laid out carefully on one of the cafe tables. Inaya checked the clock.

'We have around ten minutes to solve this puzzle before the police arrive,' she said, looking down at the pieces. 'No pressure.'

She and Joss started moving the scraps around, piecing together sentences. Within a few minutes, they had something that resembled an A4 piece of paper.

Inaya attempted to read it aloud:

FARROW ESTATES LTD

Mr McCrag,
According to our letter --- the 15th July you have refused correspondence with us for over two months now. We have repeat --------- offers to buy your property on McCrag Farmlands, Headley, Hants, SO7 6GN.

We would like to increase our offer by £500,000 for the purchase of the farm and its lands to be developed into luxury residential apartments. This offer only stands if you respond by 3rd August. Lawyers for Mr Farrow ---------- consultation with the borough and we are aware that the farm is falling into disrepair.

Please think over this offer very carefully.
Best,
Mark Farrow
CEO Farrow Estates

'So . . . this Mark Farrow guy wants to buy McCrag's farm and turn it into flats,' Joss said, crinkling her nose. 'That's so boring.'

'And it appears Farmer McCrag is *not* interested, since he was about to burn the letter,' Inaya added.

Then it happened – the light-bulb moment.

'Wait,' said Inaya suddenly. 'We met someone today called Mark. Someone who did not seem dressed for a visit to a pick-your-own.'

Joss's eyes widened in understanding – but at that moment the unmistakable sound of sirens wailed through the air. The police had arrived.

Two officers entered the cafe and asked all the guests to stay put.

'Let's tell them what we know!' Joss whispered.

Inaya shook her head. 'There's still something I can't figure out. Why would this Mark Farrow guy kill someone and bury the body on the McCrag farm?

More police flooded into the tiny cafe, surrounding Amy, Francesca, her mum and auntie, India, Harry, Mark Farrow and – last but not least – Farmer McCrag himself, who had come over reluctantly from the farmhouse.

'My name is Sergeant Singh,' a policeman with a big beard announced to the room. 'Thank you for co-operating with us. We need statements from everyone here today. We understand this must have been very upsetting but I do want to let everyone know that after a brief forensic examination, the hand in question is –'

Inaya held her breath and looked wide-eyed at Joss. Had they found more of the body?

'Fake,' concluded Sergeant Singh. 'It appears to be a plastic hand from a mannequin dummy, covered in fake blood and strawberry juice.'

There was a confused murmur among everyone in the cafe. Inaya's brain whirred a mile a minute. A fake hand . . . planted there by someone . . . someone who wanted the farm to look bad.

Inaya stood up from her chair.

'He did it!' she shouted.

Inaya and Joss both pointed at Mark.

For a split second, the smartly dressed businessman looked utterly shocked – and then burst out laughing.

'Oh, come on, girls!' he chortled. 'I think you've had a little too much sun!'

'Now I know the hand is fake, it's *obvious*,' Inaya continued. 'You want to buy this farm. We have the letter to prove it. But Farmer McCrag won't sell. So you've been trying to put him out of business, haven't you?'

'This is ridiculous!' Mark protested in a shrill voice.

'She isn't finished,' Joss said, grinning. 'Go ahead, Inaya.'

'You're the one who has been spreading rumours

about the farm online, not Harry,' said Inaya, getting into her stride now. 'You want to drive customers away. But it wasn't enough, was it? You needed something bigger, something so shocking that, even if it wasn't real, people would be talking about it for years. "*They found a bloody hand on that farm.*" That's the thing about rumours. Even if they aren't real, people still believe them.'

Joss found Inaya's hand and gave it a little squeeze in support.

Sergeant Singh tried to speak but Inaya kept going.

'We found a shovel covered in red goo in the large greenhouse. I bet you'll find Mark Farrow's fingerprints all over it. That must be what he used to bury the mannequin's hand. We saw India trying to lock the greenhouse back up earlier but the whole lock had been tampered with. It fell right off the hinges. Mark must have broken in.'

'I thought I'd just forgotten to lock it up earlier. Dad would be so angry at me if he found out, so I was trying to do it before he noticed.' India supplied, wide-eyed. 'But I was in such a state I didn't realise it was broken.

So that was one part of the mystery solved, thought Inaya.

'And you –' She pointed a finger at Amy, who was standing with one hand behind her back. 'I bet you're recording all this right now, aren't you?'

Francesca's mum peered behind Amy's back and gasped. 'She is!'

Inaya smiled. 'Of course she is. Because she's a reporter! I saw the lanyard around her neck that says JHTV. I bet that's the channel she works for. Did Mark Farrow call you here? Telling you about the set-up and asking you to report it, making sure everyone links Farmer McCrag's pick-your-own farm with murder forever? That's how you knew it was a right hand buried there, even though you claim you arrived *after* the discovery. I bet he let you come and see the crime scene before anyone else so you could describe all the gory details in your article!'

Amy turned redder and redder until finally she let out a big sigh.

'OK, fine,' she said. 'Yes, I'm a reporter. Mark Farrow called me this morning and told me to come to the farm ASAP because he wanted me to write a big piece about a so-called murder. He promised me exclusive access to the crime scene before anyone else. I'm new at JHTV, I just wanted to make my mark.'

Inaya narrowed her eyes at Mark Farrow. 'Do you still want to pretend this is all made up?'

In the blink of an eye the businessman dashed for the door, only managing to get one hand on the doorknob before two policemen grabbed him.

'OK, fine, fine,' Mark Farrow groaned. 'It was me . . .

I broke into the greenhouse – it wasn't hard, that lock must be at least fifty years old – grabbed the shovel, planted the hand and put the shovel back. I wanted to put the old man out of business. We've been offering to buy the farm for years but he won't budge! Even though this place isn't making him any money. Come on,' he said, turning a winning smile on the officer holding his arm. 'It's not so bad, is it? Just a fake hand. We'll all laugh about this one day.'

'You faked a murder and wasted police time,' Sergeant Singh said. 'We certainly *won't* be laughing about this. Take him to the station.'

Mark was bundled out of the cafe and everyone cheered.

'Congratulations on your investigation,' Sergeant Singh said to Inaya and Joss. He shook both of their hands. 'You'd make great detectives one day.'

'*One day?*' Joss whispered to Inaya when the sergeant was out of earshot. 'We already are!'

Inaya felt a tap on her shoulder.

'I owe you both an apology for being so cranky earlier,' Farmer McCrag said gruffly, standing beside his daughter. 'That Mark Farrow has been after my farm for years, and now this'll put an end to his rumours.'

'Farmer McCrag . . . India . . . have you ever thought of turning the farm into a different type of attraction?'

Joss said, a twinkle in her eye.

'What do you mean?' asked India.

Joss grinned. 'Well, there's a spookiness to the place, no offence, that would make it a great murder-mystery location. You could even turn the farmhouse into a haunted house! Or an escape room! I bet it would bring in new customers.'

A smile spread across India's face. 'We do always struggle in the winter months when the pick-your-own is closed.'

'You might be on to somethin' there ...' Farmer McCrag said, scratching his beard.

'So does this mean you're a crime fan now?' Joss asked, bumping Inaya with her shoulder as both McCrags left, smiling and talking earnestly.

'You finally got me.' Inaya sighed. 'I have been bitten by the mystery bug.'

Joss cheered and threw her arms around her best friend. 'So no more hiding away in your bedroom? You'll be out solving mysteries with me?'

Inaya's stomach filled with butterflies – the good kind. 'Definitely. I'm ready to put the creepy rumours behind me. Hopefully everyone else at school will too.'

'You always have me, Naya.' Joss smiled, putting her arm around her friend. 'And if anyone gives you more trouble, I'll put a fake hand in their schoolbag.'

Inaya threw her head back and laughed hard.

Her phone pinged with a message from her dad. Of course, now there's *finally* signal!

In car park. Why are there so many police here!?

All this was going to take a lot of explaining. But strangely Inaya was looking forward to it.

'Let's get out of here,' Joss cheered. 'Oh wait, the punnets!'

But the berries they'd originally picked were long gone – left somewhere along the way of the investigation. Inaya laughed at Joss's tragic expression.

'To be honest,' she said, clapping Joss on the shoulder, 'after all the fake blood we've seen today, I don't think I'll be eating any more berries for a *looooong* time!'

MISTLIGHT

DOMINIQUE VALENTE

MISTLIGHT

By Dominique Valente

YEAR 108 OF THE MISTLIGHT
8 JUNUS, SUMMER

DIARY OF JORMUN JAEGERSON

Twice a day, my village, Sjora, becomes an island. When the tide rises the mists arrive too, forming great curtains of fog that obscure us from view, so it hardly seems we are here at all. Sometimes there are boats who aim for us, seeing the greenish light in the mist, and thinking the lighthouse on our island will guide them over.

But few boats ever make it. They are not meant to. That's because the lighthouse isn't a guide, you see. It's not even a lighthouse at all. It's a *mistlight*.

It creates the emerald fog that conceals not just us, but our monsters too.

If those boats only knew what they might find here, when the tide changes, they would *never* try to get to us at all.

The mistlight keeps them safe but it also keeps the monsters from leaving – the sea serpents that dwell below.

We built the mistlight, so my grandma Ska says, back when there were still men living on the island. Before they had no choice but to start moving away to the mainland. That was when Sjora was a busy, bustling place full of people, not the almost ghost town it is today.

Now we send our boys away before their voices break, as part of the bargain we struck. The one we made to end the war between us and the sea serpents. The bargain that now feels like a curse.

You see, it's the cracks in boys' voices that stir the sea serpents from their slumber. It's also what sets into motion the change in the boys, so they in turn become sea serpents themselves.

It happens slowly at first, after our voices change. Just a rough scale every few months, followed perhaps by a spike or a horn, but then things speed up quickly and soon, somehow, all at once: pupils become slits, eyes turn yellow, hands and feet become webbed claws, spiky tails grow along with needle fangs and the deadly poison sacs appear at the base of our slimy throats. Soon the boys are family no more, but the monsters who keep us prisoners here.

But then, because of the mistlight, the monsters are

prisoners too, just as much as we are.

Thanks to the bargain between our worlds.

It was my great-great-grandmother Basheba who helped to forge the pact with the mighty sea dragon – king of the sea serpents.

Before the bargain the sea serpents were stealing our children and we would retaliate by killing them. At some point we started making objects from the bones and scales of the sea serpents. Wondrous things that made Sjora famous the world over, because they were beautiful and enchanted and made us wealthy. And then the men on our island began to hunt the sea serpents solely for their magical bodies, even while knowing that the sea serpents would take their revenge on us by taking more and more of our children.

This became a war, one that needed to stop.

Basheba sought out the king of the sea serpents, Lorumfur, to make a deal.

He agreed to end the conflict but warned her that the only way was to place a curse on both monsters and islanders alike. A *curse-bargain*. This way neither could hurt one without hurting themselves.

So the sea dragon cursed the boys to turn into sea serpents once they hit puberty. Basheba begged him to have mercy and to let the boys stay human if they left Sjora before their voices broke, and Lorumfur agreed, modifying the curse so that the boys who left forget where they came from, so they wouldn't be tempted to come back. If they returned they would be like the boys who remain, they would turn into monsters and the sea serpents would claim them for their own.

They shook on it and made the mistlight to keep the bargain in place.

It is what ensures the sea serpents can't ever leave our island and take anyone else's children, especially when the tide is in and the mists are at their peak – when the sea serpents are most dangerous.

It also ensures that the boys forget about their lives on the island when they leave.

But it's not just the boys who forget. The mistlight makes everyone who isn't from the island forget almost everything they ever see or do on Sjora once they leave.

When the mainlanders visit, they might distantly recall buying fish or baskets, produce that is in good supply in the village, but little else after they return home. If they form an impression of the island, it is of an unremarkable little place, a speck by the sea with dull, taciturn locals who would really rather you weren't there at all.

They don't see the hundreds of empty homes from the families who had to leave. They don't see how sad the women's eyes are either. How heavy the choice Basheba forced on them is, and how lonely we all are with most of our families having moved away. They don't see that only the women from the island can't forget because they are cursed to remember – even if they leave, which is why, after a time, they often come back to live here. It is hard to go to the mainland and visit the ones who don't remember their family.

One day that will be my fate too. To leave. To forget. Or stay and become a monster.

I still wake up in a cold sweat, whenever I recall the day my grandma – who everyone on the island calls Ska, even us – told my twin sister Elowen and I about the future that lay in wait for me. I was seven when I found out the truth.

'You'll have to leave us, Jormun, when you turn twelve.' Ska warned. 'Before your voice breaks. You must leave so you don't turn into a sea serpent. You must go and make a new life and forget about us. Like all the other boys before you.'

But do they forget us completely?

Elowen and I have often wondered about this since Ska told us my fate. We have seen the boys from the island stare out to sea. They all share the same expression, as if they are trying to remember something they can't. But it's more than just confusion in their eyes.

They look *lost*.

Then there's the stories about their nightmares.

The new parents have said that the boys wake up screaming in their new beds but can't remember why. But the pictures they draw of the monsters tell a different story . . . somewhere, deep in their subconscious, they remember something. Something that haunts them. I'm sure of it.

Though Ska always tells Elowen and I that that's ridiculous. She assures us that the boys don't remember a thing about their old lives here. That they're happy, really.

I can see why she says that, because apart from when we've seen them staring out at sea on the mainland, they do look happy enough.

Some days I don't know what to believe.

But either way, I have a plan. I'll find a way to remember somehow.

In two months' time, I turn twelve, and that's when I'll be sent away for good.

I have to do something though and fast. Because it's already started. Yesterday, I felt it on my neck.

A scale.

I can't tell anyone, not even Elowen. We're almost identical in looks but our fates are so different – she's destined to become the next mistlight keeper, to never be able to move away and to have a twin who never remembers her at all.

Neither of us can stand the thought.

Sometimes people confuse us and think I'm the girl.

That's because I'm small and scrappy and wear my hair long and loose, and she's tough and strong. But then people like to make assumptions about a lot of things they shouldn't.

Elowen cries every night when she thinks I can't hear her. I don't cry. Well, not much. What I do is go and stare at the mural that takes up one whole wall inside the mistlight tower. It shows where the feathered sea dragon Lorumfur and Basheba made their pact, and in the centre, the legend of the curse-bargain they made, written in old-fashioned script, part of which has been chipped away. The part about how to break the curse.

Ska doesn't like us to talk about it. The only thing she has said is that lifting the curse would be worse for everyone than keeping it in place. She's never told us *why*.

But we know she knows more than she lets on. We've begged her to tell us more but she refuses.

It won't stop Elowen and I from trying to figure it out on our own though.

Today, Elowen almost saw the scale on my neck. I was holding up a tiny hand mirror to try to see it when she burst into my room, right at the top of the tower.

'What are you doing?' she demanded in a mix of languages – the one we speak on the island and the sign language we made up when we were little, much of which consists of hand gestures. We made it because we were twins and a secret language was fun, but later it was helpful when Elowen started to lose the hearing in her left ear. Now almost everyone on the island can speak it.

Elowen's green eyes were fierce, but I saw a hint of fear in them too.

I shrugged, trying to pretend it was nothing, but she could see through me like I was made out of glass.

She lunged for my neck, a worried look on her face, but I scarpered away. 'It's just a bit of dirt,' I said, showing her my hand, which had a bit of grease on it from where I had been doing some repairs to the wheel that turns on the mistlight.

She frowned but let it go. We're often having to do minor repairs.

I distracted Elowen further by pointing out the window. It was the start of a beautiful summer's day. The tide was out and the mainlanders were coming over along the sandbank that would later on fill and turn us into an island once more.

The sea beyond was a bright cornflower blue, the sun high up in the sky like lemon butter icing and, as we watched, a flock of geese flew across the horizon.

I felt a pang inside my chest at the thought that one day I might not get to see this.

From here we could see the light come on inside the tiny boat bakery below. There was already a queue developing on the gangplank for people wanting one of Thesa's light and sweet orense cakes, made of the soft peach-like orense fruit that grows on the island in the summer months. I gave Elowen a look, and soon we were running to join the line. She has the sweetest tooth of anyone in our family.

I don't know why I didn't tell Elowen straight away about the scale. I suppose it's because then it would be real. More real. I know pretending something isn't there doesn't make it go away but you can fool yourself for a little while.

Also, she's worried enough as it is. When Ska is gone and I am gone she won't have any family left.

It was Elowen's idea that I keep a diary, *this diary*, so I don't forget after the leaving ceremony. The diary will remind me of my real family when I'm in my new home on the mainland.

She plans to help me smuggle the diary out. The older women check our belongings when they take us to our new homes to make sure we don't take any memories of our island life. It makes it harder on everyone that way, they say. I don't see how. They already stare back at us as if they are trying to remember something they can't. Like the melody of a song they can't name.

That's why Elowen and I will find a way, neither of us can bear to forget or be forgotten.

The mid-summer sun beat down on the beach as I watched my twin dangle her feet in the sea. Her skin is tanned and the soles of her feet are tough as leather, just like her. Unlike mine, her hair is always tied in a knot by her neck.

I took out my diary and began to sketch her as she ate the last bit of orense cake, and was so lost in my drawing that I didn't see her move before it was too late.

She was at my neck, pulling back my collar so fast I didn't have time to stop her.

'I knew it,' she cried. I could see the tears shimmering in her eyes. Her face turned red and her hands clenched into fists. 'Why didn't you tell me, Jormun?' she demanded.

I swallowed. All I could do was shrug helplessly.

'Did your voice break?'

'No.'

'Are you sure?'

I nodded, then swallowed.

I would know, right?

She punched my arm, but I was the one who said sorry.

'I didn't want you to worry,' I admitted.

She gave me a look. 'I was worried anyway, you know that.'

I did.

Then she frowned and came for my neck again. There was a strange look on her face, like she was confused. I tried to push her away but she was strong.

'Stop it I just want to see something, Jormun.'

I gave in and let her. I felt her rough, calloused finger touch the growth on my neck and shivered unpleasantly. I tried to move her hand away but she slapped mine in return. 'Don't,' she said. 'You're blocking it and I think it's something else.'

My heart started to hammer. *Something else?*

I turned to look at her, eyes wide.

She looked floored.

'It's not a scale,' she breathed.

I blinked, confused. For a second I felt myself hope, but her face looked odd. It didn't look relieved. It looked confused and maybe even a little frightened.

'What is it?' I asked desperately.

She frowned. Her green eyes looked puzzled.

'It looks like a feather.'

While I was blinking at her in confusion, I could sense Elowen was starting to think four steps ahead. She grabbed my hand, to tug me along.

'We need to go to the mistlight. We have to look at the legend on the wall!' she cried.

I didn't understand. 'Why?' We already knew it backwards and forwards. The only thing we didn't know, what we'd never known, was the part that had been cut away.

The wall spoke of the long wars between us and the sea serpents, and how Basheba and Lorumfur created their bargain.

But it was the end that interested Elowen and I the most.

One day someone will be born who will break the curse. When the sea dragon, Lorumfur, dies a new one will be born. Someone who will not begin to develop scales but f–

'Feathers, Jormun, I'm sure of it!' said Elowen, setting off on a run and dragging me along beside her. 'Just like the old sea dragon king – it's there on the mural!' She looked excited.

'We have to speak to Ska,' she said, her eyes shining. 'As the mistlight keeper she'll know more. Maybe you're the one the legend talks of: the one to break the curse! Maybe there's a way for you to stay too?'

I touched my neck. Was it really a dragon feather? I hadn't been able to see it in the little mirror. I hesitated for a moment.

'Come on, Jormun!'

I set off after her, and together we began to run. I felt

something begin to fizz inside me, buoyed by my sister's hope. How had I not thought of this myself? All those hours I had spent staring at the mural . . .

Was it true? Could I be the one to break the curse? The sheer hope spreading through me gave me wings. I began to run so fast along the beach towards home that Elowen had to tell me to wait.

Ska was making tea when we burst inside. I flung the door open so fast it swung against the wall, making a loud crash.

Ska is tall with all-white hair and the same green eyes as us. She's strong and fierce like a warrior, one who has survived many battles and has the scars to prove it. She raised us when our parents died, when we were just babies. It has always been hard on her knowing that one day she would have to send me away.

'Hey! What's all this about?' she said, looking from me to my sister, a puzzled look on her face.

We were speaking and signing, and doing both too fast she couldn't catch what we were trying to say.

'Slow down,' she begged.

'We need to find out more about the legend,' I began. 'The part that used to be on the wall – about breaking the curse.'

I watched as Ska's face changed from concerned to wary. She started to shake her head, the way she always did when we asked her about it.

'No, no, children, how many times have I explained this? It's best to leave that buried . . . you don't want to be poking about in that. *Believe me.*'

Elowen shook her head violently. 'You always say that but you never tell us why!' she roared. 'But now you have no choice, Ska!'

'Why?' asked our grandmother, who suddenly looked afraid.

'Jormun has started growing a feather!' breathed Elowen.

I turned to look at my sister in horror. I hadn't planned on telling Ska *that part.*

Ska's eyes widened in shock. 'Show me!' she demanded.

What choice did I have? I pulled down my collar and shifted so she could see it. I knew Elowen was right, and it really *was* a feather, by the way Ska gasped. She went very pale, her mouth seemed to be moving wordlessly and she started to blink a lot.

'Are you all right?' I asked.

'It's part of the legend, isn't it?' pressed Elowen. '*One day someone will be born who will break the curse. When the sea dragon, Lorumfur, dies a new one will be born. Someone who will not begin to develop scales but f–* It's feathers, right?

Is that what this means? Jormun's going to become the next sea-dragon king and break the curse?'

I held my breath. If anyone knew it would be Ska. We'd long suspected that the mistlight keeper had a few secrets no one knew about.

Ska looked at my sister, but it was as if she couldn't hear her. Then she took a deep breath and squared her shoulders. Her eyes looked sad. 'I'll ring the bell tonight. Jormun, prepare yourself for the leaving ceremony.'

We blanched. 'No, Ska!' cried Elowen.

Ska didn't look at me, her mouth was set in a firm line.

The bell was how we announced there was to be a going-away ceremony. It was usually the night of a boy's twelfth birthday. Mine was still two months away.

Tears clouded my eyes. It was difficult to swallow. I felt helpless, angry and confused. How could she be thinking of sending me away now? When there might be a chance to change *everything*.

'But what about the curse?' I asked. 'What if I could break it, Ska!'

She looked at me, finally, and her eyes looked tormented.

'Jormun, the one who begins to grow feathers doesn't just break the curse –'

'BUT IT SAYS IT DOES!' cried Elowen, who looked just as outraged as me.

Ska shook her head. 'You don't understand. It's not that simple! He will have to stay as a sea dragon forever! You might break the curse for everyone else, Jormun, but you won't be able to turn back into a boy again,' she said, her voice heavy. 'You'd become a monster. One that hunts children – they can't help it, it's in their nature, that's why we had to make the curse-bargain. If it breaks, the sea serpents will go back to stealing children again and we'll have no choice but to fight back. You could get killed, Jormun. If we take you to the mainland, you will get to live a life – you can grow up, have a family . . . If you stay, you would be giving everything up to live a cursed life – that of a heartless beast.'

My heart thundered in my chest.

'But if I go away I won't remember you or Elowen!'

I saw the pain in her eyes as she nodded. 'Yes, you will forget us, but you can make a new life. Many of the boys live happy ones, it's a blessing that they can't remember.'

I shook my head. That wasn't true. *We had seen them. Seen how lost they looked.*

I couldn't listen any more. I turned away, raced up to my room and threw myself onto my bed. I was so frustrated I felt as if I could have torn down the mistlight with my bare hands.

My choice seemed impossible: turn into a monster and break the curse, or leave and forget who I am?

I felt my twin enter the room and lie down, putting an arm around me.

We must have stayed like that for a few minutes before she whispered, 'Jormun, it's going to be all right. You'll have the diary. You won't have your memories but you will know where you're from.'

I turned over and stared at her in shock. 'You agree with Ska? You think I should go? You were just as excited as I was to break the curse!'

Her eyes filled with tears. 'I know – but I didn't know what it would mean, how the sea serpents would go back to hunting our children ... Maybe it was right to chip that part of the wall away so no one is tempted to break the curse-bargain. What other choice do we have, Jormun? Sacrifice you to the sea, or allow you to become king of those monsters?'

She was right. But I hated it all the same.

As the mists rolled in and Ska rang the bell for the ceremony, Elowen couldn't stop crying and I was struggling not to break down myself. I looked around at all the crumpled faces and thought of leaving my twin, and my heart felt like it was being ripped in two.

Ska had to pull Elowen's arms off me as I stepped into the boat.

A group of older women got in beside me, their faces stony as they waited for Ska to push us off into the crashing surf.

It was nearly midnight, the moon was high up in the sky, and the green mistlight lit the path towards the mainland.

The wind whipped my hair into my eyes and from the waves I could hear a strange hissing sound.

I watched as my sister got smaller and smaller the further the women rowed. My heart started to pound as I thought of what would happen next.

How soon would it take for my memories to go? Would it be as soon as I stepped onto the mainland? Or would it take longer, like an hour or even a day?

They never told us that.

Instinctively I moved my elbow closer to my ribs and felt the diary that Elowen had slipped beneath my slicker when she hugged me one last time, making the fabric rustle audibly.

That was my mistake.

Ska was at my side so fast that I barely had the chance to react, her strong arm lifting my elbow and wrestling the book from beneath my slicker.

In the hazy light I could see her frown. 'Oh, Jormun,' she said. Then before I could do anything, she flung the diary into the sea.

'No!' I cried, my hands reaching out hopelessly.

'It's better this way,' she said.

The other women nodded.

Anger bubbled up inside me. *Better for who? It certainly wasn't better for me. Or Elowen.*

From the sea, the hissing sound intensified.

'What is that?' I asked, but the wind whipped away my words.

My heart started to thunder in my ears. The hissing was growing louder, like a thousand whispered voices were calling my name. It was drowning out everything else. I needed it to *stop*.

My eyes started to burn. My skin began to sting like I had brushed against a patch of poison caulk. My throat was on fire. I needed water. And not just any water. Salt water.

My head felt like it was about to split apart.

The hissing was getting louder and louder, and now I could hear that it was voices.

Voices that were begging for my help.

It was instinct that made me look towards the sea but it was something else that made me leap from the boat and dive in.

The old women in the boat shouted and screamed.

But all I felt was instant relief.

The noise died down. My thirst dissipated and my

skin felt as if it was being soothed by a balm. I opened my eyes, and saw that I wasn't alone.

There were hundreds of sea serpents staring at me. They were beautiful – gold and green, blue and red, with bright jewel-like eyes – and each one was calling my name, doing shimmies in the water as they exclaimed in delight.

I frowned as I realised that I recognised some of them; I knew their voices.

'Jormunfur! Jormunfur!' they said.

At first I thought they were getting my name wrong, but then I realised they were giving me a new name as, before their eyes, I turned into a sea dragon. Stinging barbs on my skin became pale blue feathers, my fingers and toes turned to claws, and somehow, I could now breathe underwater.

'You don't know me, but I know you,' said a red sea serpent with onyx eyes. 'I am Lincurie, Ska's brother, your great-uncle.'

I stared at him in shock. I had known that many of the sea serpents were once from our village but I didn't think they remembered their old lives. We had been told that once they turned into monsters they became cruel heartless beasts, frustrated they couldn't hunt children . . . but these creatures before me did not seem like mindless monsters at all.

'Jormunfur, the humans can't understand us, but you

can, and with you here we will finally be able to break the curse. You can set us all free – humans and sea serpents alike. But to do so, we need to take down the mistlight.'

I hesitated, Ska's words ringing in my head that they would hunt children again.

'But,' I said, 'the mistlight is what keeps the children safe. I can't allow you to hunt them.'

'Hunt them?' cried a green sea serpent in disgust. He had long whiskers like a curling moustache. 'We have never hunted children!'

All around, more and more sea serpents were getting animated. 'They lied. The humans lied!'

I started at them in confusion.

'*They* hunted us!'

Lincurie nodded. 'It's true. The islanders discovered that our scales and bones have magic and can make enchanted things and they began to hunt us. We fought back by taking their children – not to kill them, but to turn them – we thought that if some of their kin were sea serpents the islanders wouldn't try to kill us, but it didn't stop. That's when we went to war and Basheba cursed Lorumfur, and cursed the men who had sacrificed the children to become sea serpents.'

I blinked in shock.

'B-but it was the other way around!' I cried. But I wasn't so sure any more.

'No! Those are more lies,' cried the green serpent. 'Basheba used the remains of the sea serpents to make the mistlight and forced Lorumfur to agree to a ceasefire. The mistlight keeps us here because it is made from the remains of our dead, and we can't leave until we give them an underwater burial.'

Lincurie nodded. 'That's why we have to take it down, Jormunfur. Then we can set everyone free from *her* curse.'

I stared at him, then nodded. 'I will help make this right.'

There were more shimmies and cries of delight now.

'It won't be easy,' warned Lincurie. 'The islanders will fight – they have weapons and have long been trained to keep us off their beach.'

I knew that.

I also knew that Sjora didn't know the full story.

They had all been lied to just as much as I had. But now I knew the whole story – the whole *truth*.

Swimming was as easy as breathing in my sea-dragon form. I cut through the waves like I was a blade. Through my new yellow eyes, I could see the old women had returned back to the island.

I felt a stab of fear.

From when we were little we had been schooled in

battle, in case of a sea serpent attack. Every woman and child on the island knew how to wield some form of weapon. And just because I was Ska's grandson, it didn't mean they wouldn't try and kill me. By now Ska would have told everyone what had happened.

They would think that the curse had been broken and that the sea serpents were free, and they would be terrified that we would be after their children.

Somehow I would have to try and find a way to tell them the truth.

My first step onto the shore was laboured, as I wasn't used to my four dragon feet. I moved slowly out of the water. My feathered body was slick and heavy.

As the sea serpents followed, slithering onto the beach that summer morning, the shouts and screams from the islanders were deafening.

A volley of flamed arrows came flying at us from the woman who ran the boat bakery. Then an old woman came rushing towards us, with a knife.

Suddenly, the sea serpents and islanders were in battle. The islanders couldn't hear what the sea serpents were trying to tell them. I realised in horror that all they heard was hissing.

My heart thundered in fear.

I turned and saw Elowen rushing to join the fray, she was loading an arrow into her bow.

With my claws, I signed her name.

She paused, an odd look on her face.

I did it again and then she signed mine in return.

I nodded.

She started to run for me, her weapon lowered. Behind her, Ska turned and saw where she was heading, and before I knew it my grandmother had aimed a flaming arrow at me, which landed in my front leg.

'Stop!' Elowen cried.

I was struggling to stand, my leg on fire with the pain.

Ska raced after Elowen.

I signed at them both. 'It's me, Jormun!'

Ska staggered to a halt, then fell to her knees and started to cry. 'You silly boy, look what you have done to yourself! I could have killed you.'

I stood up in pain, turning to address everyone.

'Stop fighting!' I roared and signed too. 'We are not at war!'

A few of the people around me paused, a look of confusion on their faces. They hadn't understood me when I spoke aloud, but they understood the sign language Elowen and I had made up when we were little.

They turned to look at me, then at Elowen. She nodded. 'It's Jormun. Let him speak!'

I thanked her and continued to sign.

'I need you all to listen to me and to stop fighting.'

Then I began to explain everything that the sea serpents had told me. About the curse and the mistlight and what had really happened.

'It can't be,' said Ska, horrified.

'It is,' I said. 'Your brother told me.'

Her eyes turned huge. 'M-my brother?'

I pointed at the red sea serpent who had been trying to avoid an old woman who kept banging him over the head with a broomstick.

'Lincurie,' I spoke and signed. He held up a claw.

Ska paled.

'Ska,' he hissed.

But of course she couldn't understand.

'Ska,' I signed.

Lincurie copied what I'd done.

Ska wasn't the only one to gasp aloud and the voices of the islanders began to overlap.

'They understand us?'

'They can speak to us?'

I nodded.

Soon we were introducing more and more long-lost family members to the villagers, many of whom began to cry as they found their brothers, cousins and friends. But it wasn't tears of sadness.

'We need to take down the mistlight,' I told the

islanders. 'We need to end this curse and break this so-called bargain once and for all.'

Then I held my breath.

I wondered if they would believe me. It was a hard pill to swallow. That it wasn't the sea serpents that had attacked first as they had been led to believe. That they weren't mindless monsters after their children . . . that in fact it wasn't them who had been the monsters all along.

But us.

Ska picked up a discarded axe that someone had dropped on the beach when we had all stopped fighting and started to communicate. She raised the axe above her head and a fierce look came into her eyes. My heart started to thump in my chest.

Elowen jumped in front of me to protect me.

But Ska didn't attack. 'Tear it down!' she yelled and began to run towards the mistlight.

There were whooping cries from the sea serpents and the islanders alike as we all rushed after her.

It took hours for islander and beast to take it apart, piece by piece. I felt a twinge of sadness, the tower had been mine and Elowen's home, and we had loved it once, before we knew what it had been built from. But together we all rejoiced as the last trace of it sank below the surface.

It was Elowen's idea to have an arrival ceremony when

the last of the mist vanished. A welcome-home party for everyone who would soon begin to remember who they were and who they'd left behind.

Elowen treated my wound and bandaged it up.

I turned to look at her and gave her a crooked smile.

'At least now they probably won't confuse us any more,' I said.

She shook her head. 'I wouldn't be so sure about that, Jormun*fur*,' she said. Then she pulled down her collar. I gasped aloud.

Because there on her neck was a feather.

She was my twin, after all.

NIZRANA FAROOK

DEATH
IN THE
TROPICS

TOP SECRET

DEATH IN THE TROPICS

By Nizrana Farook

'**G**ood afternoon. Welcome to the Palm Garden Hotel,' said the smiling receptionist in a sari of peacock-feather print.

Saba felt like she had stepped into an oven after getting off the air-conditioned coach. The air was humid and laced with the smell of tropical flowers. There were three other British families from their flight who'd arrived at the hotel with Saba, her parents and her brother Jameel. They were the Sanchos, a jolly older couple in large matching sunhats, the glamorous young Sparrows with their colour-coordinated luggage, and a surly looking mother and daughter called the Parkers.

They all went inside and settled on the lobby sofas and a waiter brought them cold towels and iced drinks spotted with condensation.

But rather than pounce on it with gratitude like Saba

did, Mrs Parker stared the waiter up and down. She was a tall and snappy old lady with a flashy, jewelled necklace that Saba had seen Mum stare at from time to time.

'What is *that*?' Mrs Parker said to the waiter sternly, looking at the drinks on his tray most disapprovingly.

The man's smile dropped as he looked back at her with confusion. 'It's tamarind juice, madam,' he said.

Mrs Parker's eyes grew wide. 'I don't know what that is, but it sounds ghastly. Please bring me a normal drink.'

'I'll have one of those!' said Gorky Sparrows, the pink-haired social media influencer who was with his very stylish-looking wife.

He took up the glass with one hand and had a long gulp. With his other he was recording himself with his phone, which he was surgically attached to at all times. Saba loved her phone like all normal, well-adjusted people, but this man was on another level.

Saba looked over Gorky's shoulder at his screen as he wrote a caption on the photo and posted it online.

'*Having the best time with friends*?' she read, incredulous. 'You've only just met us.'

Gorky turned his phone over at once.

'Thank goodness,' said Mrs Parker, now sipping an orange juice and switching on a hand-held fan. 'A proper, civilised drink.'

Her daughter Jessica sighed. She was a middle-aged

woman who looked quite like her mother. On the coach ride to the hotel, Saba had seen her looking at cat pictures on her phone the whole time.

'I quite like the tamarind,' said Jessica. 'You should give it a try, Mother.'

'Certainly not,' said Mrs Parker. 'Are our rooms ready?' She poked her daughter hard on the arm. 'Go and check.'

For a second, Jessica's eyes flashed with pure hatred, then she composed herself quickly and put her drink down. She ambled off to the reception desk.

'Well, isn't this nice!' said Gorky. He was back on his phone and typing furiously. Next to him, his wife Ruby was slumped on the sofa with her hat over her face.

'This is the first trip we've had in ages,' said Dr Sancho, patting a cold towel through her closely-cropped hair. She looked across the hotel grounds to the ocean. 'I can't wait to get in the water!'

The receptionist who had greeted them earlier came forward with four sets of key cards in her hand, followed by Jessica Parker.

She sorted out each of the families with a key, and reeled off a list of instructions about breakfast times and pool opening hours and sea warnings and closing balcony doors before sunset so mosquitos don't come in, and Saba couldn't keep track of it all.

'You're all on the ground floor together,' said the

woman with the perpetual smile, which managed to still look warm. Her badge said *Shalini*. She leaned over the coffee table and gave the first to Mr Sancho.

'Come on,' said Saba, picking up her backpack. Dad and her six-year-old brother Jam, short for Jameel, followed. Mrs Parker was getting up slowly and her daughter stood by patiently.

The Sanchos crossed in front of the Parkers at that moment, and Mrs Parker looked at them with a start. Dr Sancho glared at her.

Saba stopped in her tracks. She'd noticed a bad vibe between them in the coach too. What was going on?

'What are we waiting for?' said Saba's mum, coming up behind her. 'This way.' She walked past Saba and turned in the direction of their rooms, followed by Dad. Saba's brother Jam knew something was up and stopped next to her.

The two of them stood there in the marble corridor a moment longer, next to a large potted anthurium. Did Mrs Parker and the Sanchos know each other? Why the glares?

Mr Sancho put his arm on his wife's waist as if calming her and they turned away. Mrs Parker swept past Saba and Jam with surprising speed, not even waiting for Jessica.

'Hmm, that's strange,' said Jam.

'Right you are, brother,' said Saba. 'Something is brewing.'

At lunch, Saba had a chance to see the whole group again at close quarters. Jessica Parker was sitting at a table with her mother, and she waved at Saba's mum as they entered, inviting them to join. Mrs Parker looked annoyed and said something snappily to Jessica, which they thankfully didn't hear over the kapirinna music.

'Can we ignore them?' said Dad to Mum, stopping by a dessert table with tall fruit carvings and trying not to move his lips too much. 'I don't want to sit with Mrs Parker.'

'Don't be rude, Ahmed.' Mum beamed at Jessica and went over. After a moment she waved at Dad to follow.

Saba shrugged at Dad in solidarity. There was no getting out of it. They joined Mum and the Parkers.

A waiter came over and joined another table together to make room for them all to sit. Mrs Parker huffed visibly, much to Jessica's embarrassment.

'Thank you, Jessica, so kind of you,' said Mum, pretending not to notice her mother's rudeness.

Saba saw Dr and Mr Sancho enter the restaurant and had a fantastic idea.

'Oh, look, there's the Sanchos!' She stood up and waved jauntily. 'Come and join us.'

The Sanchos hesitated at the door, as if unsure how to respond. Saba glanced sneakily at Mrs Parker. She looked like she was about to have a heart attack.

'I'm sure the good couple would want to spend some time by –' began Mrs Parker.

'Nonsense!' said Mum cluelessly. 'We can make more room here. Come on over!'

The drinks waiter from earlier – Saba noticed his name badge said *Ashoka* – came back and joined another table to theirs. Dr and Mr Sancho looked like they'd rather be anywhere else on earth.

As they all tucked themselves in, very unwillingly, Gorky and Ruby joined them too.

'Where's the menu?' Mrs Parker asked the waiter.

Jessica smiled at him apologetically before turning to her mother. 'It's a buffet, Mother.'

'What rubbish,' mumbled Mrs Parker as Ashoka was walking away.

'I'm sorry,' said Jessica to everyone. 'Mother's a bit tired today and that's put her in a bad mood.'

Saba wasn't so sure about that. Mrs Parker's bad mood seemed permanent.

'No need to apologise,' said Gorky Sparrows genially. 'Not everyone is comfortable with constant travel. Personally, I could do this all day every day, me.'

No one took any notice of him.

'Do you like my mother's necklace?' Jessica suddenly asked Mum.

Mum went very red. 'I-I just think –'

'Oh, don't worry, I don't blame you!' said Jessica. 'I just noticed you keep looking at it. It's very pretty.'

'And very valuable,' said Mrs Parker archly, giving it a little pat.

'I bet,' said Dr Sancho from across the table.

Mrs Parker paled slightly.

Saba kicked Jam under the table, as if to say *watch me*.

'So,' said Saba, biting into a bread roll. 'How do you know each other, Mrs Parker and Dr and Mr Sancho?'

Everyone looked startled by Saba's question. Dad stared at her.

Mrs Parker pretended not to hear. Mr Sancho cleared his throat. 'It was a long time ago. We had a very short-lived business venture together.'

'How interesting,' said Gorky's wife Ruby, much to Saba's delight. 'What sort of business?' She was just being polite, of course, but Saba waited eagerly for the reply.

'It's not that interesting,' said Mrs Parker hastily. She got up and pushed her chair back. 'It was over and done with very quickly.'

'Except . . . ' Dr Sancho stared at her. 'It wasn't, was it? You never gave us our money back.'

Mrs Parker had gone white. Everyone seemed to freeze over the noise of clinking cutlery. Then Mrs Parker sighed as if trying to remember something, although it looked totally fake to Saba. 'Is that so? My memory isn't what it used to be.'

Jessica Parker was watching this exchange with interest.

'Oh, I doubt that very much,' said Dr Sancho. 'I think you remember it perfectly.'

'Come along, Jessica,' said Mrs Parker, walking away. 'Could you get me something to eat from this wretched buffet?'

'In a minute, Mother,' Jessica said, stopping to talk to Ashoka who was walking by. 'I love how you serve these king coconut drinks in the shell itself. So good for the environment!'

Ashoka smiled pleasantly, though he looked harried.

'What do you do with them at the end?' asked Jessica.

'We compost them, madam.'

'Oh, how amazing!' said Jessica. 'Can I see where? I have a special interest in this sort of thing because of . . . er, my work.'

'Of course,' said poor Ashoka, leading her away. Mrs Parker sullenly went off to get her own food.

Later that afternoon, Saba and her family were getting ready for a swim. She sat on a deckchair with a book and waited while Dad rubbed sun cream on Jam's arms. Inside, Mum was filling a backpack with some of Jam's beach toys and measuring instruments. She stared quizzically at a slide rule before putting it inside.

From the next room, the glass door slid open with a huge screech and Jessica Parker walked outside. 'Good heavens!' came Mrs Parker's voice as she followed her out. 'Will you give them a ring at reception and complain about that door? The sound of it could wake the dead.'

'It's fine, Mother.' Jessica slid the door shut, and it made the same horrible noise again, making even Saba wince.

Mrs Parker settled down into a seat on the terrace outside their room and Jessica arranged a pillow for her head. Mrs Parker moaned about it for several minutes and had Jessica fluff it up and place it in different angles before she was satisfied.

'Where are you off to, Ahmed?' Jessica called out to Dad when she'd finished, and settled down next to her mother.

'The beach. Jam has been talking about building a structurally sound sandcastle.'

From the room next to the Parkers, Gorky had come out with his wife Ruby. He was holding out cashews on his palm to chipmunks in the trees and Ruby was filming him at his request.

Dr and Mr Sancho came out too. They'd changed into floral-printed clothes and were on an animated video call with their family members back home.

Ashoka walked past with a tray of drinks. He went

to Jessica and Mrs Parker and put down a king coconut drink on the table. As always, it was in its shell like Jessica approved, with a frangipani flower and straw.

Music started up and a hotel entertainer came to the poolside with a mic, announcing some kind of inane show that made Saba sigh. A local dance troupe was performing on the lawn beside the pool. Jessica Parker stood up and moved closer, leaving Mrs Parker sitting on the terrace. Other guests watched from the water and pool bar, and the British party from their places outside their rooms.

Saba looked back at the others for a moment. Gorky was filming the dance, with Ruby watching by his side. Dad watched from his deckchair, Jam leaning on his shoulders. Dr Sancho was swaying and clicking her hands to the music, with Mr Sancho close by taking pictures on his phone. Mum – enjoying the performance from her position in the shade – stood closest to Mrs Parker, who was at the very back, sitting on the terrace with a newspaper and a king coconut drink on the table in front of her.

Saba turned back to the entertainment. OK, so it wasn't too bad. She was beginning to enjoy it even.

The drums crescendoed and the dancers stamped their bare feet on the grass and everyone began to clap. Mr Sancho put his phone in his pocket and ran up, joining the dancers and raising a laugh from the crowd. People cheered and copied the dance moves of the troupe.

Suddenly, a high-pitched scream cut through all the noise and brought the dancers to a standstill. Everyone looked around, unsure of what was going on. Saba turned. Mum was standing by Mrs Parker, a look of horror on her face.

Saba gasped and ran up. Mum tried to shield her from the sight. But it was too late. Saba had already had a good look. Mrs Parker was in her chair, staring sightlessly at the sky. She was dead.

Saba's mind was in overdrive. *A holiday murder!*

She cornered Jam while the adults were talking to the police.

'This is just like last time with our Christmas murder. Do you remember, Jam?'

'Vaguely,' he said, while sitting on the deckchair doing a crossword in the local English language paper.

'That was back in the day when you were a normal five-year-old. I'm sure we can find the murderer this time too.' She began pacing up and down the poolside. They'd cordoned off the room and surroundings. There were policemen here and there skulking in the background, noticing everyone's comings and goings, and acting as if no one could see them. It wasn't a great look for a holiday resort.

'What do we know so far?' asked Jam, pushing his glasses up his little nose.

Saba hesitated. Jam was only six but he'd always been her partner in crime-solving so she ploughed on.

'The police think she was suffocated. It happened quickly and there were no signs of a struggle, but she's quite old. And her necklace is missing.'

'Oh. So she was killed for the necklace?'

'Seems a bit over the top somehow. I feel like there's an air of revenge about the murder.'

She shook away the mental image of Dr Sancho and the argument of the previous night.

'It has to be one of our group,' she said. 'No one else was anywhere close. Other hotel guests were on the other side of the pool.'

Jam frowned. 'Could someone have come into Mrs Parker's terrace from her room?'

Saba shook her head. 'Remember how the door screeched when it opened? We'd have heard if those sliding doors had moved.'

Jam nodded slowly. 'Who benefits from her death? There's our person.'

Saba shrugged in frustration. 'I know you're thinking of Jessica. But it seems a bit unnecessary. She's Mrs Parker's only child, I heard her telling Ruby on the coach.

Mrs Parker's ancient. She'll die soon anyway. Why steal the necklace that she's probably going to inherit?'

'So the Sanchos and the argument earlier then?'

'That makes more sense. Though it was a long time ago, maybe the Sanchos are still stewing over it and want their money back. The necklace would reimburse them nicely.'

'There's no proof that's what happened though.'

'That's right. Only Gorky and Ruby are safe. Let's start our investigations with them so we can rule them out definitely.'

Saba looked around. The police must have finished questioning Gorky because he was out on the grounds dressed fully in black and filming himself on his phone. Ruby watched from a distance. Gorky looked glum and sombre – the same face Saba used on teachers when she'd not done her homework.

Gorky and Ruby walked down towards the bougainvillea garden.

Saba left Jam doing sudoku and crept behind them.

'I don't agree with it at all!' Ruby was saying.

'Honey, it couldn't be avoided,' said Gorky. 'I don't think you get how much trouble we're in. My follower numbers were dropping like flies. How else do we pay for more trips like this?'

'What rubbish,' she hissed. 'This is beyond the pale and I won't be a part of it.' She turned and stormed back to the hotel.

Saba went back to Jam. 'Guess what? I think Gorky killed her.'

Jam's eyes widened. 'Why?'

'He said something about losing followers and having money troubles.'

'So he killed her for the necklace?'

'That or to create a big drama for his socials.'

Jam tapped his pencil on the paper. 'So we can rule out only Mum and Dad?'

'About that . . .' said Saba. It was never a good idea for a detective to show any bias. 'Mum was looking at Mrs Parker's necklace *a lot*. Jessica noticed too.'

'Looking isn't a crime.'

'But looking . . . quite *enviously* and then the wearer being found dead is a bit sus, isn't it?'

'We can't suspect our own parents!'

'Not parents! Just parent. Although Dad could have been an accomplice.'

Jam shook his head at her in disappointment.

'We can't eliminate people because they're family. Also, Mum was physically closest to Mrs Parker. Oh, look, Jessica's here now. I'm going to talk to her.'

Jessica Parker was sitting on the other side of the lawn with a pot of tea and a plate of sandwiches.

Saba went up to her and said, 'I'm very sorry about

your mother, Jessica.'

Jessica Parker looked up. 'Thank you, Saba.'

'Do you need some company?'

Jessica started shaking her head then stopped. 'Actually, why not? I'd love someone to just chat to about anything other than the murder.'

This was the very opposite of what Saba wanted but she sat down politely anyway. 'Are you going back to the UK now?'

'Not immediately while the murder inquiry's going on.'

Saba nodded. 'You must be eager to go home.'

Jessica laughed. There was a bitterness to her voice. 'I lived with Mother but I don't know where things will take me next.'

'But surely . . .' Saba hesitated at the rude personal question but plunged on for the sake of the case. 'Won't you continue living in the same house?'

A shadow passed over Jessica's face.

'I'm sorry, Jessica. I shouldn't have asked that.'

Jessica sighed. 'It's OK. I've had to explain this to the police too. My mother isn't leaving anything to me.'

Saba knew that wills were secret grown-up things, but it looked like Jessica knew about her mother's. She kept quiet, hoping she would say more.

'These are really nice,' said Jessica taking a bite of a sandwich. 'It's like tuna but a very different local fish.

Caught just this morning, I'm told.'

Saba smiled politely. She wanted to move the conversation back even if Jessica was more interested in the fish. There was the small matter of her mother's murder to clear up. 'She's not leaving you anything?'

Jessica looked sad as she picked up another sandwich. 'She's left everything to a home for cats.'

This confused Saba no end. She couldn't imagine Mrs Parker was an animal lover. 'She liked cats?'

'No,' said Jessica, taking another bite. 'She hated them.'

'Any leads?' said Jam. Mum and Dad still weren't back. Jam had been left to his own devices for hours. Any other six-year-old might have trashed the place, but Jam had gone to town doing a full-page cryptic crossword. He had his own pot of tea and plate of sandwiches too, like a proper grown-up.

'Here's the thing,' said Saba, plopping herself on the ground. 'Jessica *doesn't* benefit from Mrs Parker's will. She's left everything to a cat charity.'

'That must hurt,' said Jam.

Saba took one of the sandwiches. 'Yes. Stealing the necklace means that she could have that at least without the cats getting their paws on it.'

'Look, Dr and Mr Sancho are going down to the sea.

The police must have finished with them too.'

'Be right back, Jam.'

Mr Sancho was jogging on the beach, slightly away from his wife. She was kneeling on the sand, examining a seashell on her palm.

'That's a lovely shell,' said Saba, coming up.

Dr Sancho looked up. 'Isn't it just? So beautiful.'

'Are you going to take it back as a souvenir of your trip?'

Dr Sancho sighed. 'I don't want a souvenir of this trip. I want the police to give us the go-ahead to leave, actually.'

'I'm sorry your holiday was ruined.'

'I don't care about the holiday, Saba. I'm more sorry about Jessica. Even though we had our differences with Maggie, I wouldn't have wished such a thing on anyone.'

Saba stared at her. Dr Sancho sounded quite sincere. She smiled and walked back to her brother.

'Guess what?' said Jam. 'I was listening to two of the policemen talking. I acted like a six-year-old and heard stuff.'

'What stuff?'

'The necklace hasn't been found. They've searched all the suspects' rooms and the suspects themselves. But no necklace.'

Saba frowned. 'Super strange. They're in a new country, it's not like they could have passed it on to anyone.'

Saba poured a cup of tea. Even though she didn't

drink it, it was the sort of thing a detective might do while thinking about a case. She took a sip of the tea. It was all right.

'I think,' she said. 'The necklace is at the heart of everything. If we find out what happened to it we'll be closer to figuring this all out.'

Mum and Dad walked over to them then, looking tired. Mum hugged them without a word.

'Everything's fine, alhamdulillah,' said Dad. 'The police are doing their jobs, hopefully we'll be in the clear soon.'

'Could you tell me what you saw, Mum?' said Saba.

Dad sighed. 'Saba –'

'I don't mind,' said Mum. 'There's nothing much to say. I was going to pop back to the room quickly, to get my phone for a photo, when I nearly slipped on some wet grass just by Mrs Parker's terrace. I looked at her for a moment and realised something was wrong. That was when I screamed. That's it really.'

'Come on,' said Dad, taking up Jam's backpack from the table. 'They've given us another room away from . . . all this.'

On the way to breakfast the next day, Saba saw Gorky skulking by the pool. There was something immediately different about him. It took Saba a moment to realise

– it was because he was without his phone. It was very disconcerting. As if he were half a person.

'Good morning,' she said to him.

He mumbled something in reply and Saba was shocked at how down he looked. Was it guilt?

Breakfast was a very muted affair. The group sat together again, as if taking comfort from each other. Mrs Parker's absence was very pronounced.

Saba's eyes roved around the table. Everyone looked like they had something they regretted. Except Jam, who was reading the financial news while eating eggs on toast.

After breakfast Saba and Jam wandered off and got into a hammock together. People had started coming out after breakfast and a family was in the pool. The splish-splash sounds blended with the noise of people moving deckchairs, scraping them across the grass. The police cordon had been removed, and although the rooms were still closed it looked as if the murder had never happened at all.

Ruby came out to the lawn with Jessica. Gorky trailed behind, still without his phone. Ashoka the waiter walked by with a tray.

Saba took out her phone and looked up Gorky's social media. His last post was a video, posted the previous evening. It was the same one she'd seen him film, with him dressed in black. She watched a few minutes of

Gorky explaining that there'd been a murder of a dear friend and he was caught in the middle of a murder investigation. There were video clips of Mrs Parker from the coach and the previous day played as flashbacks.

She clicked through to the comments and gasped. She showed the screen to Jam.

Comment after comment condemned Gorky for the video. They said it was distasteful and mawkish, and people were unfollowing him in droves.

A picture was slowly beginning to emerge for Saba. She understood Gorky's motivations at last.

Mum and Dad came by and saw them in the hammock.

'Well, this is lovely!' said Mum. 'Since we're going tomorrow, anyone for a swim in the sea?'

'Sure!' Saba climbed out of the hammock. Just because she was on a case didn't mean she couldn't have some down time. They spent the next hour or so on the beach and swimming in the sea. Jam finally built his sandcastle, but it was very boring and technical and Saba zoned out. It was very hot, even when they sat in their wet swimsuits in the shade. Dad went to the pool bar and got them drinks of king coconut.

Saba picked up the frangipani flower on the coconut and put it in her hair while she sipped her drink. Mum took out her phone and snapped a photo of her. Saba looked at the photo that Mum held out.

A memory was jogged from somewhere. A king coconut drink and a frangipani flower.

Saba sat bolt upright.

'What is it?' said Mum.

'We need to get the others together,' said Saba. 'I know who killed Mrs Parker.'

Dad held up a sandy hand. 'Wait a minute. Aren't you going to tell us who it was first?'

'I don't want any spoilers,' said Jam. 'I'd rather know as it happens live.'

Everyone looked nervous in the conference room of the Palm Garden Hotel.

There were eleven chairs arranged in a circle when Saba walked in with Jam. Mum and Dad had set it up with a lot of convincing. Jessica Parker, Gorky and Ruby, the Sanchos, and Mum and Dad sat there, along with two officers in khaki uniforms who looked like they thought this was a waste of time. Mum introduced them to Saba as SSP Almeida and his assistant PC Peiris from the local police force.

Shalini the receptionist stood by the door. On a side table Ashoka arranged food platters and tea.

'Has there been some kind of progress?' asked Jessica Parker, looking to the police.

'Saba has something to say,' said Dad.

'So, er, hello, everyone,' said Saba quickly before anyone could protest.

She saw Gorky's hand go to his pocket automatically, but Ruby stilled him with a look.

There was no point beating about the bush. 'I know who killed Mrs Parker and why.' There was a murmur around the room and Saba plunged on. 'Please allow me to walk you through how I came to my conclusion.'

'We're listening,' said SSP Almeida, though he looked impatient and annoyed.

'Mrs Parker was killed with all of us right there behind our backs,' she began. Her words echoed around the large room. Even Shalini and Ashoka were listening.

'It had to be one of our group who did it. We were the only people close to her. If any other guest had crossed over to where we were we would have seen it at once.'

Dad nodded encouragingly.

'Of course, all eyes were on the dance performance by the pool,' she said. 'But of the people nearby there were just seven suspects. It should be easy enough to narrow it down to one. The first thing was motive. Who stands to gain from Mrs Parker's death?'

All eyes moved to Jessica Parker.

She raised her hands up in a shrug. 'I already told you, Saba, and I've told the good inspector here. I get absolutely *nothing* from her. Mother left everything she owned to the Shkrimi Kitty Cat Home.'

There were startled faces around the circle. Dr Sancho muttered under her breath, 'What a piece of work.'

'So it wasn't a case of inheritance,' said Jam.

'Which brought me to the next thing. Revenge.'

'Let me stop you right there,' said Mr Sancho angrily.

'I know she's wronged you and your wife, Mr Sancho,' said Saba.

Dr Sancho shook her head. 'She has, but we weren't prepared to kill her for it!'

'I was very sure it had to be a revenge-motivated killing. The Sanchos had just met Mrs Parker after ages and their anger at her was still there. They hadn't got over it.'

Mr Sancho glowered at her.

'But then I changed my mind,' said Saba. 'This is not at all how a detective detects, but there's also room for instinct. And my instinct told me the crime didn't make sense. The Sanchos are successful, healthy and very happy. Clearly Mrs Parker's scamming hasn't affected their life. I've seen their phone pics with their children and grandchildren. I saw their happy video call with their children and grandchildren. Mrs Parker's own daughter doesn't seem to like her.' She mouthed a sorry to Jessica. 'Why would the Sanchos risk all their happiness for a pointless crime like this?'

Saba wasn't sure if she was imagining it, but SSP Almeida was nodding slightly as if he was impressed.

'Which brings me to a not-so successful suspect.'

Gorky looked up.

'Gorky Sparrows is in financial trouble. His social media content is boring and he needed something big to happen to build up his flagging follower count. People are known to do desperate things for attention. Even murder.'

'Look here!' Gorky stood up. 'Are you suggesting that I killed her to boost my followers?'

'I overheard a conversation between you and Ruby the other day. I thought Ruby was angry because you killed Mrs Parker so you could bolster your career through that. But what you were doing was less evil, just opportunistic. She was angry that you were using the death of Mrs Parker to lure people back.'

'That's right,' said Gorky. 'I'm not evil.'

'Just stupid,' said Ruby.

Saba agreed with that. 'It didn't work anyway. It had the opposite effect as people saw it for what it was.'

'At least I'm not a murderer.'

'No. You're not. Neither is Ruby as she has stronger morals than you.'

'So this means . . .' Jessica looked incredulous. 'Your *parents* did it?'

Saba stood up and walked slowly to the middle of the

circle. 'No, they didn't. *You did.*'

Jessica gasped.

'You'd just cleared her!' said Mr Sancho.

There were angry mutterings from around the table.

'QUIET! Let her speak!' barked SSP Almeida.

'My parents had no reason, no motive to do this. Yes, there was the necklace, which is very valuable and which my mother was looking at with considerable envy.' This time she mouthed a sorry to Mum. 'But coveting something isn't illegal and it's not a sign that someone's going to commit murder.'

Mum and Dad looked only slightly relieved.

'The crucial thing for me was the missing necklace. Where did it go? Someone had to have removed it from the scene. As it happens, there *was* an outsider wandering through the murder scene.'

Again, Saba turned and pointed. 'Ashoka the waiter.'

There was a thud as Ashoka dropped a saucer on the carpet. He looked completely bewildered.

'What nonsense!' said Jessica.

'You used him, Jessica. And he doesn't even know it.'

'You've got some –'

SSP Almeida waved Jessica away. 'Can you explain that?' he said to Saba.

'When Jessica told me that her mother had left her fortune to charity, and confirmed the name of the cats' home just now, I realised that she'd recently found out about it. Possibly just before the trip. On the coach ride to the hotel I thought she was looking at cat photos on her phone. But I remember the name on top of the website, it was the Shkrimi Kitty Cat Home, her mother's soon-to-be beneficiary. The slight was fresh in her mind.

'I'm guessing from Mrs Parker's behaviour that all Jessica's life she was bullied by her. And in a final dig at her daughter she was leaving everything to animals she hated. Jessica was ready for murder. And what's more she'd take the necklace and use that to start her new life.

'Mrs Parker was wearing the necklace when she was sitting on the terrace. When she was found dead it was missing. Jessica couldn't have taken it because it wasn't on her. So this means Ashoka *must have.*'

SSP Almeida interrupted here. 'The staff were searched too, and their quarters.'

'Something else went missing along with the necklace,' said Saba. 'There was a king coconut drink on the table in front of Mrs Parker earlier. It wasn't hers, of course, she wouldn't drink it so it must have been untouched. But when she was found dead it was gone, with just the flower left on the table. Who else but Ashoka would have taken it away as he moved in and out serving guests?

'Anyone who's had these king coconut drinks knows that there's a small square cut into the coconut for the straw and it's hollow inside where the water is. It's the perfect hiding place for something like a necklace as it can't fall out easily.'

Jessica's eyes had gone very wide.

'So *this* is what happened,' said Saba. 'Ashoka brings a king coconut drink that Jessica's ordered to the terrace and puts it on the table. Mrs Parker ignores it. Ashoka then moves on. Jessica moves forward as if to watch the performance by the pool. When all eyes are on the dance she slips back to her mother. Pretending to adjust her mother's pillow, she pulls it out and suffocates her. She removes the necklace quickly. She then pours out the coconut water and drops the necklace into it, then goes back to her previous position, the whole operation taking just minutes. She signals to Ashoka to collect the empties while bopping along to the dancing. Ashoka comes by moments later. He does his job automatically and doesn't realise Mrs Parker's dead as he collects the shell onto his tray and goes away.'

SSP Almeida had leaned forward in his chair. Everyone was watching intently. Jessica looked down at her lap. The fight had gone out of her.

'My mum then wants to get her phone and makes for our room. She nearly slips on the wet grass where Jessica emptied the coconut. Mum then notices Mrs Parker dead and screams.'

'So where's the necklace?' asked Ruby, looking from her to Ashoka.

'It's in the hotel compost bin. This was what Jessica was trying to find out from Ashoka under some pretext that first lunch, acting like she was interested for environmental reasons. She was going to retrieve it tonight. She would have done it earlier but was thwarted by being constantly watched. I think, Mr Almeida, if you were to look there you'll find it.'

Jessica closed her eyes.

'It was the perfect murder,' said Saba. 'All eyes were on the dancing and Jessica could carry this out unnoticed. It was seeing the Sanchos and their old grudge, and Mum staring at the necklace that gave her the idea to strike now.'

The two policemen got up. PC Peiris handcuffed Jessica and she made no struggle. Almeida said something to her about consular assistance but her expression was blank and Saba wasn't sure if she was taking anything in. She was led away by Peiris out of the room, passing a sombre Shalini on the way.

'Well, that was something,' said Dr Sancho. 'An unmasking of a murderer!'

The life had flowed back into Gorky's face and he looked like his old self again. 'I know, right! I wish I'd filmed it.'

Ruby stared at him witheringly. 'If you'd done that there'd be another murder here.'

Dad laughed. 'Our Saba does it again.'

'We're proud of you,' said Mum.

'I concur,' said Jam.

'Thank you for clearing that up,' said Shalini the receptionist, coming to them and smiling warmly. 'I hope you had a pleasant stay at the Palm Garden Hotel and will leave us a lovely review.'

THIRTEEN
WINTER
MYSTERIES

THE
VERY
Merry
MURDER
CLUB

FROST
FAIR

Edited by
SERENA PATEL & ROBIN STEVENS
Illustrated by HARRY WOODGATE